Deep Hanging Out

RICHARD GWYN

Snowbooks acknowledges the financial support of the Welsh Books Council

First published by Snowbooks in 2007

2

Snowbooks Ltd.
120 Pentonville Road
London
N1 9JN
Tel: 0207 837 6482
Fax: 0207 837 6348
email: info@snowbooks.com
www.snowbooks.com

British Library Cataloging in Publication Data
A catalogue record for this book is available from the British Library.

ISBN 1-905005-56-3
ISBN 13 978-1-905005-56-7

Manufactured in the EU by LPPS Ltd,
Wellingborough, Northants NN8 3PJ

Author's Note

An earlier version of Chapter Fifteen, 'Stratis' Nasty Tale' first appeared in *Totem* magazine. Chapter Two, 'A Boat Trip' was first published in *The New Welsh Review*.

"It seems as if it was intended to be experienced as a wonder-creating journey of the soul."

Rodney Castleden: *The Knossos Labyrinth*

"No arsenal or no weapon in the arsenals of the world is so formidable as the will and moral courage of free men and women."

Ronald Reagan, American President, 1981

"Even the use of one nuclear bomb would inevitably lead to an all-out nuclear exchange."

Leonid Brezhnev, Soviet President, 1981

1. *Cosmo and Ruben*

He shared a narrow, three-storey house near the old harbour with Ruben Fortuna, an Argentinian photographer. They had, in their separate ways, taken refuge on the island when the cold war seemed about to turn the planet into a toxic, windswept desert. All round them were the artefacts of military action.

Seen from a satellite, Crete was a strip of russet in the eastern Mediterranean, but also a strategic nexus between three continents. Its long rectangular shape broadened at the western end, sprouting two peninsulas. Viewed imaginatively, and in the context of the island's ancient culture, the peninsulas might have resembled twin horns. The town of Xania lay just to the east of them.

He arrived on the evening flight from Athens. Once he had hauled his bag upstairs, and finding Ruben not at home, Cosmo sat in the kitchen and prepared tea. He needed calming down. The flight had been turbulent, and Cosmo disliked flying. He preferred to take trains, where possible. Under normal circumstances he would have caught the overnight ferry from Piraeus, but had accompanied Alex, his companion of the past eight days, from Corfu to Athens, to catch her connection with Dublin, and had then opted for the Olympic Airlines service to Xania out of a desire to get home fast. Now that he was here he needed a while to settle; to see his things around him and to gain the sense of having truly arrived that air travel so distorts.

The departure from Alex had not been a happy one. There were missing details, entire days gone adrift. They had spent a week on the blighted paradise of Corfu, and by the time Alex caught the flight home to her job as a psychiatric nurse, she was both sad and relieved to part company from this man with multiple and compound personalities, all of them, it seemed to her, on a sharply declining trajectory.

First he had appeared to her as a dishevelled, vaguely exotic stranger whom she had recklessly seduced and straddled on the upper deck of the Brindisi night ferry. Then came deterioration, in daily stages, punctuated by gratuitous and unprovoked rows, one overnight stay in hospital for Cosmo after walking into a moving taxi (concussion) and another after challenging four bald Cockneys to a fight (cracked ribs and eight stitches above his left eye). It was all pretty grim for Alex. She had taken this holiday to get over her Dublin boyfriend, himself borderline schizoid, and wandered into something just as perilous, and all the worse for not having spotted it in Cosmo's face that first night. By the time he had downed the smoky potion several times over and become transformed into a wild-eyed nemesis, it was too late. She was already contemplating the appalling possibility of staying in Greece with another terminal berserk.

But Alex's diagnosis of Cosmo was prejudiced by her choice of profession. Cosmo was not a psycho; he had simply been on a binge and she had happened into him. The rail journey from Bologna down the length of Italy had started it, or rather the five-hour wait at a bar near Bologna station, downing grappa with an itinerant Slovak cheese salesman, while around them the famously gorgeous women of that city took their evening stroll. Cosmo had slept through most of the journey, enduring painfully erotic dreams alone in his compartment, and by the time the train pulled into Brindisi he was refreshed, breakfasted, and ready to interact. Alex had then put into practice the kinds of fantasy that the previous evening's street-gazing had stimulated.

For Cosmo, Alex was already history. Among confusing memories of splintering glass, a large dent in the bonnet of a car, and a remorseless pummelling of blows to the head and body, he retained clear recall only of her very long blonde hair and an enthusiastic talent for fellatio. But beyond the thrill of the first caress, the ecstatic moment that could occur once and once only, Alex had merely confirmed for Cosmo what he already knew to be true: where women were concerned he was a failure in the art of sustained relationship.

The cat had been following him around the house since Cosmo unlocked the front door, purring and rubbing her shanks against Cosmo's ankles. Now that he was seated, she took advantage of his lap, turning in a circle twice before finding the most comfortable position. Cosmo's upper thighs gave off an odour of intimate human stuff, which the cat briefly enjoyed. Her nostrils twitched, she performed a third and final circuit of his lap, then opted for the table top, where she stretched out full-length, allowing Cosmo to stroke her chin. Through half-open eyes, she watched a moth batter repeatedly against the lampshade that overhung the kitchen table.

Cosmo was asleep in the chair, perfectly motionless, when Ruben let himself in shortly after midnight.

– *Che!* I was expecting you last week.

Ruben stood in the doorway, wearing a brown suede jacket and blue jeans. A Nikon hung from a shoulder-strap, uncased. He was in a good mood. An attractive man with a mass of long black curls, he was a *Porteño*, a Buenos Aires kid who had moved to London by way of Mexico, and had not looked back.

Cosmo raised his head and blinked.

– Ruben. *Amigo mio.* I was detained. Unavoidably.

Ruben had moved across from the door and was studying his housemate up close.

– Shit. What they do to your face?

Ruben traced a finger tenderly over the stitches on his friend's eyebrow.

– A little misunderstanding over something the nature of which I forget. Like most everything else that happened while visiting Corfu.

– Corfu? What you doing in that dump? Place full of *Inglesi* wankers.

Cosmo indicated his forehead with a stabbing finger.

– I rest my case.

– So what you do? Try to start a war?

– Hey *hombre*, you know me. I come in peace.

Ruben swivelled astride a chair, arms resting across the high back.

– You're going to need those stitches out, when?

– Couple days.

– You look like shit.

Cosmo started to get up, intending to make some more tea, but was stopped by a riveting pain in the ribs. Now that the alcohol had worn off he was beginning to feel every tiny spasm, every shift of tissue on bone, every billiard-ball kiss of internal movement. He tried to enfold his body in his arms, as if to smother all sentient programming.

– What else they do? Smash your ribs?

Cosmo nodded.

– Here, said Ruben. I'll make the tea.

He picked up the pan from the table and filled it with fresh herbs and water.

– Got any painkillers?

Ruben shook his head.

– Finished the downers. Apart from the purple fuckers some crazy person left behind, and you don't want to try them. I was gonna throw them out. Raki?

– Yeah, I'll have a glass.

Leaving the water to boil, Ruben returned to the table with a large bottle of clear spirit and two small glasses. He retrieved the cork with his teeth and tipped out two measures of the raki, handing one to Cosmo. They clicked glasses and downed the shots. Cosmo felt his mouth burn, then a draft of scorched air raced through his limbs and lodged in his stomach.

– Where you been, Lyrakia? His verbs often fell apart in conversation with Ruben.

– Working, man.

Ruben indicated the camera.

– Any luck?

– Luck doesn't come into the equation. Patience, yeah. Luck's for those who never learn to wait.

– A fallback strategy.

– Precisely.

– Man, can you talk the talk.

Cosmo stretched back in the chair. The pain in his ribs seemed duller, less punitive.

– I'll have another one of those.

Standing, Ruben poured a second round, then turned to fetch the pan of tea.

– News from the Unspeakable? Cosmo asked.

He was referring to a restaurant, where they regularly hung out.

– Let's see. The Dutchman has been barred, again: good. Nikos has been put on sentry duty for a month, a year, a long time, possibly for ever, for stealing explosives: bad.

– Crazy Nikos, the sailor?

– The same.

– And the explosives?

– He won't tell, apparently. His purpose in obtaining them is obscure, as are most things with Nikos. I believe, and this is ultra confidential, that he intended to blow up a hotel.

– Here in Xania?

– In his village, near Sitia.

– Any reason? Or just for the bang?

– Nikos thinks Greeks should take responsibility against the new colonialism that is tourism. He is busy forming his anti-tourist terrorist outfit. So, with two fellow villagers, cousins no doubt, he was set to take proactive action. Can you say that? Only they haven't finished building this new hotel yet. He was going to wait till it was due to open, then blast the place to fuckery.

– Nikos told you this?

– In person. While you were away. But being who he is, he was collared by the Military Police. *In flagrante.* The cooler for a while, then sentry duty. His mate, Yannis, told me this last night.

–Yannis with the reggae habit?

– Mister Marley.

– So your connections with the Greek Navy remain with the enlisted ranks?

– Not many officers visit the Unspeakable.

– With good reason. The food, for one.

– True. And the wine.

– The wine is rough.

Cosmo leaned forward and carefully poured the tea.

– You ever been to Florence?

– No. Roma. Napoli. In Napoli the Fortuna are big.

– You mean there's more like you, or they are gangsters?

– Big gangsters. Camorra. Mafiosi.

– You joking?

– No way. Very serious bad. Horse head in the bed level bad.

– Come on, man.

– No kidding. My grandpa came to Buenos Aires with a kick in the ass from same Camorra. Now Fortuna fight back, hold their ground. Nobody fucks with the Fortuna.

– The Family is Everything.

– And God. The Motherland.

– The Holy Trinity.

– In Argentina it's the same. Or worse, under the Junta. How was Firenze?

– Same as in the postcards, only more so. Talk about the blight of tourism. I stayed with locals, in a villa back of

Santa Croce. The guy's a friend of a Serious Collector. Their son and I got on OK. He told me that it never eases up, the tourist flow. 'Like a sewage' were his words. No, I told him, just 'like sewage.' 'That's what I say,' he said, 'a sewage, like.' Forget it, I said: say 'a sewage' if you want. This guy, Bruno, has a heroin habit. He was clean while I was there, except the last two days. Then he borrows money off me. Better say I give him money since I know I'm not gonna get it back. He lays this stuff on me, this China White. We shoot up in some church painted by, like, Michaelangelo. Jesus, I said, never ever give me that again. 'Don't you like it?' Like it? Man I love it. Far too much. In fact we had some more that night and the next day, then I had to call it quits.

– Because you liked it too much? You thinking you'd get hooked?

– No. The hiccups.

– Huh?

– Fucking hiccups. Every thirty seconds for two days. I tried everything. Drinking water with my head the wrong way up. Holding breath, counting to a hundred till my veins were popping. Went in this bar, this *Fiascheteria,* my local pub. The guy there, Roberto, a really good guy. Ideal landlord. He sees me doing the hiccup thing, then sneaks up behind my back, bangs a ladle on a tray. Jumped out of my fucking skin.

– This was his intention.

– Shock therapy.

– Did it work?

– No.

– So how did you get rid of the hiccups.

– On a two step programme. Getting drunk in Bologna. Then getting laid.

Cosmo liked sharing a house with Ruben. They gave each other space. The top floor of the house provided Cosmo with a studio, a bedroom and a bathroom, while Ruben was quartered on the first floor and had converted a large storage area at the back of the kitchen into a darkroom. When he was working Cosmo usually spent the mornings painting, rising at dawn and working through until it was time for food and a siesta. Since cutting short his studies five years earlier, he had been able to make a comfortable living, quite beyond his expectations. He had attracted the interest of two or three Serious Collectors and had held exhibitions at good venues, most recently in New York, London and Florence, from which last he had just returned with sufficient money in the bank to sustain his stay in Greece indefinitely. He was becoming a name to look out for in the international art world, but didn't like the idea of people knowing who he was, nor where he lived. He didn't even like to talk about his work. He left everything in the hands of an agent who had phoned him at his father's home in Paris while still a student, and since his teachers told him that this was an exceptionally good agent who only took on new clients if he was convinced of their talent and marketability, never had reason to look for another. He simply did what he had always done, paint rough, raw, with lots of colours. He knew he had been lucky, that he led a charmed life, and it made him a little uneasy, but only a little.

Cosmo's parents had separated when he was six years old. His formal schooling in north London had been a disaster and he had left at the earliest opportunity. But there had been compensations; his mother's extended Irish family provided rumbustious contrast to his father's solitary Paris existence, and moving between the two cities as a teenager, Cosmo grew up fast. He was a compulsive reader and autodidact, and when he eventually settled in Paris to attend art school, moving into his father's large and high-ceilinged apartment, he had been given not only a studio space of his own but access to a library that spilled over into several rooms.

Streetwise and self-assured, Ruben had grown up in the sprawling outskirts of Buenos Aires, working night shifts while pursuing a degree in politics and anthropology at the city's university. Then, midway through his studies, the advent of the military junta had rendered his course meaningless. Knowing that his political leanings would make him a prime target for the inevitable inquisition, he immediately left the country on an Italian passport, worked on oilrigs in the Gulf of Mexico and, most important, discovered photography. Ruben believed in his art, and worked hard at it, and, being a good researcher, he spent a deal of time doing what he called Deep Hanging Out. This, according to Ruben, indicated a close empathy with and knowledge of his chosen subject, which, as a photographer, included most of humanity and its constructs. He was, in his own manner, an ethnographer of the human condition, embarked on a Big Project, which involved watching the world, and paying attention. Cosmo, too, liked doing Deep Hanging Out, although he thought of it as *loafing*: an essential pre-creative process that usually involved drinking a lot of wine. Ruben said there was a difference: Cosmo was not sure. But he was happy to call it Deep Hanging Out.

Ruben had come to Crete, he told Cosmo, because it lay between three continents and was a long way from Argentina and its rota of assassins: Videla, Agosti, Massera, Galtieri. He had always loved the name of this sea, *Mediterranean*, the centre of the earth, and of this island in the middle of it all: Kriti. He felt as though he was at the geographical crossroads of things, and yet hidden, almost out of sight. Seeing but unseen. This linked him to Cosmo in a way that made their friendship all the more inevitable. They came to share a sense of being both invisible and yet of having penetrated to the core of a precariously held secret; witnesses to an event that was always imminent, yet just beyond their understanding, and almost certainly beyond their power to influence or change.

It was the beginning of the 1980's. The cold war was heating up. Visions of mushroom skylines and solar winds overwhelmed the popular imagination and to mollify their citizens Western governments mailed out instructions telling them to cover their windows with newspaper and hide beneath the kitchen table in the event of nuclear attack. Prognoses were apocalyptic: countless thousands would die from the immediate effects of nuclear attack through the triple onslaught of flash, blast and radiation. Terrible winds and firestorms would destroy what remained. Monstrous atmospheric explosions would deplete the ozone layer irreparably. Everything would burn or be broken. Everything would be contaminated for a very long time.

Here in Crete, however, Cosmo and Ruben conspired together on an adventure which they considered to be entirely of their making. Thus they were drawn together not only by the shared delusion of invisibility, but by a common quest.

2. *Pre-Military Activity*

The town edges down towards the sea, and it is the sea that made the town, the sea that draws a ring around it, furnishes the arched alleyways and narrow conduits of the Venetian quarter, perfumes the air with resinous seaweed, purges it with salt. The outer suburbs slope away into the orange groves to the south and west. A few hotels rise above the skyline. But the town's gravitational pull is downward, ever downward, towards the sea, the older buildings' crumbling sandstone witness to a heritage of assault, resistance, plunder. For six thousand years of continuous settlement this has been a living city, its archaeology revealing its diverse lineage, from the Minoan through the Hellenistic, Roman and Byzantine, Venetian and Ottoman eras. Remnants of Venetian fortifications, the *kastelli,* rise above the old harbour, with its long jetty leading out to the lighthouse. This blinking eye has overseen Barbary Corsairs, Turks and Germans in their various raids and occupations. The road that follows the harbour front shreds off into alleys and dead-end streets, narrow arteries named after figures from classical mythology – Icarus Street, Daedalus Street, Minos Street – which converge in the upper reaches of the zone, known as the Splanzia, with streets whose titles derive from the wars of independence; a proliferation of significant dates and the names of revolutionary leaders. In this way ancient myth is welded to historically documented events, creating a continuum that blurs fact and fiction, sacrificing both concepts to an overarching principle of Greekness. Here, more than in most places, it is hard to know what is myth and what is not; harder still to distinguish between an object and its shadow. It was here, in the Splanzia, that Cosmo and Ruben lived.

To the west of the town a succession of beaches stretches all the way to the peninsular of Kissamou in the distance: Cosmo and Ruben were out at Neachora, the nearest of them. It was one of those early summer afternoons before the tourist onslaught, with a clean shoreline and a still sea. They swam, and lay on the sand for an hour, reading and dozing. For a week since Cosmo's return from Italy they had been on a regime of daily swimming and early nights, easing up on Deep Hanging Out in favour of more healthy and cerebral pursuits. Cosmo had started painting, while Ruben spent the mornings working on the engine of a seven metre fishing boat the two had bought the previous year. The old fisherman they bought it from had sold the vessel – the *Agios Nektarios*, or Holy Nektar – with a degree of sadness, since he'd had it for twenty years, but he liked the new owners and respected the way they, or rather Ruben in particular, lavished his attention on it. Over the winter they had hauled the *Nektar* up onto the quay for a complete strip-down. Ruben had removed the engine and taken it apart, cleaning everything by hand with an oiled rag, replacing old or inefficient parts. It was a skill he'd learned while doing military service in Argentina, he told Cosmo: he'd been assigned to the engineering corps. They had already taken the boat out to sea many times during the spring. Now they planned an evening fishing trip.

In the late afternoon they started back into Xania, a twenty-minute walk. There was a strip of restaurants on the last stretch of beach, then the road rose slightly, taking them past the ruins of a large Venetian fortification and a small harbour where fishing boats bobbed on a gentle breeze. Away from the seafront the pavement widened and cedars grew at intervals along the roadside.

A pair of American naval officers stood chatting under a tree. Nearby was a small building site, one of hundreds of such places suspended in a perpetual state of non-completion that strew the landscape of Greece. The men were dressed in white uniforms and one of them nodded towards the ground, towards a plot of new-looking cement and a metal covering or man-hole set among the rubble. Ruben pulled Cosmo back and whispered to him to wait. He had raised his camera and was snapping shots. Then the trapdoor lifted and a head appeared. Another man climbed out from the shaft and held the cover open while a fourth officer emerged. From the way the others deferred to him, it appeared that the last man out of the trapdoor was the senior officer. The first two men moved over to the opening and appeared to secure it. The four then stood talking for a short while before walking over to a white Honda car and driving off. They had been out of earshot and neither Ruben nor Cosmo had been able to pick up any stray fragments of their conversation, but the little scenario seemed altogether strange. These blue-eyed, tanned Americans in their crisp white shirts were inspecting something, their energies concentrated on protecting knowledge of the thing they guarded, making it doubly obvious to any passer-by that what was guarded was a secret, buried in the rocks below the ground. But if this were so, how could they be so brazen about their presence there? Surely they could not rely on the inactivity of the siesta hour to grant them invisibility? If they were monitoring the construction of something secret, why appear in uniform, with only the civilian car as concession to their anonymity? Why were they not disguised as builders, or as architects surveying a site under construction?

Once the naval officers had driven away, Cosmo and Ruben continued walking into town. Ruben was preoccupied.

– What was that about, you reckon? asked Cosmo, to break the silence.

– Who knows? They act like they own the fucking place.

– Well, sure. They do. *Apart* from that.

– What would your guess be?

– Let's see. Nuclear shelter?

– Precisely. But why here, in a part of town nowhere near the naval base?

– We don't know. I mean, we don't know who else lives near here.

– Sure. But look around.

Cosmo looked around. A luxury hotel, in the final stages of construction, was the only building of any size between here and the main part of town. The Hotel Marco Polo was the first of a new brand of five-stars, catering to a different market from the package-dealers.

– Maybe a shelter for visiting VIPs. A way into the shelter.

– A way in and a way out.

– And the hotel is strategically positioned. A vantage point over the bay.

– *Bueno.* We're doing well. Let's go eat.

– Why do you want the pictures?

– Evidence. Pre-military activity.

– You a spy?

– No. I do research.

They skirted a high wall, once part of the town's defensive structure, on which was daubed familiar graffiti: GREECE FOR THE GREEKS, then walked along the harbour-front and up past a jumble of cafés. A few customers lingered over a late lunch, but mostly these places were deserted now, the odd waiter dozing at a shady table. Café Costas had its usual contingent of battered travellers and crusties lodged outside, drinking beer and exchanging stories no one wanted to hear. Cosmo nodded at an acquaintance and Costas himself yelled a greeting from under the awning, tray in hand. Ruben carried on walking without raising his head. He despised the clientele at Café Costas.

They turned into narrow Skridlov Street, where the leather merchants were beginning to display their goods on the pavement after the siesta break, and stopped at the Unspeakable. They called it this in homage to an item on the restaurant's menu, *Ta Amaletita*, which in Greek means the 'unmentionable' or 'unspeakable,' and is a euphemism for sweetbreads, or pig's testicles. On a blackboard outside the bistro was painted a menu, offering mainly fish and seafood, in Greek, English and French. With a lack of finesse that reflected unpromisingly on the target clientele, *Amaletita* was rendered into English as 'Pig's balls,' and it was by this term that the place was known among the town's itinerant population. 'Pig's Balls' was a description that Cosmo and Ruben eschewed. The official name for the restaurant was in fact *To Diporto*, meaning 'two doors', so called because the place was lodged between two parallel streets, with entrances on either one.

The owner of the Unspeakable was Tassos Manolakis. He employed a single waiter named Igbar Zoff, a drunken polyglot who could no longer remember when, or why, he had arrived in Crete. Tassos spoke only Greek, and relied on Igbar, who was unemployable elsewhere, to take orders from the customers and wait at table. Tassos did all the cooking and his wife washed the dishes. Igbar managed to keep up a semblance of propriety as a rule, but occasionally took a week off to concentrate on uninterrupted drinking, during which time Tassos would employ one of a family of Romani to take his place until Igbar had sobered up sufficiently to return to work. So it could be said that Tassos made allowances for Igbar, but also that he depended on him rather more than he would have cared to admit. Theirs was a symbiotic relationship. Working for Tassos, Igbar ate two square meals a day and earned, with tips, a fair salary. In turn, Tassos (whose establishment was insalubrious in the extreme) was able to lay claim to a certain international *savoir faire*, by proxy. Igbar had studied Fine Art at the Slade in the 1960's and had made a promising start as a painter before becoming a professional alcoholic. (There was a picture of his, entitled *Le cocktail dans le cauchemar*, hanging in Cosmo and Ruben's kitchen, in which two desultory figures were dwarfed by a cocktail glass whose contents, lurid and malignant, blazed with hyperactive colour). He maintained that he had needed a break from the vicious and incestuous dealings of the international art world, but in reality he had never known much success. Now, in his late thirties, he entertained international dropouts and members of the Greek and American armed forces with his unique skills as a waiter.

It was Igbar who came to serve them now, a stained dishcloth in one hand, with which he made a rapid and fruitless sweep of their table. He was unshaven, with an oversize moustache and eyes that flickered with the embers of a keen intelligence. He produced a tattered block of orders from his pocket and a pencil from behind his ear.

– What'll you be having, gentlemen?

– Please don't stand on ceremony, Igbar, said Cosmo. Just tell us what's fresh. If anything.

– The calamares and the red mullet, both. This morning from the harbour.

– Bring us a plate of each then. And a Greek salad. And chips.

– Chips? Igbar looked crestfallen. Cosmo knew what was coming next.

– Chips, explained Igbar, can pose a problem for Tassos. He needs a big order in order to justify the preparation of fried potatoes. Or else he waits until the individual orders for chips have accumulated to the extent that their preparation could become feasible. Something that can take hours. Especially at this time of day.

– Two portions of chips then, said Ruben.

Igbar, despairing, looked to Cosmo for support.

– I'm going to wash my hands, said Cosmo, and moved into the dark and narrow interior of the restaurant.

The decor of the Unspeakable was impervious to the demands of fashion or political correctness. It had remained essentially unchanged for three decades. On one wall a large print of the primitivist school of painting showed the parachute invasion of Crete by the Nazis in May 1941. In the picture, a fierce and patriotic Cretan prepares to smite a descending German with a shepherd's crook. Around him lie the bodies of the fallen, mostly slain invaders tangled in the webs of their chutes, while jubilant greybeards, women and children, armed with spades and axe-handles prepare to decimate those others who fall out of the sky around them. In the background the peaks of the White Mountains leave no doubt as to the setting.

The body of the restaurant narrowed further where the fridge and counter jutted out into the room. One had to slip through here in order to reach another room on the far side of the cooking and serving area, where there were more tables and a jukebox that, when working, blared out ancient Rembetika songs. Tassos Manolakis, slouched behind the counter, watched Cosmo approach. His eyes were dark and riotous. Only a person with a developed sense of the absurd would have employed Igbar as a waiter.

– *Kalispera* Cosmo, he called out, pulling himself vertical. Cosmo was a moneyed customer compared to the regular flow of international flotsam, hookers, pimps, naval ratings and scroungers that constituted the bulk of Tassos's clientele.

Cosmo returned the greeting. His Greek was good, though not fluent. He inquired after Tassos's family: Anna, his wife; Thespina, his daughter, who was a student in Athens; Stavros, the son, on military service in the Peloponnese.

– We want fried potatoes, said Cosmo, once the

formalities were done. To complement the red mullet.

– Of course. No problem.

– We'll have some calamares, a large salad, and a litre of cold white wine. Not retsina.

– Not retsina, repeated Tassos, memorizing. *Endaxi,* Cosmo. Ten minutes.

Cosmo continued on through the cooking area to the back room. To the left was a door that led to the toilet and a store-room. A rat hurried past him into the toilet and shot down the drain. Cosmo stepped back, taken by surprise. Sighing, he unzipped his pants and aimed at the hole in the ground down which the rat had fled. On the wall, scratched in flaking penknife script, was written a new and querulous scrawl: *Why does it hurt when I pee?* The toilet stank of ammonia.

On his way back past the cooking area, Cosmo brushed close to Tassos, who was deep-frying fish and potatoes in olive oil.

He whispered: – There is a rat in the *toualeta.*

Tassos turned around, frowning, shrugged apologetically, muttered a profanity, and returned to frying fish.

Since Cosmo and Ruben were the only customers, Igbar had pulled up a chair at their table, nearest to the door and was lighting a cigarette.

– One of your clients may have a venereal disease, said Cosmo, taking a seat.

– Indubitably. Igbar exhaled a lungful of smoke.

– Lunchtime custom good?

– Spare. The Dutchman came back, asking for credit. With his girlfriend. Tassos gave them short shrift. Some regulars. American ratings. This one chap from Detroit built like a Sherman tank: 'I'll have some of them there *Pig Nuts,*' pointing at said gonads in the fridge display. He's been before. Courtney. Most effusive chap. You probably know him. Always has his Pig Nuts. Where have you two been?

– Working. Swimming. Enjoying life, Cosmo answered. Observing the pre-military activity.

Ruben glanced up. Cosmo wasn't sure whether his friend wanted him to go on.

– Meaning?

Cosmo caught Ruben's gaze and changed course.

– What exactly are the Americans up to here in Crete?

Igbar pondered his reply.

– The naval base at Souda provides NATO with its most powerful presence in the eastern Med. Discounting Turkey, which the Greeks would rather do in any case. As Churchill knew, holding Crete is a strategic necessity. Why the interest in cold war politics?

Igbar filled Cosmo's glass, then drank it himself, down in one.

– Well then, Igbar, who's your latest suspect?

Cosmo was referring to Igbar's insistence that Xania must be home to a Soviet Intelligence Operative. It had developed into a sort of game, called 'spot the spy,' usually carried on at night in the Lyrakia, Igbar's favoured drinking hole. Most of the population had good reason to be in the pay of the KGB, if Igbar's analyses of local life were anything to go by.

– You are. Or Ruben with his bloody camera.

Tassos appeared in the entrance, blinking at the sunlight. He carried plates of food, but when Igbar got up to help him, Tassos hissed at him: – *Katsi,* seedow. It was the only English phrase Tassos ever uttered: *Seedow*, delivered almost as an expletive, but leaving little doubt as to its meaning, prefixed by the Greek word and accompanied by a flat downward movement of the hand towards a chair. Groups of foreign tourists, regardless of their language of origin, were treated to the same disdainful imperative by Tassos until Igbar appeared from whatever task he was engaged in to take their orders.

When Tassos had finished delivering their food, he took a seat at the table the other side of the entrance: or rather he took two seats, in the local fashion, sitting back on one, while his feet rested on the other. His dark, mesmeric eyes scanned the street's activity.

The shops were open now and visitors emerged from hotel rooms and coffee shops and beaches. Some of them consulted guide-books to confirm that they were in the right place, scrutinizing the street signs and shop fronts, puzzling over the Greek script. They sauntered down Skridlov Street dressed in shorts and sandals, red-faced and bare-legged, poking the leather goods, shielding their eyes from the lowering sun.

– There was a girl in here earlier, French. Hippy type. She'd been out picking melons on a farm near Maleme. Usual thing, day labouring. She was with a group of bozos who hang out down at Café Costas for the early cattle market, seven a.m. Frightfully nice girl. Pascale. Very comely.

Igbar's professed fondness for teenage boys did not prevent him from these eulogies to a certain type of *femme fatale.* Cosmo suspected that both attitudes amounted to little more than posturing, and that, in sexual terms, Igbar was pretty much an empty room.

The waiter blew out smoke and looked up, dreamy, confused. There was a long silence. He appeared to have forgotten what he was talking about.

– Come on Igbar, cut to the quick. You are wearing the expression that warns of an anecdote that has no purpose or direction.

– Quite so. Sorry, Cosmo. Igbar stirred himself, straining with the effort to recall what he had begun to begin.

– Pascale, prompted Cosmo. The comely.

– I know, I know. It seems there was some NATO exercise this morning. A parachute drop on the fields of Maleme. *German* Paras. How insensitive can they be? Almost forty years to the day, well, month, since the Nazi invasion, and in the same bloody place. One trooper lands in Pascale's melon field and before he has time to unharness his parachute she lobs a melon at him. Catches him full-on in the gut. Girl's from Toulouse, you see, knows her rugby. Scrum-half torpedo throw. Brilliant. The parachute chappie takes it in good humour. *Ach, you haf vinded me!*

Ruben said, – Winded or Wounded?

– What? Winded. *Vinded.*

– He'd know this word?

– Why not?

– My guess is he said *wounded.*

– No. Definitely *winded.*

– I doubt it.

– Dammit Ruben, he said *winded.*

Igbar, rattled, poured himself a glass of Cosmo's wine and shot a glance behind to check that Tassos was not watching: but Tassos was watching, he was always watching everything. Igbar sat with Cosmo's glass poised inches from his lips, caught in transit.

Tassos scowled. *Sigah, sigah,* Igbar. Take it easy.

Igbar necked the wine anyhow. Tassos turned away, hurt.

– As if real invasions were not enough, they now have simulated ones. Carried out by the sons of men who carried out the last one, continued Igbar, – Do they really *need* any more invasions? They have the tourists. And the Americans at Souda Bay. NATO.

– Us, added Ruben.

– Us?

– Us. We're part of the sequence too. We just choose not to see it that way. What do you think all the Graffiti is about? GREECE FOR THE GREEKS.

– Steady on, said Igbar. Remember that Greece has only recently come out of seven years of military dictatorship. Those slogans appeared just before the last election. They were part of the Socialist Party campaign to get rid of the American bases. They weren't aimed at travellers. Or tourists. Are you equating us with the Ottoman Empire, the Nazis, the tourist industry and the American Navy, NATO? That's quite a lot to take on board. Historically.

–We're talking about a sequence of disasters in the history of Crete. We might think we don't fit into the agenda, the historical *process*, but we do. Sometimes I think our sense of being on the outside looking in is just a little trick. A matter of perspective. Truth is, we *are* a part of it. And perhaps could do some more to change the course of things.

– Maybe that's what Nikos is about, with his explosives, said Cosmo.

– You've heard then. About Crazy Nikos and his dynamite?

– Sure. I'd hoped not everybody knew, said Ruben.

– People don't. Civilians. And even I don't know why they banged him up, other than he stole the stuff and wouldn't tell them why. I suspect he told you though.

Ruben declined to say more.

Some customers arrived and Tassos retreated to his kitchen, while Igbar shuffled into action. A circumspect waiter at the best of times, he had a knack of confusing his customers into a state of near torment. Since nothing in the Unspeakable was quite what it seemed – many of the items on the set menu being unavailable and others, unlisted, materialising on tables where they were not requested – there was an almost mystical quality surrounding any visit to the restaurant. The regulars knew this, and took it in their stride, if not as an added attraction. But to those unfortunate strangers who risked entering the place, their only source of information was likely to be Igbar, who managed well enough, when he felt like it, in Greek, French and German as well as his native English. He had also learned the regional and dialect terms for all the varieties of fish served by Tassos in several other European languages, mainly as a source of entertainment to himself. But the opportunities for discussing what he grandly termed Ichthyological Terminology were few compared with the more mundane run of questions that were posed to him daily. Why, for example, did half-litres of wine come served in old Amstel beer bottles? Why was there a thirty-minute interval between the delivery of a plate of calamares and the accompanying salad? Why, if moussaka had been ordered, did the surly Cretan who scowled from the recesses of his kitchen command them to sit down – *seedow!* – rather than confess that moussaka was not (nor ever had been) available at this restaurant? Why did the salt shaker contain rice granules but no salt? Why were there cockroaches in the corridor to the back room? *Why does it hurt when I pee?*

Igbar's talent lay in providing laborious and convoluted responses to these and other questions. He had a flawed genius for the art of waiting tables. Given his artistic credentials, it might have been considered something of a comedown for him to spend his time serving boiled shrimps to package-deal holiday-makers and fried eggs to vagrants. But Igbar did not see it that way. He had, after his fashion, found a vocation, and if it signified the end of the road for him in terms of career opportunities, this did not appear to trouble him. Within the two doors of the Unspeakable, he was both dissolute prince and lawmaker.

While Igbar set about making the new customers feel uncomfortable, Ruben and Cosmo finished their wine and left. They were going fishing.

3. *A Boat Trip*

They cast off from the boat's berth in the old harbour, the *Nektar* nudging past anchor ropes and buoys in the calm water. Here they were protected from the breeze that had blown up while returning from the beach at Neachora, and only an occasional, distant flurry of white specks interrupted the unbroken blue of the sea.

Cosmo sat cross-legged on the prow. He wore stained army pants and a vest and was baiting a line with small squid. Ruben steered the tiller. Before long the indolent chugging of the diesel engine accelerated into a more punctuated rhythm and the *Nektar* bounced and swaggered through the waves. She rode low in the water at the stern, but was quite seaworthy and the work that Ruben had carried out on the engine gave her an extra couple of knots in speed. They passed the lighthouse at full throttle, leaving the main harbour with its pastel-coloured houses and its trail of striped awnings and headed into the lowering sun and a rising wind, in the direction of Kastelli.

Cosmo dropped his hand into a large rusting tin at his

side and threaded more squid onto hooks as the boat began to dip and rise through the mild swell. Ruben, the wind now blowing his locks across his pirate's face, single gold earring glistening, was in his element at the helm. Before long, salt-spray had flecked their hands and faces with a fine white lustre.

Once they had passed the promontories and scattering of rocks that lay to the west of the town, they veered seaward. They were moving slowly north-west when movement in the water ahead told them that a shoal was active near the surface. The presence of half a dozen gulls confirmed this. Cosmo, hunched over, moved down the boat towards the stern and trailed his line through the water. Almost immediately the fish began to bite.

– *Gopes*, said Ruben.

Gopes are long thin fish, like sardines, but less oily. They were a poor man's dinner, but still a welcome catch. It was rare to come across a shoal so quickly in the ungenerous waters of this stretch of sea. Cosmo pulled in more than a dozen fish from the first line, and threw out a second, while Ruben cut the engine to a subdued drone. Then the two of them knelt in the stern and tossed the *gopes* into a bucket, where they thrashed about, drowning in air.

When they had nearly filled the bucket Cosmo leaned inside the hatchway to the covered hold that housed the engine and brought out a block of ice, wrapped in sackcloth. He splintered the ice with a small pick and re-arranged the fish in the bucket around the ice. Ruben was baiting another line with shrimp when he re-emerged.

Cosmo sat back against the upright of the hatchway and lit an unfiltered cigarette. The tobacco tasted sweet in the salt air. There was very little wind now.

– You going to drop another line?

Ruben looked up. Other than his single word on identifying the catch, it was the first time either of them had spoken since leaving land. They had been working at their individual tasks without communicating, and their actions were co-ordinated: each knew what the other was doing, or about to do. To hear his friend's voice almost took him by surprise.

– I'm gonna catch a Big Fish, he said. His smile showed very white teeth. Definitely a pirate's smile. *Beeg Feesh.* Although Ruben could do formal English when it suited him, he sometimes performed in an exaggerated Latino patois.

– Not here you won't.

– Tuna. Dorado. Bonito.

– Wrong sea.

– Well, fuck it, man: a shark.

– A shark would be nice.

– Tassos would appreciate a shark. He would be ecstatic.

– Many others in his line of business would pay more than him.

– It's not the money I wanna see. More the look on his face. Walking through his door with this big fucking shark thing hanging on your shoulder.

– Or draped around your neck.

– A shark with big teeth. *Beeg.* Like Bowie knives.

– Dream on, *gaucho.*

Cosmo pulled at his cigarette and watched the distant roadway that led through the coastal villages. There were many reasons why he had chosen to settle here, rather than almost anywhere else he could have wished, but what he saw now, the colours at this hour of the day, provided the best he could think of. Behind the road there was a plain, and then the mountains rose abruptly, a majestic backdrop to the jumble of rooftops that was all that could be seen of Xania: the White Mountains, which even now were snow-peaked, but whose rocks shone white throughout the year, hence their name. They were not white now: the setting sun was reflected on their western slopes, lending them a sheen of golden peach. This was offset by the deep green of the lowlands, with citrus groves all the way down to the sea, and then the darker green of olives, scattered across the foothills. Every evening when he watched the sinking sun's shadow flit across the great white sierra, casting up these tableaux of shifting colour, he believed he had found a crossing point to a tragic, flawless world that lay always just beyond his powers of perception.

He stood up in the boat and pulled off his clothes. Diving out from the bow, Cosmo swam underwater for as long as his breath allowed him, surfacing twenty metres from the *Nektar.* The water was cold and deep. He was a confident swimmer and set off without hesitation, at first taking long strokes in a steady crawl, then stopping and treading water. Here he was utterly alone, a small stranded land-creature afloat in deep sea. Along with naked exhilaration, he felt the tremors of a profound vulnerability, the shocking jolt of fear that he sought when diving from the boat. He turned his head towards the shore. From here, the towering mountains, girdled now in rose-pink, seemed to be floating in air above the water. The waves were choppy, and he felt a low wind coursing from the west. The wind thrilled him with a faint, ominous whistling. This being alone in deep water: he could easily believe the sea was inhabited by unknown forces, unseen spirits. All that stealthy movement beneath the surface. A swish of fins. The touch of something cold and smooth on skin.

He started swimming back towards the *Nektar,* which was little more than a distant spot on the seascape, and which disappeared completely when he swam through a trough between waves. As he made his way towards the boat the troughs deepened and the crests of the waves grew higher. The boat didn't get any closer. Cosmo was afraid, but that fear only stimulated him, made him feel more alive. He had chosen to dive into the water, to swim away from the boat. He hadn't said a word to Ruben. Lifting his head between strokes, he noticed that a bank of black and indigo cloud was chasing inland at his shoulder. The sea was turbulent and the world had very quickly darkened, the weather so sharply changed it was as if he had emerged in a different location entirely. He concentrated on his breathing, and on taking long rhythmic strokes. He felt the butterfly flutterings of impending panic in his stomach and knew that he was nothing here, a piece of weightless flotsam. And with each downward plummet after peaking on a wave he sensed the vastness below him, and imagined, in the turbulence, how many sets of eyes the sea held hidden.

How many sets of eyes and what dull shimmering shapes? Christ the awful fear of being dragged, weighted now, down into the deep; the thalassic folds, the great briny, Davy Jones' locker: but what, hey what if that depth were to continue, downward, and the depth of the world was the terrible depth of its oceans, and that the oceans continued down towards and beyond the earth's core, and it was all water, the whole planet a vast pelagic sphere, a watery bubble-planet wheeling through space, the land surfaces mere islands floating on a ball of water, and everything subject to the furious and inhuman thrall of the sea and its salt water – which flows in our veins, and which is also the world – a huge water-bead hurtling through oblivion

He was tiring fast when he heard the faint growl of the *Nektar.* The spotlight was on, raking the area slowly. As he rose on the swell he caught sight of Ruben, standing rigid by the tiller, face tense, scanning the waters closely. Cosmo yelled out and the boat immediately disappeared from view. When he rose on the next wave the *Nektar* was almost on him. Ruben turned the tiller sharply and leaned over the side. Cosmo caught his arm, and scrambled on board, falling exhausted in a heap by the bow-rails.

– Hold this, said Ruben, indicating the tiller.

Cosmo rolled over onto the balls of his feet and sat shivering by the wooden tiller, struggling to keep control of it against the force of the swell. Ruben was back in seconds with a blanket, a long black jersey, and a flagon of raki.

He threw the blanket over Cosmo's shoulders, and took control of the tiller, steering confidently into the troughs and riding the crests.

– We might as well aim to make it back to Xania. No good place to stop off on the way in this weather. Here, First Aid.

Cosmo took a slug from the flagon, and then a long drink of water. He sat up on the deck.

– By the way, thanks, he said.

Ruben clicked his tongue.

– *Che,* I thought you were drowned.

Cosmo felt invigorated by the drink, but was still shivering. He used the blanket to dry himself off, then slipped into his army pants and the big woollen jersey. He took another drink of raki.

– Eat something, man. There should be some food in the hold. It's gonna piss down soon.

The boat plunged through an oncoming breaker and lurched from side to side just as Cosmo grabbed onto the entrance to the hold. He slipped, then regained his balance as the *Nektar* straightened out. Inside he found a plastic box that contained the remains of Ruben's breakfast. He grabbed a handful of salty black olives and a hunk of bread. Clinging to the hand-rail, he sidled back towards the stern. He sat there chewing, still slightly dazed. Then the rain came down, in torrents. Ruben had to raise his voice against the hammering of the rain on the wooden slats of the deck and the crash of water against the bows as they hit a wave.

– Shit. This isn't going to help. You go up front, for ballast. And keep an eye out for rocks, starboard. I don't know how close we are to shore. Try not to get swept over.

It was not yet night but the dense cloud had hastened the onset of darkness: a smouldering violet storm-grey sky and lashing rain that hammered on the deck as Cosmo edged forward. The wind was behind them now, and they were being driven at a pace through water, in the direction of home, their sole concern reaching the harbour ahead of another squall. Cosmo climbed onto the raised section of the prow, and held fast to the rail. The added weight helped to steady the *Nektar,* but every time they passed through a wave he was soaked from head to foot by the wash that crashed over the lowered prow. He turned to watch Ruben, an image of the sea-wracked mariner, wet hair hanging to his shoulders, both arms struggling with the tiller as he steered the boat out of a decline so as to avoid being met side-on by the next wave. Ruben strove always to take the waves head-on. The system worked, up to a point, and the point was to make sure that the *Nektar* could not be rolled by a side-swipe from a big wave. As they approached the island of

Thodoropoulo before the bay of Xania, Cosmo tried to make out smaller rock-shapes ahead and to the right. He stood warily, and turned the spotlight to starboard. There was the promontory and the cliff that lay below the Hotel Marco Polo, but the boat was too far away to be in any danger from outlying rocks. The rain had eased a little, having lost its initial violence, but still came in a steady downpour.

They began to cross the wide entrance to the harbour and were abruptly propelled forward by a new blast of wind from aft, making it too difficult to turn landward without crossing waves at a dangerous tilt. Ruben's face was taut, focussed on a spot just beyond the flashing lighthouse. Cosmo lay forward on his belly, trying to spread his weight. He watched the hypnotic beams from the beacon as they splayed the water, the shock of light passing rapidly around the bay and bouncing back at them from the walls of the ruined Venetian warehouse above the harbour.

Ruben was steering them towards a breach in the harbour wall, a narrow arched waterway of only four metres' width that led directly into the calm waters of the inner haven. It was risky, but the only choice available to them now that the wind had forced them on beyond the main approach.

Once past the lighthouse Cosmo could see the archway carved into the wall. Ruben had taken them wide in order to make a clean run towards it. It was a question of riding a wave and trusting that they were not battered against the stonework while making the approach. They needed to take the first wave that broke, and Ruben did so, the *Nektar* skimming at speed towards the breach. But they seemed to be aimed too far leftwards, and were heading for the wall. Cosmo braced, waiting for the splintering impact, just as Ruben wrenched the tiller with both arms and the *Nektar* straightened out, ploughing through the chaotic water of the short tunnel way, and gliding into the inner harbour unscratched.

Ruben leaned forward and flicked his fingers in front of his face like a conjuror.

– Close enough for you, man?

He laughed and picked up the flagon of raki and uncorked it with his teeth, steering

with his free hand. He took a drink and wiped his mouth on the sleeve of his sweatshirt. He had turned the engine down to that stuttering chug that Cosmo so associated with the *Nektar*; the sound she made at low throttle when starting out and coming home. A cheerful, lazy sort of sound that seemed to make the boat entirely animate, as if she were breathing slower after the exertions of her sprint through the high surf.

Cosmo had the landing rope ready and they steered the last few metres to the *Nektar*'s berth. The harbour was quiet: the nightlife of the town happened further down the quayside. A solitary street lamp illuminated the deck of the boat now, and peering inside to retrieve the catch and the remains of the ice, Cosmo found himself face to face with an enormous angler fish. Its head poked out of a black plastic bin and ice was packed around its body. The fish wore an expression of outrage, and its extended antenna hung across one eye like a loose dreadlock.

Ruben was at his shoulder, beaming.

– You see. I catch a *Beeg* Fish. When you go drown yourself.

– With shrimp?

– Si Señor.

– I didn't know monkfish were partial to shrimp.

– Nor me. Nor did he. What you call it?"

– Monkfish. Angler fish. I don't know if there's a difference.

– Angler fish I understand, said Ruben, tweaking the antenna. But monkfish? He don't look much like a monk to me. Ugly fucking fish. We call it *rape.* Spelled r-a-p-e. Ra-pay.

– Ra-pay. Good. It's quite a catch. But not a shark.

– No. It tastes better than shark.

The bloodshot eyes of the fish glared at them under the flickering of the streetlamp as a passing beam from the lighthouse held it in full spotlight for a split second. The rain had stopped. From a disco further down the quay they heard the pounding of a repeated bass line.

Cosmo retrieved the soaking blanket from the stern of the boat and tossed it across his shoulder. He closed the hatchway to the hold and Ruben pocketed the ignition key. The lighthouse beam once again scanned the houses above them and the ruins of the Venetian warehouse as they stepped off the boat and onto the harbour road.

4. *The Lyrakia*

In the Lyrakia, a session was in progress. A man with eyes shielded by dark glasses was strumming a Cretan lute with mechanical indifference, while at his side an ancient virtuoso with curling moustaches and dressed in mountaineer's black – shirt, breeches and long boots – sawed frenetically on the fiddle resting on his knee.

The Lyrakia was untouched by concessions to the tourist population, but proclaimed its international connections with a display of maps around the walls. Many of these maps would shortly be out of date, representing states and borders which were to dissolve at the end of the decade, or else were re-drawn as arbitrarily as they had been last time around. Some of the maps displayed a decrepitude analogous to the shifting World Order, the wide spaces of the seas piss-coloured with the stains of cigarette smoke, the pinks and blues of dislodged empires muddied into an indistinguishable khaki.

The place was run by the man currently playing the lute,

bad-eye George, who wore dark glasses at all hours of day and night. George was reputed to have inadvertently caused a number of Bad Things to happen to people with his Eye. As a precaution against unintentional accidents, he always wore shades. They lent him the aspect of a *mafioso* quite out of keeping with his laconic nature and scruffy appearance.

Ruben and Cosmo had been here for two hours. Having deposited the bulk of their catch at home, bathed and changed into dry clothes, they had headed for the Lyrakia with a bagful of *gopes,* which they presented to George for general distribution. As they had foreseen, George insisted on first cooking them a plateful of the fish, along with a pile of *spanakopites*, or spinach pies, and a carafe of his finest *proto* raki. Cosmo was stretching back in his chair, aching from his strenuous swim and feeling strangely dislocated from his surroundings. He was listening to a conversation between Igbar, Ruben and two customers from the Unspeakable whom Igbar had brought along with him. More accurately, Cosmo was *watching* one of the newcomers, a young black woman seated alongside the diminutive waiter.

– My *father* was Greek, a Cretan, though he left Crete young. My mother is Somali. And I'm from Cardiff, so that makes me Welsh.

– Somali women don't marry non-Muslims, non-Somalis even, said Igbar, confused.

– My mum was a Catholic, brought up in Aden. Dad worked as a ship's engineer. Their marriage was a consequence of Empire.

– A very happy one, if you are a consequence of the consequence.

Cosmo surmised that the girl was a little tipsy, but not as drunk as Igbar.

– So they wound up with a chip shop in Tiger Bay?

– Yeah, well. A café. That was after Dad stopped working on the ships. Mum ran the café. It was popular with the sailors. Bit rough, like. My primary source of education.

– Girl went to Oxford, said Igbar, as if presenting a protégée to Cosmo.

– Previous And Only Other Person to go to Oxford from my school was in 1947. And in 1975 I was the token prole. She had a voice like gently corroding steel rope. Her education had squeezed much of it out of her, but when she had been drinking her vowels went all over the place. Cosmo had never heard Cardiff spoken before.

– Modern Democracy in Action. Equal Opportunity for All, said Igbar.

– Bollocks. Oxford was *brutal*, honest to God. All that carrot-up-yer-ass posturing.

Again, Igbar interceded.

– Gets a scholarship to Princeton to do doctoral research on Greece. Lovely, isn't it?

– Doing what? asked Cosmo.

– Yannis Ritsos and the phantom of Greekness, the girl answered, in a way that should have sounded like an explanation, but to Cosmo meant nothing at all. Across the table he could hear Ruben engaging the other female newcomer in an animated dissertation of the finer points of dynamiting fish.

There was a break in the music as a different accompanist took up George's lute. The landlord plodded over to their table with a fresh carafe of raki, another portion of fish, and a saucer of peanuts in their salty shells. A man of few words, he slapped Cosmo on the shoulder and wandered off behind the bar. This random delivery of foodstuffs and alcohol was a specialism of George's. It complemented the anarchic atmosphere of the Lyrakia, where bouts of inspired Cretan dancing might sometimes be broken up by fistfights and the smashing of chairs, only to be resolved five minutes later in an orgy of loud reconciliation and raki quaffing.

The girl seated next to Igbar turned abruptly towards Cosmo and smiled. Cosmo, jolted, drew breath.

– Hi, she said. – I'm Alysa.

– What brings you to Xania? Cosmo asked her.

– Working holiday.

God she is so lovely this trembling in the guts has nothing to do with the sea well not that sea out there this parting of airwaves is a giant tide channelling a path between the mountains of water in my chest cavity overspilling on both sides like the parting of the Red Sea it was the Egyptians who were in pursuit perhaps she was their princess then cruel and majestic and terrible and this knowledge this recognition of like by like connects directly between my eyes and her face her eyes and my face. The way a loose strand of hair straggles and she brushes it behind an ear. Like that.

– I've never been quite sure what a working holiday was. You work, but you have fun doing it, or you work so that you can have fun when you're not working?

– Well, Alysa answered slowly, – I don't have to be anywhere, so thought I'd do some research.

That word again. Everyone was doing research these days. Ruben and his photographic cataloguing of the human species. The art collectors and gallery owners and reviewers of his own exhibitions. The Americans and Soviets with their spy satellites and submarines. Even Igbar and his ichthyolgical bloody terminology. He was staring at Alysa's hair, which was tied in loose plaits, fastened by oval wooden beads. Around her neck she wore a golden chain and double axe-head, symbol of Minoan Crete, but also, in these days, of arcane significance for certain women, though Cosmo wasn't sure, precisely, what that significance was.

A part of Cosmo's cognitive apparatus was still riding the waves, a mile from land, but now something like a small ship's propeller was churning through the sea of nerves behind his stomach. He knew he had to speak, but the words, when they came, sounded distant, as though spoken by someone other than himself.

– Deep Hanging Out.

– Pardon?

– What you call research, we call, Ruben that is, my housemate, sitting there attempting to charm your friend; what Ruben, who you haven't been introduced to yet, but who I live with, or rather, speaking hyper-correctly, with whom I live, calls Deep Hanging Out.

Alysa squinted at Cosmo, a half-smile forming.

– Er . . . you mean Café life? Propping up the bar? Soaking in the atmosphere?

– A little more to it than that. You have to Hang Out. Deeply.

– Can you give me an example? The concept is interesting but I would appreciate some elaboration of details.

She leaned over the table at him, grinning now. Eyes like black pits, shining nuts of anthracite. Simmering with secret intelligence. Waiting for him to speak.

– Sure. It's a bit like being an explorer. Or an anthropologist, but definitely without the scientific method and usually without the tape recorder.

– Anthropologist speak with forked tape-recorder.

– Quite. The idea is simply to absorb without judgement or judgementalism. To accept that there's always more than one perspective on what's going on around you. I think I understand that as a painter already. Doing Deep Hanging Out is the Research Element.

Cosmo was very pleased with himself for managing to get the word Research into his explanation, but in getting there he had let slip that he was a painter.

– Oh, of *course*: you're *that* Cosmo, the artist. I read about you in the New York Times. There was a photo. I thought you looked very handsome.

Alysa said this quite without affectation, then laughed nervously and glanced at Cosmo.

– That's nice, he muttered, embarrassed. – I'm almost famous. He hoped she wasn't an Art Groupie. A few months earlier a garrulous student had stalked him, ruining his Christmas. But instinct told him that this girl was safe.

– You know that painting by Velazquez, the Royal Court scene . . .

– *Las Meniñas*?

Of course, she would get it in one.

– Exactly. Where Velazquez brings in the figure of the painter, that is, himself, as an element of the thing being observed. These figures in the Court of Phillip II, the *Infanta* and her dwarves.

– I, er, read an essay about it by Michel Foucault, a French writer and celebrity.

– Ah. Monsieur Foucault! My father knows him well. They take tea together, of a Thursday. He shaves his head. Or is he completely bald? Foucault, not my father, who has a full head of hair and sports a goatee. I haven't read the essay. But in *Las Meniñas* the painter is both actor and audience, observer and observed. Scientific method aims for invisibility. Objectivity. As if. Probably a waste of time, aiming for invisibility. You're always present however hard you try to erase yourself from the equation and your presence changes the thing being observed. The observer's paradox. Heisenberg's principle. So impartiality and invisibility become a kind of mystical quest. You are always present, always complicit in some way. Like the painter in the painting. You watch, but you are being watched even as you watch. This painting shows us how in depth and detail. Deep Hanging Out acknowledges this paradox and doesn't pretend to be what it isn't.

Cosmo felt himself drifting into inarticulacy. He was tired and his body ached, but he carried on talking anyway.

– So you're tired and your body aches, but you're comfortable and the company is good. So you hang about. I mean hang out. Deeply. That's it. Drink some more.

Alysa interpreted this as a directive, which it was not, and filled their glasses.

One of the *Lyrakia's* regulars, a lithe and hirsute brigand named Andreas, was preparing to lead a dance. Tables were pushed aside to clear a space. He linked to the second dancer with a kerchief in his hand and as the music started up, Andreas took the group of four into slow, geometrical orbit around the centre of the room. They swayed in trance-like unison and their feet drew patterns on the ground; simple patterns that became more deliberate, more filled with meaning and intention as the dance progressed. In his long black boots, Andreas held his head high, concentrating exclusively on his movements, in a way which, to Cosmo, was defiantly

Cretan, displaying both dignity and recklessness. His dance was a form of *hubris* – it made the gods ashamed. He was defying them, the gods, by rejecting any lower status that being mortal might confer on him. When Andreas leaped, as he did now, his feet clicking together well above the height of the tables, there was an outright challenge, but no preening self-regard. The high jumps followed one another in succession and then a lowering of the eyes to the ground, a conditional resignation, to pacify the gods, the condition being that he would do it all again, for as long as he could walk or breathe. Pulling away from the outstretched hand of his second dancer, skimming, turning, he joined the tail of the quartet so the dance could continue, with his cousin, Adonis, now taking the lead.

Adonis did not have the athletic grace of Andreas, but there was a quality to his movements that was at once erotic and tragicomic. He could not jump as high as Andreas, perhaps no one on the island could, but what he lacked in physical virtuosity he compensated for in watchability. His face was childlike and he smiled a great deal, unusually among his tribe. He was not smiling now, but neither was he as utterly absorbed in his role of dancer as Andreas had been. He moved smoothly and gently though the steps with feline gravity, as though engaged in a task of love. When he jumped, there was a wild joy to his leap, and the dance for him was not in any way a challenge to the gods, more a celebration of his body, done with pathos; irony even. Finishing his turn as lead, it seemed to Cosmo that the dance was, for Adonis, a way of laughing at the world.

Cosmo watched Alysa watch the dance. She was transfixed. Eyes wide, head raised to see above the heads of people at the next table, she looked very young, but there was something else in her face, a sense of composure, or *belonging*, that unsettled him profoundly. She felt Cosmo's eyes on her and fixed her gaze on the dance.

Cosmo got up and pressed past the crowded tables to the entrance. He needed air. The Lyrakia looked out directly on the harbour. The clouds had passed and there was a half moon high above the black waters. A couple of large fishing boats were berthed here, crewed by Egyptians from Alexandria. Half a dozen of the sailors were outside the Lyrakia, at a table set up on the pavement speaking in Arabic. Cosmo could hear their voices from where he stood, the rasp of their consonants, the thick gutturals. He lit a cigarette and leaned against the wall.

There is something in this woman something fierce and bright something that is not within my understanding but it swirls and hovers on the periphery just out of reach just beyond cognition it excites me and is more than just a little terrible is it anger is it some exquisite but destructive energy flooding off her spilling from her pores in a million frenzied molecules and how do I know that whatever it is it is her body that will express it that much is certain her body her physical being holds this secret fight or flight and bubbling hot and unrelenting perhaps it is a capacity for cruelty why did I think that thought makes my spine shiver and my soul ache perhaps it is this taste of something salty on my lips perhaps it is simply I am tired and she is of a dangerous mettle forbidden fruit perhaps it is the way she looks at me perhaps it is perhaps . . .

– This is a great place, Alysa said, on his return. – I didn't know they still had places like this.

– It's doomed. It'll turned into a disco one day or become a parody of itself, an ethnic funhouse. At the moment it's the last bastion of authenticity in Xania. You know, they don't even sell Coca-Cola here. How many places along this coast, in the world, could you say that of?

– That's good.

– It's good, sure. It's a question of sticking to your roots. George is like that, but he's a dying breed.

– George?

– The owner. Stocky man with shades.

– The dancing is something else.

– The dancing makes me want to weep.

– Is that why you went out?

– I just wanted air.

Cosmo looked around the table. Ruben and Alysa's friend, whose name, he learned, was Jade, were making closer acquaintance. Igbar was engaged in conversation with another long-term resident, Jean-Jacques, about the little island of Gavdos, to the south of Crete. Around them the volume of talk was rising. The air had been electrified by the dance and people in the room were in a state of expectation for the next event.

– Did you know Gavdos was uninhabited for centuries, simply a stopping place for Barbary pirates? Igbar asked Jean-Jacques.

Cosmo looked up. He knew nothing of Gavdos, had only seen it marked on a map.

– The story goes that in the nineteenth century it was settled by a family from Paleochora, in the bottom south west corner of Crete. This is how it happened. The father was the village drunk, and his family didn't know what to do with him. He brought them shame; he kept losing money on wild ventures; he kept passing out. His sons stuck him in a boat and sailed to Gavdos, left him there with just a barrel of water and some food. They intended for him to dry out and they'd come back in a week. It just so happened there was a shipwreck, and some casks of brandy drifted onto the beach where the old man had been abandoned. He woke up to find himself in a drunkard's paradise. Got stuck in. When his sons came back days later, they found their father perfectly wasted, shitfaced, and with no intentions of leaving. They decided that this was their father's destiny, and as he was head of the family, their duty was to be with him. It was God's will. They returned to Crete and picked up their families, their goats, their chickens. Set up home in Gavdos.

Igbar beamed: a wish-fulfilment story.

– Good patriarchal values, said Alysa. The man's a complete loser so the entire family has to move to a desert bloody island and watch him get pissed.

– You make this up? Ruben asked Igbar.

Igbar looked suspicious.

– No. Read it in a book.

– You made it up. It's local history according to Igbar Toff.

– Zoff.

– As you wish. It's a fabrication. A falsehood.

– In a book. *The History of Crete.*

– A book, a myth. *The History of Crete.* Whose history? As if the whole thing could be laid to rest with the use of the, uh, definite article. A rural myth, an insular myth. You are a purveyor of cock and ball.

– Cock and bull.

– Precisely. *Caca de vaca*. Cowshit.

– Why do you do this, Ruben? Why are you so gratuitously rude?

– Because I love you, man.

Igbar moaned and knocked back his drink.

Alysa watched the conversation, eyes darting from Ruben to Igbar and back again.

– Are they always like this? She asked Cosmo.

– Frequently. Then he asked, – Where are you staying?

– Some pension run by a man who looks like he might be a serial killer. The Piraeus?

– Ah yes. A reasonable description of Bad Babis.

– That's reassuring.

Cosmo found a moment of inspiration.

– Would you like to come to a party?

Alysa flicked her hair from her eyes.

– Where?

– Our place. Ruben's and mine. Refreshments provided. Come as you are.

– Sounds all right. I'll ask my friend.

Alysa got up and skirted the table, pulling up a spare chair alongside Jade.

There was a commotion a couple of tables away and a tall, unsteady figure headed towards them. Before Cosmo had time to protest, the Dutch beggar, Kees, had slumped into the chair that Alysa had just vacated. He was in a belligerent mood, but his wish to be considered a commanding presence was undermined by an inability to pronounce words containing the letter R.

– Lend me a hundwed, please, he said. It was not framed as a question.

– That seat is taken, said Cosmo. –All the seats are taken.

Kees began to contest this, then thought better of it.

– Just a hundwed. I *weally* need the money. I owe George. I'm an alcoholic.

– *I'm* an alcoholic, said Igbar, bristling, as though it was a matter of falsely claimed status. –A *waving wino.* But I'm not promoting it as a virtue. And at least I'm not a parasite.

Kees glared at Igbar.

– Calm down now, boys, said Cosmo. – This isn't a competition. I'm not giving you a hundred drachmas, Kees, because I don't like you. Simple. Whether or not you're a parasite is a separate issue, but one that doesn't interest me. I don't care what you are.

This was probably true. Cosmo, on a normal day, usually gave to beggars. He simply had an aversion to Kees, and his shuffling, whining remonstrations.

Kees had helped himself to Cosmo's cigarettes. He leaned back in the chair.

– All of *you* are pasawites, pawasites, he said, struggling.

– Bravo, said Cosmo. – *Now* will you go back to your friends?

Kees didn't budge. Ruben was watching him in a manner that Cosmo recognised. His eyes were sparkling and he was drumming lightly on the table-top with his finger tips. Cosmo didn't want the evening to degenerate into ugly brawling, especially as he had just met Alysa, and particularly in the Lyrakia, where a fight inevitably led to many fights, whether the participants had an interest in the initial altercation or not.

Kees looked around the table.

– I tell you what you are, he said, breathlessly.

– I beg your pardon? asked Igbar.

– These others. This four. His hand waved at Cosmo,

Ruben, Alysa and Jade. The English waiter and the Frenchman I know too. But you four. I know your *woots*.

– Fire away then, said Cosmo. – If you must.

– This might be interesting, muttered Igbar, leaning across Alysa. – The man's an ass.

– You. Kees pointed a quivering finger at Ruben. An Is-wayli intellectual.

Ruben bowed his head, caught, as he was so often, between conflicting desires towards mirth and violence. He nodded at Kees, as though he'd been uncovered.

– You are *I-wish*, Kees went on, pointing at Cosmo. – Probably a tewawist, on the wun. He considered his own pronouncement for a moment, then added: Which is why you are *witch*.

He shook his head sadly, as if the strenuous nature of his psychic revelations were taking their toll.

– You are Jamaican, he informed Alysa. – And Blondie, she is an English wose.

Jade, who was American, stifled a giggle. Kees looked at them, bleary-eyed but proud.

– See. I can tell a person's *woots*. I've been around. On the woad.

– Clearly, said Igbar, you've been around the block. No mistaking that.

– I don't look remotely Jamaican, said Alysa, from across the table. – Who is this creep?

– Now look, said Igbar. You're upsetting the ladies. Run along and bother someone else.

Ruben was measuring up, thinking about it.

George appeared at the table, looking angry. He tipped the back of Kees' chair and the Dutchman went sprawling onto the ground. He got himself up immediately, leaning on the table, but George had him by the arm and ejected him physically through the open doorway to the street. He yelled some choice abuse after him and closed the door.

Alysa had made eye contact with Cosmo and was nodding her head.

– Light entertainment. Let's leave before things get too exciting here, Cosmo said, getting up from his seat. There was still the sound of dispute coming from the group that Kees had re-joined. A couple of women travellers were arguing loudly. One of them was Kees' girlfriend. The other Cosmo did not recognise. Andreas the dancer called out a valediction to Cosmo from further down the room. George was leaning on his broom, a signal that he wanted to close. But he would have to wait: his clientele showed little inclination to move on.

Outside, the half moon cast its reflection on the black water of the harbour. As Cosmo waited for Igbar and Jean-Jacques to buy wine, Alysa slipped her arm around his shoulder. It pleased Cosmo that they were the same height. They walked slowly down the sea-front, past the boatbuilder's yard and past the ruined fort. Their footsteps echoed in the cool night air.

5. *Omalos*

Late the next morning Cosmo and Alysa were drinking coffee on the roof terrace adjoining Cosmo's studio. The sun was high and the Splanzia was busy, or as busy as it ever got. The terrace had a view over a small, dusty square, shaded by a single plane tree. The square was bordered by four or five houses, a brothel, and a long single-storey building with a corrugated tin roof. This last, a mess of breezeblocks and wooden planks, housed a large family of gypsies. Next door, a single-roomed whitewashed cabin provided a home for Igbar. As Cosmo peered down onto this corner of the square an ancient motorcycle with sidecar pulled up. Tassos dismounted and beat on the door. Igbar appeared, shading his eyes against the bright sunlight. He was hungover, as always, but a tumblerful of raki and orange had already kick-started him into working mode. An orange juice mixer was the closest Igbar ever got to a conventional breakfast.

A narrow street curves upward to the town: the other way lies the seafront and the old Venetian fort. Since the streets are little more than alleyways in this quarter there is no noise from traffic, apart from the occasional motorcycle or stuttering *machinaki*, a species of rickshaw powered by a lawnmower engine. From the church of Aghios Nikolaos, the priest's insistent recitation slices through the morning, the ancient amplification system spitting out a crackling soundtrack to a cloudless day.

Cosmo knows this scene as though it were an infallible reality.

A woman sweeps her porchway across the square. Her back is turned, so he cannot see her face. But he can see the face of another woman from one of the red-light houses, who leans from an upstairs window, yawning, and a group of cats who watch one another, tails flicking and eyes blinking in the sun.

Although the sun casts little shadow at this time of day, to walk these narrow streets is to walk in shadow. A man unknown to Cosmo ambles across the little square, carrying a white stick and flicking it from side to side ahead of his path. He seems almost translucent in the bright sunshine, but that is a trick of the light: people who move stealthily act as though they were always in shadow. Cosmo watched him sit on the park's solitary bench and turned to Alysa.

– We could catch the afternoon bus up to Omalos, he said. – Camp out on the plateau, and get to the gorge early, before the coaches arrive. Or we could walk across the mountains, to Sphakia. It's serious walking, that.

– I'd like to see the gorge, said Alysa. – And its famous mountain goats.

– We'll need provisions.

Cosmo lit a cigarette and leaned back, bare feet on the terrace wall. It had been a strange night. Shortly after returning home, he and Alysa had come up to his studio. He had lain down on the studio couch while she inspected his paintings: half a dozen completed canvasses and two large works in progress. A diptych of wildly uncompromising colour, with a density of texture enhanced by strips of gauze, silk, seeds and nutshells, labels, tickets, tobacco, latex, all pasted into the paintwork to create a sculptural effect. He watched her as she moved about the studio, marvelling through half-closed eyes at her easy manner, the brooding quality of her gaze. He felt as though she had put him under the influence of a benign opiate. The exertions of his swim and the soaking he'd received in the storm had brought on a slight fever, and he fell into a deep sleep where he lay. Alysa searched in the small adjoining bedroom for a blanket, covered him, and returned downstairs to join the party. Only when the others had left, and it was apparent that Jade was going to spend the night with Ruben, did she return to the studio, and, leaving Cosmo asleep on the couch, climbed into his empty bed. And it was there that she had awoken, hearing the scrape of his palate knife as he applied thick dabs of acrylic, before turning over and returning to a warm, provocative waking-dream. The next time she awoke, Cosmo was leaning over her, inviting her to step onto the terrace for breakfast. Resisting a strong inclination to pull him into the bed with her, she got up and followed him outside. She felt an almost unbearable anticipation. He excited her, but she decided to hang on, to delay gratification until something burst. And she wanted it to be him to let go first.

She had expressed a desire to go up into the mountains: Omalos was a high plateau surrounded by the snow-capped peaks, and a path led down through the gorge to the Libyan sea.

While Alysa showered, Cosmo took the breakfast things downstairs to the kitchen. Jade and Ruben were sitting at the table, drinking coffee.

– I need to pick up Alysa's stuff from the Hotel Piraeus, Cosmo said to Jade. – Will you come with me? They won't give it to me otherwise. Like Alysa, Jade was a research student at Princeton, where they had been dorm mates. Demure and languorous, she was raised in West Virginia. Her face was feline in its contours, with a broad triangular structure, widely-spaced cheek bones, and framed by auburn hair, cut quite short.

The Hotel Piraeus was only ten minutes' walk from the house. The serial killer was not behind the reception desk, but his nephew was. He refused to charge Cosmo the full rate for three nights, since the room had been unused for one of them. Undeterred by this self-defeating logic, Cosmo settled the bill, and when Jade protested, told her she could buy him lunch at the Unspeakable when he returned from his excursion with Alysa. He carried Alysa's bag, and they started back towards his house.

– How long have you two lived here?

Jade exuded a native inquisitiveness that appealed to Cosmo. She seemed *present* when she spoke to people, maintaining eye contact, as if filtering every new piece of information before storing it for future reference. But that was harsh, he thought; made her sound too calculating. Perhaps it was a part of her intellectual training; or perhaps it was simply a part of her, insatiably curious. He wondered what she had in common with Alysa, other than their studies; what their friendship brought to each of them. They seemed, outwardly, so different: Alysa striking, streetwise, with a quality veering on arrogance; Jade collected, composed;

but, he also intuited, gently, mockingly subversive.

– We've been in the house two years. Ruben was here six months before me though. I found the house and Ruben at about the same time. He'd been sharing Igbar's hovel for a week and was being eaten alive by bugs. I was looking for someone to share the rent. So we did a deal, and Ruben was just right.

– He *seems* just right, she smiled. She stopped on the pavement and removed her backpack, propped it against a wall, and adjusted the shoulder straps.

Cosmo decided to test the waters.

– He's a maniac.

– I daresay. He has that air.

Jade remained impassive.

– He has an army of admirers. Harem-loads of rejected lovers.

– That I can believe. And?

– There are recent rumours that he works for the KGB. The coordinator of a chain of operations stretching from Istanbul to Naples.

– You can't scare me.

Jade was wearing a pale green patterned dress, a colour which returned the observer's gaze to her quite astonishing emerald eyes.

– Tell me Jade, do you have any Irish in you?

– Not that I know of. Hungarian, French, English. A bit of a lot of things. Might well be some Irish knocking about, causing trouble.

– Oh, I think so.

– Would it make me more, let's see, *acceptable*?

– Not at all, at all.

– So, uh, why is it an issue?

– It isn't. Just making conversation. I don't like the crap that goes along with nationalities.

– You don't? It isn't the kind of thing you like or dislike, is it? It's something you're, well, *born* with. Like me being an American. That isn't always easy, you know. Getting stick wherever you go in Europe on account of policies made by my country's government but which I personally oppose. That sucks. Not *everyone* voted for Reagan for Christ's sakes!

– Point taken, said Cosmo.

He liked Jade. He wondered for a moment what would have happened if he had met her first, rather than Alysa, then abandoned the line of thought as it became too complex for him to contemplate. He simultaneously recognised and shied away from that sense of detachment that regarded the women he met, as in the dream world, to be potentially interchangeable, almost as though different refractions of his own personality.

Later, Cosmo and Alysa visited the market, which was shaped like a cross and lay in the middle of the town, between Skridlov Street and the bus station. The market was a vast emporium of scent, sound and colour: the soup stalls with overcrowded tables spilling onto the aisles; butcher shops with carcasses of goat, lamb and offal hanging bloodily from meathooks; herbalists with hanging sheaves of sage, thyme and oregano and fruit barrows laden with plums and citrus. Everywhere, the pervasive aroma of cinnamon and roasting coffee beans. Cosmo and Alysa weaved between the shoppers, and when they had crammed their bags with food for two days' walking, they headed for the station.

Waiting for their bus, Cosmo was greeted by a large,

beaming, and off-duty American sailor, the Courtney whom Igbar had described as harbouring a fondness for pig-nuts. Cosmo knew him as an acquaintance: he was friendly with Ruben and had been around to their house a few times to smoke Ruben's hash. He was an expressive yet laid-back type, with something of the philosopher about him, as well as a glint of the trickster. Cosmo and Courtney had established a bantering camaraderie over previous meetings.

– How ya doin' Mister Cosmo, Miss? He spent a long time taking Alysa in.

– Fine, man. You on shore leave? What am I saying, I forgot: you can't have shore leave cos you never get on those damn boats, sorry, ships – they're just for display. Cardboard cut-out ships, right? Spend the whole time around the bars in town tracking down pussy.

Alysa looked at Cosmo, querulous; raised an eyebrow.

– Ho ho! You're a funny man, Cosmo. Like I get the time for such, uh, *frivolities* when I gotta be defendin' the entire Free World.

Courtney howled at his own joke with such contagious enthusiasm that Cosmo found himself joining in.

– So what you planning on today then? Do a bit of Culture?

– No way. I have *exhausted* all the possibilities of this town's three museums; namely the maritime, the archaeological and the, she-it, I forget the third, it must have been *that* good, man.

Courtney exploded in a second fit of laughter, before recovering his thread.

– Besides, I get a cultural *experience* whenever I happen into you. And every single time I visit that goddam restaurant. In fact right now I think I'll go get me some of your man

Igbar's pig-nuts, and enjoy a glass or two of Amstel beer. Is my amigo Ruben at home by any chance?

– He was, when I left. But he's bound to be going to the restaurant at some point.

Courtney swept a handkerchief across his brow and sighed. It was a warm day. Cosmo picked up his backpack. – Our bus, he said to Courtney, by way of explanation. He stepped down off the pavement and shook Courtney's extended hand.

– Have a good day in town, mate, he said. Paint it red!

– Oh, me; I just want a quiet life, man.

As the Omalos bus pulled out of town Alysa pressed her face to the window, while Cosmo perused a large, unreliable map of the island that he had bought the previous year. On the map villages had been relocated at the whim of the cartographer, streams and rivers burrowed up hillsides and mountain peaks were scattered at random with little regard to their actual geographical position. But it was, incredibly, the only large-scale map available, and Cosmo considered it, at worst, as a coded intelligence test for foolhardy foreigners, and at best, an exercise in the art of the approximate. It was a decidedly Cretan map in this respect, reflecting a healthy scepticism in the face of empirical evidence. History had shown the islanders that fixed points of reference were subject to shift and change, that nothing was permanent, and the map was just another symptom of terminal uncertainty. Cosmo was sure there must be a more accurate British or German equivalent, but guessed that its circulation was limited to the military.

They eventually arrived on the plain of Omalos after a seemingly endless ascent through, first, orange orchards, then olive groves, and finally past a long series of hairpin bends. With the last villages behind them the landscape became rocky and infertile. Occasional shocks of bright red and misspelled anti-American graffiti appeared on strategic roadside cliff-faces: ΕΞΩ ΟΙ ΑΜΕΡΙΚΑΝΟΙ - YANGEES GO HOME. By now the bus was empty apart from Cosmo, Alysa and a couple of shepherds. All four passengers got off outside a café in the middle of the plain, a solitary outpost on the road to the gorge. Within fifteen minutes the bus would be back, laden with tourists and walkers returning to Xania.

The plain of Omalos was an oasis, billiard table green beneath the sheer faces of the surrounding mountain peaks. Cosmo and Alysa took a coffee beneath an overhanging vine, and asked the proprietor to fill two large plastic bottles; one with water and the other with wine. They crossed the narrow road and set off towards a peak on the eastern side of the plain. After walking for twenty minutes they came to a small shepherd's hut. The door was fastened with a padlock that was held in place by a rusty chain. Behind the hut stood a number of large boulders, marking the edge of the plain where it began to rise steeply toward the mountain. The boulders seemed to be growing organically out of the ground, megaliths left behind in some prehistoric cataclysm. The sun had disappeared from view behind the peaks and a chill had fallen on the plain, in prelude to the night.

They had set a blanket on the ground and were beginning to cut into the bread and cheese when a large wolfish dog approached them, sniffing the air. He came close, curious, and not in the least intimidated, investigated Cosmo's army surplus jacket and then raised his head abruptly in response to a loud and piercing whistle. A young shepherd was coming down the hillside to the side of the hut, swinging a crook and moving with long easy strides. He called out a greeting as he passed the hut.

Cosmo returned the greeting, and answered the predictable opening questions that all travellers face in the Greek countryside: *where are you from; what are you doing; where are you going?* The dog had moved away from the bread and cheese and was scratching himself energetically at his master's feet. Once the shepherd had satisfied his curiosity about Cosmo and Alysa, he produced a key from the depths of his coat and unlocked the door of the hut.

– *Ela!* said the man. Come.

He showed them inside. There was a simple bed of upturned crates and mattress and a space in the corner to set a fire. A blackened pot hung on a nail above the ashes, and a small pile of cut logs lay alongside. There was nothing else; no furniture, no lamp.

– It gets cold at night, he said. And there are *kapri.*

– *Kapri?*

– Wild pigs.

– He means boar, whispered Alysa, whose Greek was better than Cosmo's.

– In the morning, lock the door, the shepherd went on, – and leave the key here. He gestured them outside and indicated a loose tile above the doorway.

And then he was gone, the dog loping behind him. He walked quickly, and as far as Cosmo could tell, in a direction where no villages lay. He simply melted away, into the system of evening.

Alysa and Cosmo returned to the blanket and ate the sharp feta cheese and black earthy olives. Cosmo was leaning against a rock and Alysa nestled against him, her back against his chest. He played with her hair and kissed her neck as the first stars began to dot the deepening indigo of the sky. They drank wine straight from the bottle. It was rough and strong, and they took deep draughts.

– You know what? said Cosmo, when the last suds of daylight had been wiped from the sky.

– What's that? She half-turned her head towards him. But she was harbouring a different response to his question inside her head. *You know what? If you don't fuck me soon I'm going to die.*

– I think we should take our clothes off and go to bed.

– Okay, she said. But I want you to undress me. And – here she turned to stare him in the eyes – don't be gentle.

Once they were inside the hut, Cosmo made a fire in the corner with brushwood and added a couple of logs. The smoke was sucked through a vent in the thatched roof. Alysa pushed the door closed and the bare room was transformed into a magical cave, flickering with orange light. She lay back on the bed and Cosmo pulled off her clothes, starting with the white blouse, his hands searching and caressing, her skin glowing copper in the firelight. She grasped his head in her hands, and kissed him deeply, biting his lower lip as he pulled away. He could taste the blood on his tongue. Sliding his hand under her pants, he cupped her warm sex, fingers teasing. She pulled roughly at his arm and he sensed a simmering urgency in her, something close to hunger, closer still to violence.

In the dead of night, the fire now reduced to a few vermilion embers, the door of their cabin crashed open, knocked off its hinges, and was trampled by a hundred-kilo boar. Both Cosmo and Alysa sat up at once, startled out of an exhausted, sex-drenched sleep.

Alysa stared at the intruder, aghast. Seconds later a sow came stampeding through the doorway in search of her mate.

– Sweet Jesus. The boars of bloody Crete.

– Fuck me dead, said Cosmo, an expression he had picked up off Ruben.

The first pig had found the unfinished loaf, which Cosmo had bagged and tied to a nail just above floor level, hoping to keep it from the ants. This, he hadn't foreseen.

– Oy, fuck off.

He shouted the inane insult, climbing from the bed.

The sow, who wasn't eating, looked at him without interest. The boar continued to eat. It made hideous chomping and snorting noises as it demolished the remains of the loaf. When finished, the boar glared up at Cosmo, drool spilling from its jowls. The tusks were nasty-looking. Cosmo felt very naked. He covered his genitals with his hands and jumped back onto the bed.

– Sorry, he said to Alysa, – but I am no hero.

The two of them watched, horrified, as the pigs snuffled and rooted through their bags, which they had left strewn in the far corner of the hut. Aware that the rest of the food would be found also, Cosmo rallied himself for an attack. He looked around for some weapon, a stick, anything, with which to beat the intruders from the room. Finding nothing, he resigned himself to the loss of their provisions.

The boar, however, fortified by food, decided it was time for love. With a prolonged snort, he clambered onto the back of the sow, who let out a shocked squeal. Skidding across the dusty floor of the hut, his front trotters scrambling for purchase on the sow's broad neck, he gave a few brief thrusts and then let himself down onto the ground, sated. As he dismounted he slipped, and rolled onto his side.

– Is that it? asked Alysa. – Bloody typical, that is.

– Ah, come on now, began Cosmo, his pride pricked. – It hardly applies . . .

There was a discarded tin of white beans lying on the ground near the bed and Alysa scooped it up and hurled it at the pig, hitting the back of his head. The pig snorted, disgruntled, and buried his snout in the tin, tempted by a post-coital snack. But the tin was empty, and the pig's snout became lodged deep within it. He tried to ease it free with his front trotters, but only succeeded in wedging it more firmly in place. With a sigh and a muted snort, he turned on his side and fell asleep, the upended tin fixed to his snout, his mouth ajar, a trail of saliva hanging from his jaw. Disgusted, his mate stomped from the hut pausing only to let out a long fart from the doorway, before disappearing back into the night.

Alysa and Cosmo looked at each other and broke down laughing.

– What a *rude* awakening!

– *RUDE,* man. *Pure* rude. Dirty rasclaart.

– I had no idea they were so completely lacking in decorum.

– That's why they're called pigs. Look at that, will you?

The swine had rolled onto his back, front trotters splayed, the can still perched on his snout like a makeshift gas-mask.

Cosmo pulled on his pants and went to feed the fire, hoping that flames might drive the unwanted visitor from the hut. The dry brushwood caught at once and tall flames leaped upward, but the pig only grunted and turned back on his side. Cosmo added a log to the fire and returned to bed, clutching raki and cigarettes. They sat up in bed, drank and smoked, Alysa unzipping Cosmo's fly and resting her hand inside his trousers. But the antics of their visitors prevented either of them from wanting to take things any further. Cosmo fell asleep, drifting into a fragmented and perverted dream, waking shortly before sunrise, when the sow returned in search of her mate. As before, she entered with a noise like a landslide, clattering over the fallen door and burrowing her snout into the boar's chest. He looked up suddenly and got to his feet, the empty can of beans falling from his snout as he did so. Then, turning, he bit the sow savagely on the rump and chased her, screeching and honking through the open entrance, their hooves smashing against the flattened boards of the door as they went.

After this second awakening, Cosmo and Alysa decided it was time to leave. Cosmo boiled some water on the fire for tea. Alysa fetched her rucksack from the corner where the boar had lain. She let out a disgusted groan: the bag was smeared with a snailtrack of pig drool. She reached inside, wincing, for a small pot of honey, from which they added spoonfuls to the brew. Clutching enamel mugs, they went outside and sat against the wall of the hut. To the east the sky was stained with a trace of tiger-lily orange. A cool breeze swept over the plain.

A wooden sign at the entrance to the gorge gave clear warning to visitors in both Greek and English. Among the instructions were:

IT IS FORBIDDING THE INTRODUCTION OF DOGS AND PARROTS

IT IS FORBIDDING THE INTRODUCTION OF DRING AND DROOGS

IT IS FORBIDDING THE NUDISH

– Parrots? asked Alysa.

– There is a lot of paranoia in Greece about parrots. Parrot fever, or psittacosis. There was an article in the *Athens News* about it not long ago. A couple of teenagers in Saloniki were found to have a horde of twenty parrots. They were punished with great severity. Parrots are big crime, apparently.

– But why would anyone want to bring their parrot on a hike down the gorge?

– They wouldn't.

– So why the sign?

– It's a mystery. You tell me. You're half Greek. The Greeks invented logic after all.

– And were not averse to the nudish.

– Not at all. Consider the Olympics.

– And the Minoans did a lot of nudish.

– Well, they had those little skirt things. Personally I blame God. The Orthodox religion. Guilt and shame. Misanthropy, misogyny – both Greek words.

– God has a lot to answer for.

– Those pigs have a lot to answer for. Our sex life may be blighted forever. We won't be able to do anything without remembering *creatures* rutting in the hut.

– I think we'll get over that. Alysa pulled Cosmo close and slid her hands down the back of his trousers and traced a finger along the cleft of his buttocks.

They had arrived long before the first tourist coaches and had a head start down the steep side of the gorge. They walked quickly, the early sun dappling the pathway through the leaves of overhanging trees. By the time they had reached the stream at the bottom they were hungry and breakfasted on what the pigs had left them. They took a quick swim, naked, in icy waters, and continued downward between the majestic, towering cliff-faces on either side.

At midday they found a green spot a way back from the stream, near the ruins of a chapel. The cliffs of the gorge rose sheer to either side of them. Their limbs were aching with the speed of the descent, but they felt good, and the air was clean. They had a siesta beneath a quince tree, sleeping for an hour. However, by now the keener walkers from the tourist coaches had caught up with them, and they no longer felt that they were the only humans in that extraordinary landscape. The loud voices of two blonde hikers broke into their slumber and roused them. They got to their feet, stretched, and set off on the final leg. It was late afternoon by the time they arrived at the small village that lay between the exit from the gorge and the sea.

6. *Ruben and Courtney Make a Deal*

Ruben had spent that previous night engaged in Deep Hanging Out, then progressed to researching Premilitary Activity. While Igbar Zoff treated the existence of a Soviet agent in Xania as a game, whose purpose was to make his life more interesting and promote him in the eyes of the travelling population as something of a *savant*, for Ruben the entire infrastructure of cold war realpolitik had zoomed in on the balance of power in the eastern Mediterranean. He realised that the American Base at Souda was central to any regional military manoeuvres, and for an archivist of the contemporary world such as himself, this was irresistible, more so since he had chosen to make Xania his home.

After spending the early afternoon at the beach, Ruben and Jade had returned home for an energetic siesta. Rising in the evening, Ruben cooked the monkfish, and after eating, they set out for a stroll along the harbour, before deciding to drop in at the Unspeakable for a drink. They arrived to find the place in full swing. As always when the restaurant was busy,

Igbar was flustered, but welcomed them as allies. He was at his best and worst when working under pressure; bemused, laconic and, where the opportunity arose, slyly belligerent.

There was a group of young French backpackers indoors with a New Age travel publication open on their table, guilefully marketed to an audience reared on vagabond chic. It was the only guide to make mention of the Unspeakable, which was a source of considerable amusement to Igbar, given the generally unhealthy appetites and inclinations of his clientele.

– It even refers to the place as *chouette*, he said, hurrying past Ruben with an armful of plates. – Cute: what an epithet for a dive like this.

Ruben and Jade took the only spare table, near the counter, and shared a bottle of beer. Minutes later, Igbar had returned.

– I do envy Cosmo, he said, leaning on their table while waiting for Tassos to fry a portion of squid. – Taking to the hills; striking out on the mountain track. Very wholesome.

Igbar never walked further than half a kilometre at a time if he could avoid it. Less, if there was a bar en route. Ruben could not let this go unremarked.

– When did you last walk in the White Mountains, Igbar?

– Last year, when my sister was visiting.

– They hired a jeep!

– Well, we got there by jeep, yes. Then we walked around for miles, you know.

– Walked around?

– There's a little *kafeneion* up there. For the shepherds.

– So you walked. From the jeep. To the café.

– In a manner of speaking.

– And then back into the jeep.

– What's your point, Ruben? Are you suggesting that I lack your rude health and stamina, or something more nefarious?

– Simply that you are a very idle person.

– Dammit man! I suffer from asthma. My constitution doesn't allow me to enjoy the Great Outdoors as once I did. I can't even walk from my house up to Splanzia Square without a blast on the inhaler.

Igbar, as ever, was rising to the bait, his face turning a nasty shade of purple.

– Hey, Jade said, sweetly. Stop bullying him. You Israeli intellectual.

Ruben guffawed, a full-bellied laugh that ascended into a whoop.

– *Mossad Man*, added Jade, for good measure. *South American Assassin*.

Tears streamed down Ruben's face. He was having a grand time. He reached for the bottle of ouzo on the counter and poured three small glasses.

Tassos called for Igbar to serve more *calamares* and with a scowl at Ruben, the waiter turned and attended to his customers. A group of English tourists were expecting service at the table behind. Apparently, what they thought they had ordered did not correspond with what had been delivered to them. They were a group of four, comprising two couples; contented middle management burghers, intent on enjoying a little local colour. But they were not prepared for the unusual exigencies of the Unspeakable and its unpredictable waiter.

– Excuse me, one of the men called to Igbar as he passed their table.

– One moment, replied Igbar, without turning. I'm

busy.

The customer raised his eyebrows. Igbar did not appear to be busy, at least not in any conventional sense. He had paused at Ruben and Jade's table and was knocking back an ouzo.

The Englishman raised his voice. He clearly believed that Igbar was a *foreigner*, and as such – like dogs and maniacs – would understand him only if the words were delivered at high volume.

– Look here. Do you speak English? *Milas Angleeka?* The phrasebook Greek sounded strangulated.

Igbar's eyes narrowed and he adopted the manner of an erudite pedant.

– Quite well, actually.

– This fish is not a cod-fish.

Igbar turned. He inspected, from a distance, the article of white fish that the customer was prodding with a knife.

– Decidedly not, he replied.

– You told me it was a cod-fish, the customer persisted.

– I told you nothing of the kind. Igbar took time lighting a cigarette, then folded his arms. These were the high-spots of his professional life. – I told you it was a *glossa*.

– *Glossa?*

– Glossa. I would never use the term 'cod-fish' in any case. It is an aberration. I would have said 'cod'. But never cod-*fish*. You must have been reading too many Greek menus.

The man looked at his company, perplexed, and tried a new approach.

– What is this *glossa*?

– What you are eating. And, in a sense, what you are

eating *with*. It means tongue.

– This is a fish.

– But it is shaped like a tongue. Hence its name.

– In English please?

– I beg your pardon?

The man's wife, who resembled an indignant heron, was waving a phrase book under his nose with flapping gestures, indicating a particular phrase with the index finger of her free hand. The man dipped into his shirt pocket for spectacles and read.

– *Tee inay aftoh pisaree*? he managed, laboriously, like a low-IQ military conscript being asked to recite from an advanced weapons manual.

– Um. I imagine it is plaice. Frozen and imported from northern Spain. Technically, however, it should be sole, since 'glossa', that is, the shape of the tongue in its entirety, is something akin to the shape of the sole, that is, the fish, as well as the lower part of a boot or shoe, to which it bears a keen resemblance. In shape, if not in texture. However this is not a sole, but a plaice. The term *glossa* can been used a trifle too loosely, I'll admit. But this is, after all, Greece.

– Are you saying this word *gloss-ah* can mean either a sole or a plaice? Or a tongue. Or a boot. Am I eating a boot? You don't take me for a complete idiot do you?

– Not at all complete, sir. It's a complicated matter.

– The naming of fish is complicated?

– That also. Frequently. Ichthyological terminology is something of a linguistic jungle.

Igbar lingered just long enough to register the terminal confusion on his victim's face, then turned towards the kitchen area to collect another order from the beckoning Tassos.

Ruben wandered through to the back room, visited the infamous washroom, and checked out the clientele on his way back. There was a group of Greek sailors at one table, Maria, a neighbourhood hooker with her companion Stavros, a seedy-looking man with the darting eyes of a shit-house rat, and next to the jukebox, a couple of off-duty American servicemen. He singled out his friend Courtney, an Unspeakable regular, the large sailor from Detroit with a proclivity for pig-nuts, and approached the table.

– Hi fellas, said Ruben.

– Hey, Ruben, said Courtney. Give us five and pull up a seat, man. This is my good friend Marvin.

Ruben shook hands with Marvin.

– Ruben is a *South American*, explained Courtney to his colleague, as though his origins implicated Ruben in an act of felony. – Say, man, I caught sight of your buddy Cosmo today with some black chick up by the bus station. Was she *hot!* She *English*?

Ruben nodded, not prepared to provide Courtney with an account of Alysa's complex roots. – She's Welsh.

Marvin looked puzzled. Courtney came to his rescue.

– Wales is a part of England. Like Scotland, man.

Marvin registered complete and utter incomprehension. Both men had been drinking all afternoon and with Marvin it showed. Ruben decided to address the question uppermost in his mind.

– Tell me Courtney. I was coming back from a swim yesterday and I saw some of your guys, officers, coming up out of a hole in the ground. Just outside of town, near Neachora.

– Hell man, what d'ya expect from officers? Maybe they *live* underground like *moles* and was just comin' up for air.

– But what are they *doin'* down there? They got some kind of brothel hidden underground?

Courtney looked around the room and hushed his voice.

– I'm telling you man, cos you're my buddy. My *Latino Amigo*. They got themselves a noo-cleah shelter, so when them Russkies push the button they goin' ta hide their sweet white asses *underground*, and leave us niggers to face the music an' the winds of hay-ell.

Marvin looked at his ship-mate groggily, wearing a lopsided smile.

– Man, you shouldn't talk like that. This guy ain't *personnel*! You know the rules.

– You questionin' the integrity of my amigo? Or you doubtin' Courtney's *judgement* of good *character?*"

– Aw, hell man. Don' go gettin' sore. Marvin belched and poured more beer.

But Courtney was not so easily placated.

– She-it. You sayin' we should all bend over an' ask Uncle Sam to fuck us in the ass? We slave our guts on some stinkin' tub, and when the pressure gets too hot you watch 'em man, they'll jump ship like mothafuckin' rats. Head straight down their noo-cleah bunker. With all the brass, all the V.I.P's. You think there's gonna be one goddammed nigger down there, boy, you are *deluded*.

Marvin conceded this with a melancholic shaking of his head.

– Too right, man, Courtney continued. – There is a peckin' order in our line of work and you and me are at the place where what you get to peck is jack shit.

– Hey I'm agreein' with you brother. I didn't say

nothin'. Jus you gotta be careful who hears you talk is all.

Courtney scrutinised the back room of the Unspeakable with an exaggerated furrowing of the brow.

– What d'ya see brother? A wino hooker with her pimp. A few Greaseballs on shore leave. What the fuck you so *paranoid* about?

– Cool it, man. I was jus *sayin'*. I was jus' bein' the voice of reasonable caution.

– Well don' bother. Courtney is a man of considerable discretion.

– You boys hang on right there, said Ruben. I'm going to get some more beer.

He returned to his table by the bar, where Jade was chatting with one of the French backpackers, signalled to Tassos, and helped himself to three bottles of Amstel beer from the fridge.

– Hey, my man! said Courtney as Ruben rejoined the sailors and set up the beers. Amstel is the only beer in this goddam country. It ain't *Bud* but sure beats the competition. You ever have a *Fix*?

Ruben nodded.

– Fix, man, said Courtney to Marvin. You imagine callin' a beer a *Fix*? 'Hey guys, let's get down Jimmy's for a Fix!' *Hell!* Ah could never bring myself to ask for one of them. It's jus' a bottle o' suds man. They make it sound like an *inter-venus necessity*.

The two men laughed loudly, causing the Greek sailors at the next table to turn and stare.

– Careful, man, warned Marvin. Musn' go upsetting the Native *Personnel*.

– Our *allies*, man.

Both men laughed again, but more quietly.

– So, Courtney. They offerin' guided tours of this nuclear shelter? You think I might procure a ticket?

– Man you talk kinda funny for a Dago. No offence.

– None taken, buddy.

Courtney lowered his voice.

– You want something doin'? There are limits even to my entrepreneurial skills, but one of the Great American Virtues is that most things are available at a price. What d'ya say?

– Like I said. I'd appreciate a ticket for the subway.

Courtney sat back in his chair, legs sprawling into the space between two rows of tables. He was a big man; long limbed, barrel-chested. His face mustered an expression of Profound Attention, but there was a playfulness about his eyes that ensured the preoccupied pose didn't quite fulfil its purpose. His face gave the message of a physical and existential anomaly: here was a person capable of breaking you in two with his bare hands, but without the slightest intention ever to do so. He toyed with a pack of Lucky Strikes for a few seconds, then looked up.

– So here's the deal, Ruben, my man. You procure for me some fine cocaine, I'll see what I can do.

– You like a snort? I never had you down as one for the charlie. More a drinking man.

Courtney tapped the side of his nose with a forefinger.

– Strictly business. In this life a man gotta make ends meet, you get my drift? The price of ice is runnin' high just now. I happen to know of an officer with a cravin' for a little white powder.

Ruben had contacts, it couldn't be denied. He was surprised, however, at Courtney's intuiting this. Perhaps the sailor had merely assumed that, being a South American,

Ruben would be on friendly terms with Colombian drug barons.

– I'll see what I can do, he said.

– I'll be wanting five grams. That's my fee, replied Courtney, quiet and serious now.

– That's enough to get a man life in this country. Several times over.

– That's my fee, man. It's my ass on the line too. You could be a goddam spy.

Courtney grinned widely, with a display of surprisingly small, fine teeth. Marvin was gazing into his beer as though some profound truth might be found within the contents of the glass.

– And don't go cuttin' it with no *unnecessary* shit, man. Rat poison or Plaster of Paris or shit.

Ruben's face did a 'What you take me for?'

They fixed a day and a time.

7. *A Strange Harvest*

After descending the gorge, Alysa and Cosmo spent the night on the beach a mile outside the village of Aghia Roumeli. They had passed a quiet two hours at a restaurant there, resting their tired feet and watching the day-trippers embark on the boat that would take them up the coast to the resort of Palaeochora.

The beach was deserted where they decided to make camp. Cosmo collected driftwood for a fire and they settled beside it, wrapped together in Cosmo's blanket. Further down the shore lay the ruins of an ancient castle, probably a defence against the pirates who had once made use of this stretch of coast. All that remained of it now was overgrown and abandoned, its sole inhabitants the crows that circled above the battlements in the darkening sky. As the moon rose, they undressed and walked into the sea. They dived in the shallows, surfacing together. Weightless, soundless, Alysa eased her body onto his, enfolding him, and their tongues lapped at each others' skin, tasting the salt on shoulder, neck and lips. She slid more tightly around him, guiding his movements as they swayed slowly in the water, only their heads and shoulders above the surface. The moon shone down on them like a giant magnet, absorbing them in its pool of silvery light.

At sunrise Cosmo re-kindled the fire and filled the long-handled pot with water and herbs. Leaving the infusion to boil he took a quick swim, striding into mercurial water, colder than the night before. After the first icy shock of entrance, he warmed with the movement of his limbs and swam purposefully for a couple of hundred metres. He caught sight of a school of porpoise leaping and skimming through the water at some distance towards the orange furnace of the sun and strained to watch them, but staring towards the sun caused his eyes to smart, and he turned back to the shore. He kneeled by the fire, prepared the tea and sat close to Alysa. She was already awake, watching him. She smiled a greeting, and they sipped their drinks without speaking, at ease in the silence.

The morning's walk involved a steep climb through sparsely-wooded slopes, rising to vertiginous heights above the sea. By mid-morning they had covered enough distance, according to Cosmo's map, to start heading inland, but still the only track led obstinately along the south-facing mountainside. They had entered a world of rock-fall and scree, the consequence of centuries of erosion and landslide. At times the path narrowed to goat-track, bordering on a sheer drop of four hundred metres. From this height the water was a diaphanous turquoise, and Cosmo felt as though they had become the sole inhabitants of a mythic landscape. Even the small, bent and withered trees that had scattered the ascent thus far did not grow here, finding no purchase among the mass of shattered limestone.

And then the meagre track was simply gone. They retraced their steps for ten minutes, but found nothing that resembled a path. They had somehow to negotiate the mountain, and so began clambering over the stacks and shards of scattered rock towards the skyline. The sun was high now, burning down on them like a white contagion, suffocating and dry in the blinding brightness of the rockscape. They stopped to drink from their flasks, conserving their supply of water by washing it around their mouths before swallowing. Cosmo took out the map again and sighed.

– We're lost, huh? said Alysa.

– We're in a real place, but have a fictitious map. I guess that counts as lost.

Alysa tied her locks back from her face with a red and gold cord. She looked radiant. Their predicament did not seem to bother her at all. Cosmo couldn't imagine her losing her poise. Standing against the backdrop of sea and rocky mountain, in blue jeans and khaki shirt, it struck Cosmo that her ancestors might have walked this mountain track five thousand years ago, when it was a densely wooded Eden.

Who were they the Minoan people with those great sloe eyes you get on the ceramic vases and their brown bodies and wasp waists... what did they eat what did they do with their lives four thousand years ago here in these mountains and were there lions then bears wolves. . . did the people stick to the lowlands did they have any fear of invasion were they a people primed for the pursuit of pleasure were they a matriarchy were they peace-loving? . . . it would go against intuition it would go against the grain . . . Minoan civilisation as a lotus-eating paradise didn't tally with the architecture or the era nor even with the geography on an island renowned for its years of hardship and occupation and the ferocity of its fighters . . . were they then a people who lived entirely at peace and what about the symbols the bull's horns or the double-headed axe? . . . the double axe makes me think of the Unspeakable the Two Doors two sides to everything two perspectives two ways in and out doors to different worlds maybe inside-outside world-underworld . . . where does history end and the invention of possible histories begin? . . . is Crete a victim of serial abuse catering now to a new and terrifying expansionism a new world order based on nuclear warheads corporate interests and the baleful dictatorship of cashflow tourism?

– Are you a gift, he asked, continuing his train of thought, – from King Minos?

– A very dangerous speculation, she replied, – given the gifts he gave to others.

– Which were?

– A wooden cow to his wife, so she could climb inside and have sex with a bull that may have been a god. He gave his other daughter, Phaedra, to Theseus, after Ariadne had been swept away by Dionysos. I think he gave his magic dog and javelin to Procris, a most unprincipled hussy, so he could sleep with her. No doubt there's more.

– Then you're an envoy, not a gift. Where did you learn all this stuff?

– We had lessons. There were classes out of school for Greek kids to study the language and culture of the motherland.

– Didn't you have Somali lessons too?

– My mum was a bit of an outsider there. Being brought

up as a Catholic in a mission school in Aden. The Cardiff Somalis took a dim view.

– I see.

– Look, are we going to climb this hill or what? I'd like to find some shade. There's nothing here but rocks.

Eventually, after scrambling over several towers of fallen rock they found a path, which began to weave inland. They left the vista of sea behind and followed a level track between dry-stone walls and groves of gnarled olive. After the white heat of the ascent, this relative verdancy came as a balm to the eyes, and was accompanied by a slight breeze blowing off the higher mountains of the interior.

They had been walking for an hour or so when they made out the whitewashed facades of houses enfolded beneath the mountain to their left. The path forked and they followed a rocky track between low crumbling walls. From a nearby grove, a ferocious barking signalled the approach of a group of half a dozen wild-looking dogs. Cosmo scanned them nervously. He had heard rumours of bands of dogs roaming the mountain areas. One story ran that prior to evacuating the island in the winter of 1944, the occupying forces had let their dogs go free: these fierce dogs had formed packs and, trained to attack, had caused the deaths of several villagers, mainly children. In the intervening years their progeny had been hunted down, but never wiped out.

Approaching, hackles raised, the dogs circled them, running along the low walls at shoulder-height before jumping onto the path to their rear, snarling, goading, worrying their ankles. Cosmo felt a sharp nip on the shin as one dog pushed his chances, and he swung around, making as if to pick a rock from the ground. The dog backed away, but, like the rest of the pack, continued to provide a furious and deafening escort along the path to the village. Alysa and Cosmo walked without hurrying, knowing that any display of fear would incite the dogs further.

Just as Cosmo and Alysa came to the first houses, the dogs vanished into the trees as suddenly as they had appeared. Cosmo was sweating profusely, the muscles in his neck and shoulders tense.

The village showed no signs of life. True, it was afternoon, and people might have been taking a siesta, but Alysa and Cosmo did not pass a living soul. There were twenty or so houses, a church and small schoolhouse, but no sign of any café. They found a well, but there was no bucket or pulley attached, so they sat in the shade of a nearby plane-tree and waited to be noticed, but still nobody appeared from a doorway. However, both of them sensed that they were being watched.

They had a distance to go yet, and unless they pressed on to the village of Anopolis they could easily be out on the mountain pathways when darkness fell. The wild dogs did not make that an appealing prospect.

Again, the map proved misleading, the distance between this village and Anopolis being double that indicated by the scale, but the wild beauty of the landscape more than compensated and they found the thin trickle of a stream to fill their flasks. The path they took was paved in intricate zigzag shapes, small rectangular stones fitting together in a pattern that reminded Cosmo of designs on Aztec masonry. They descended into gullies and crossed dry streambeds, ascending steep paths that wound up almost vertical mountainsides. They passed a white-haired shepherd, carrying a colourful *sakouli*, or woollen knapsack, on his back, ascending the path with a swiftness that quite belied his age. He greeted them and stopped in answer to their question: how far to Anopolis. His answer was 'three cigarettes.' This was a means of measuring distance that Cosmo had come across before with older Cretan men, but he had always resisted the temptation to ask them the question that he now asked Alysa.

– Does that mean three cigarettes smoked one after another, or three cigarettes with a reasonable space between them?

– I think it means one after another, chain smoked. It's a unit of time after all. You can't gauge what a 'reasonable space between them' might mean.

– Okay. I was just wondering. So if it takes five minutes to smoke a cigarette, we should be in Anopolis in fifteen minutes. But we won't be, because we can't see it. And it isn't hiding behind a hill. I've been there before, though not from this direction. So I guess this unit of time makes provision for a reasonable space of time between cigarettes. In fact I have my own theory. One cigarette indicates a unit of between twenty and thirty minutes. Three cigarettes is somewhere between an hour and an hour and a half. That way, you can make allowance for faster or slower walkers.

– I didn't have you down for such a geek.

– This puts you off?

– Kind of, yeah.

– Come on. Let's look at this rationally. Mr Rational, me. Every guidebook or study of rural Greece makes mention of this rather quaint and no doubt expiring custom of measuring distance in cigarettes, but nowhere does anyone question whether the cigarettes are smoked end to end, or with a reasonable space in between. I've asked load of Greeks. They just shrug their shrug, you know. Or they're embarrassed about being considered archaic and twee. But

I'm convinced that the measurement of time in cigarettes make allowance for space *between* cigarettes. What I want to know is: what is a 'reasonable space' between cigarettes?

– What is 'reasonable force' when restraining a prisoner in custody?

– My point exactly.

– What is reasonable?

– What is space?

– No. Oh no. I'm not having that.

– Okay then. I'm having a cigarette. I'm going to sit down on this rock, smoke an Assos *sketo* and then, after a reasonable pause, continue on my way.

The afternoon was edging into cooler evening as they made the approach into Anopolis. Darkness fell quickly and they were grateful for the shelter that the village provided. It was a place of shepherds, many still dressed in the traditional black Cretan outfit with tassled headband and long boots.

The owner of the village café offered them goat meat and bread, washed down with small carafes of raki. A fire burned in the brazier, and with the darkness, the place filled with more shepherds. They sat in twos and threes, smoking. Most of them ignored the blaring television, set high on the wall to the side of the bar. But Cosmo spotted one old man with a white moustache who watched the TV with an angry scowl. The programme was presented by the talentless son of a dead movie star. It involved a banal parade of acts introduced by this inane presenter, himself surrounded by a cluster of half-dressed young women who cooed and coddled him in a simulated state of sexual enchantment. Nobody but this old shepherd was watching the programme. He was trembling in rage, his hands clasping the table's edge, his eyes perplexed. He strained to read some subtitled prattling, then stood, quaking in his leather boots and overcoat. He treated the occupants of the bar, and of the world, to an explosion of furious dialect, and then he left. He, for one, was not embracing compromise.

Cosmo and Alysa were warmed by the meat and strong spirit, and rejecting the café-owner's offer of a room for the night, set out to find a place to sleep under the stars. They had a good sleeping bag and woollen blanket, as well as the prospect of each other for warmth. Walking out of the village towards the east, they soon found a moonlit olive grove.

They wandered through the trees, trying to find a comfortable place to settle. There was a dense growth of weeds and grass in this grove, unusual in itself. Harvested olive groves need to be well weeded, since moisture is scarce and what little remains in the soil is needed by the trees. This orchard had not been farmed for years.

When Cosmo found a soft, flat surface he threw down the sleeping bag and prepared to arrange it on the ground. Alysa was looking about her, thoughtful, preoccupied.

– No, not here.

– It seems as good a place as any.

– And yet . . .

– Go on.

Alysa sat on the ground, hugging her knees.

– Are you cold?

She nodded.

Cosmo unfolded the blanket and draped it over her. He sat down next to her, but she made no attempt to move.

– If you get inside the sleeping bag it'll be warmer.

Alysa was rocking gently back and forth on her heels.

She was quietly crying, tears glistening on her cheeks. He put his arm around her.

– What's up? What's upset you?

Alysa continued with the rocking motion. Her lips were trembling and the tears kept coming. She spoke with difficulty, as though forcing the words out in isolated breaths against a tide of incoming and receding water.

– Sad? Cold? Not a sadness. Not a coldness. Something colder than cold.

And then she was truly crying, great heaving sobs, pressing her face against his shoulder, and shaking her head from side to side.

– We have to move. This is not a place to sleep. I can't explain. I don't know . . .

She stood, leaning heavily on Cosmo. Picking up the rucksack and sleeping bag, Cosmo took her hand and together they left the olive grove. They walked for five minutes and found a small house under construction back towards the village. The ground was white with cement dust, but at least the place provided shelter. And by this stage Alysa seemed impervious to location, impervious to everything. Once they left the grove, she had slumped against Cosmo, as though she had expended some extraordinary effort and now was drained. Wrapped in the sleeping bag, she fell silent, and from her regular slow breathing, Cosmo could tell she was asleep. He pulled the blanket around his shoulders, back against a concrete pillar, and smoked a cigarette. It was only then that he became aware of the barking; from all parts of the plain, between the higher outlying peaks to where the land fell away towards the sea. In this star-vaulted mountain village, the only sound was this outraged, polyphonic concert of dogs.

With the pale grey dawn, while Alysa still slept, Cosmo could wait no longer. He had to return to the olive grove before the full light of day dispelled whatever demons had ambushed Alysa. He walked quickly, because it was colder now. Entering the orchard, he saw that the trees had been allowed to go to ruin. They had been left untended and the broken branches of some dragged like dead limbs across the grass.

He found the spot where they had first thrown down their bags. There was still an imprint in the dewy grass where they had sat. He got down on his hands and knees, guided by instinct rather than any process of reasoning. His hands brushed through the grass and he flicked away twigs and accumulated leaf-mould. Then, like a rare mushroom, whose cold metallic nub pressed into the palm of his hand, he discovered a heavy bronze torpedo shape. He uprooted others as his fingers dug deeper into the cold damp ground. While no expert, he knew that this strange harvest bore no resemblance to the ammunition used by present-day hunters.

These were old machine-gun bullets. Forty years on, artefacts of the last world war lay scattered on the ground even as the island and the world braced for the next.

Whatever happened in this place she has somehow got wind of it how I cannot guess . . . through some peculiar ability to tune into a feeling or to decipher ghosts in an orchard I have no idea . . . in this awful place where the branches scrape the long grass and the sun has not yet cleared the peaks I am kneeling in weeds and in my hand are these heavy little missiles that can cause a person's head to split apart spilling brains and blood and splintered skull and this happened right here once upon a time right where I am kneeling perhaps at this time of day the officer in a hurry to go and get his coffee and schnapps the men grumbling the naked prisoners trembling in the cold but proud the soldiers set up the machine gun here and they faced those trees over there where the Cretans stare arrogant in the face of their killers one of them asks for a glass of wine and to sing a mantinada *before you shoot me and a soldier is dispatched because it is very bad luck to deny a condemned man his last wish so long as that wish is insignificant and unthreatening but what can be the harm in a glass of wine and one of their miserable dirges and the soldier returns with wine and the officer smiles thinly when the prisoner begins to sing he is eighteen years old the other one is more like sixteen but they destroyed property belonging to the Reich and lied about the number of sheep they had and then the younger boy makes a break for it one minute he's there then he's gone how do they do that the men shoot at random through the trees and two set out in lumbering pursuit but the boy is fleet of foot and even with his hands bound has made distance tell leaping flying naked through the orchard how am I going to explain this to the colonel oh shit let the other one have it boys and they cut him to ribbons with the Maschinengewehr and his blood runs and now I can have my schnapps . . .*

He collected the bullets and put them in the top pocket of his jacket. Then he returned to the building-site to sit with Alysa.

8. *Ruben has Several Conversations*

Ruben had left Jade sleeping in order to catch the early morning flight to Athens, and now he could hardly wait to get back to Xania. The city was at its sulphurous worst, percolating a rank and acid stench that assailed him the moment he stepped off the plane. He took a taxi to Koukaki and visited a house shared by two friends, exiles from Argentina like himself, and a Greek chemist from the *Polyteknika*. He then took a Metro into town, intending to visit some other acquaintances for lunch, but half-way there a rush of hormones changed his mind, as he remembered Jade's warm skin and the sleepy kiss she had planted on his lips before he left her that morning. He got off at the next stop, made a quick call from a payphone, cancelled his lunch appointment, and took a taxi to the airport. He had, in any case, achieved what he had set out to do in Koukaki. So it was that he was back in Xania by early evening.

Now Ruben lay with his head resting on Jade's thigh as she stroked his hair and shadows lengthened on the whitewashed walls.

– You get done what you wanted in Athens?

– Mmmmmm. Ruben's tongue was tracing the little channel between Jade's inner thigh and the swell of her *mons veneris*. He lifted his head and kissed her belly button.

– Hate the place, Athens.

– Good. I'm glad you hate it.

– So I came right back.

– I'm glad.

– I got a hard one in the Metro.

– Hard-on.

– That's what I said.

– No, you said *hard one*. The correct term is *hard-on*.

– No kidding?

– Honestly.

– Then I rephrase. On the Metro I experienced a hard-on.

– Yes? Jade's fingers played with his long black hair.

– And that was it.

– You caught an aeroplane because you got a hard-on? What a man! Many would have sought instant relief in some dark and sordid place. But you kept it for me.

– I'm glad you appreciate it.

– Oh I do. You have no idea.

Jade was long-limbed, graceful and used to getting her own way. She appreciated comfort and attention. But Ruben knew, from occasional remote warning signals, that she was not to be crossed. She was one of those people, sweet and demure, whose subversive potential the undiscerning will invariably miss. She spent much of her time reading, curled up on Ruben's bed, but her studiousness was in some ways a subterfuge: at heart she was an unwilling pragmatist. She could hide behind her reading in the same way that a cat avoids confrontation by washing itself. Now, after a couple of hours of vigorous, then lazy sex, she was happy to return to her books for the rest of the evening while Ruben went out to rendezvous with Courtney in the Unspeakable.

On meeting the American, Ruben was relieved to be unburdened of his package. Just carrying the stuff around had been making him nervous all day, and was the second, undisclosed reason he wanted to get back to Xania without delay. He took a stroll with Courtney around the back of the Unspeakable. Courtney took an idle look inside the envelope that Ruben gave him: enough to confirm the presence of the wares. He nodded at Ruben and put the envelope in an inside pocket.

– Aren't you going to check the gear?

– I trust you, man.

Followed by a look that offered the inadvisability of being proved wrong.

He handed Ruben a key and a code that would give him access to a restricted area of the US Military installations on the island of Crete.

– This code, like you tap it into the electronic keyboard on a second trapdoor *inside* of the manhole. Courtney handed Ruben a scrap of paper. – And this is the key to the outer cover, right? Don't ask me how I got this stuff man. I gotta be crazy.

He paused, then added in afterthought, – You're in luck man, they haven't installed laser yet.

Ruben glanced discreetly up and down the street.

– Buy you a beer?

– Thanks, but no. I'm goin back to the base to check out a certain lieutenant before he finds there's something missin' from his bureau. I am not officially here.

– You're AWOL?

– A brief absence only, my security guaranteed. Someone coverin' for me.

It was a clandestine affair, that exchange in the alley. There was a fine rain falling, and while Courtney had not appeared unduly rushed, it was clear that the sailor was anxious. He did not show obvious fear – that would have been against the code – but he was agitated, eyes darting, and there had been something like false bravado in Courtney's claim about his unscheduled absence from the base.

– Are you OK, man? You seem pretty jumpy.

– Hey man, just worryation.

– Worryation?

– Yeah man. Worryation and Botheration. I jus' got a *bad* vibe coming in today.

Courtney was weighing up whether to say more. Ruben watched him closely.

– It's nothin'. Thought this guy was following me is all. An older guy, hitting sixty I guess. Looks in good shape. Thought he was one of our spooks.

– What this guy dress like? Trilby and trenchcoat?

Courtney forced a small laugh.

– Like a regular John Doe. Baseball cap, Yale sweatshirt, jeans. Not so white. Probably Dago blood. No offence.

– None taken.

– But I kinda got it in my head that this guy was *watchin'* me, and I can tell you, that gives me *not* such a good feeling.

– You seen this guy around before?

Courtney shook his head.

– Man, I don't want to seem over *zealous* or nothin' but you haven't *mentioned* this to anyone have you? Not even your buddy, the one with the hot chick?

– Not a soul. My lips are sealed. And my mate's out of town someplace.

– Well that's cool. That's cool. Courtney seemed placated. – You know what, man? I can't wait to get outa this uniform once an' for good. Do my seven years' service, that's two left, save a few bucks, buy a nice little condo down in Florida and watch the sun go down, drinkin' piña coladas. Maybe a couple of fat, happy kids runnin' about the place. An' a sweet chick an' a long stretch of beach in back of the place an' one of them English MGBs for wheels an' maybe I'll do a little business from time to time, but man, I won't have to obey another fuckin' order in my life and for that small mercy I will praise the Lord till the end of my days.

Courtney looked thoughtfully down the road over Ruben's shoulder.

– You sure you're OK?

Courtney nodded. – The only thing I beg of you, with a pretty, pretty please, is that Courtney's name is not dragged into any investigations that might, in the worst case, arise from this, whatever thing it is you plan to do. I am actin' at least partly out of principle here.

– Principle laced with cash.

– You mock my style. *Hasta la vista, amigo.*

– *Hasta luego.*

Ruben returned inside the Unspeakable. He wasn't hungry, but didn't feel like returning home yet. It was late and the restaurant was nearly empty. Tassos was preparing to close up. So Ruben waited for Igbar, and the two of them walked down towards the harbour to get a drink at the Lyrakia.

– That French girl was in here again. Woman, I mean.

Pascale. Canadian boyfriend, unfortunately. But Pascale. God, Ruben. You ever get that feeling? If *only*?

– If only what? If only you were straight?

Igbar ignored the jibe.

– If only. Another time. Another place. Destiny. You never get that?

– No.

– No. I suppose you wouldn't. You're used to women crawling over each other's dead bodies to get to you. She's a drunk, of course. One of those sullen brooding female alkies. Breaks my bloody heart just looking at her.

– If she's a drunk, she probably pisses the bed.

They had passed the harbour square and its crowded cafés, and they took a right along the sea-front. A pandemonium of sounds drifted across the waters of the harbour: disco, pop, heavy metal and the crooning of a Greek balladeer.

– She has a boyfriend then, said Ruben, although he was not really interested.

– Yes. Don't you listen to anything? A tall Canadian.

–Tall, you say?

– Tall. Six two, three.

– Whereas you are short, yeah?

– I'm a tad on the diminutive side, you might say. What's your point? Igbar looked at Ruben suspiciously.

– If you had been tall yourself, would you have bothered to refer to the Canadian as tall?

– Perhaps not. But if I was tall and he were short, *and* he was Pascale's boyfriend, I might have referred to him as 'that short-arse Canadian git.'

– That's the spirit. Very English. Dunkirk. Singapore. Crete. Run away but talk tough. What I'm saying Igbar, *amigo mio*, is that if you were both tall, or both short, or even both of medium stature, you would not have brought height into your assessment of him.

– Probably not. But I still don't follow you.

– Fuck you, Igbar. Of course you do. You call him the 'tall Canadian' as a pre-emptive act of cowardice. You don't like the guy. But your *reasonable* side tells you you ought to make the effort to be civilised. Really you'd like to cut his balls off and ravish this Pascale, right?

– I say. Steady on. That's a bit too South American for me. Besides . .

– Yeah I know. You'd rather be buggering teenage boys.

– That's not what I was going to say. As it happens . . .

– But by calling him the *tall* Canadian you are doing yourself a disservice. You are, like, *disempowering* yourself.

– Christ. I suppose I am. Thanks for that insight. You know what I most dislike about the tall Canadian, Ruben?

– No. What's that?

– He keeps saying: *Oh man, what a crock of shit.*

– A crock of shit?

– Just so. A crock of shit.

– A crock is?

– A lavatory bowl.

– I see. And?

– Well. Whenever he says it, I hope you don't consider this to be invidious, I mean, you're my pal and all that, but, well, whenever he says it . . .

They had reached the Lyrakia. Igbar stood in the doorway, feigning thoughtful, before launching the remainder of his sentence.

– I can't help but think of you.

Ruben pushed Igbar into the noisy, smoky tavern.

The atmosphere of authentic Cretan revelry cheered Ruben immediately. A large and deranged-looking young man with bulging eyes scratched out snatches of half-recognizable tunes on a fiddle while George sustained his usual staid accompaniment on the *lyra*. The music spilled out furious, an orgiastic blend of frenetic rhythms. Ruben bought raki and carried the carafe and two glasses over to a table facing the musicians, where Igbar had taken a seat and was looking absently at a map on the wall.

– You know, he began, as Ruben settled in his chair. – I don't believe the Minoan labyrinth was ever at Knossos. I think that's all a red herring.

– What brings this on?

– Look at the map of Crete.

On the wall facing them a yellow-stained map showed the familiar contours of the island.

– I'm looking.

– Well, the western end, near Kissamos, just to the left of Xania. What does it remind you of?

– Two peninsulas. A large bay. A peninsular on either side.

– No, not a description, you moron. What does the profile remind you of?

– A two finger salute?

– Or a bull's horns, right?

– Or a bull's horns. Just about.

– Seen from above. Seen, let's say, from fifty miles above the earth, the western end of Crete resembles a bull's head. Or the head of a bull-man: the Minotaur.

Ruben would have asked if Igbar was implying that

the 'horns' were first observed by alien visitors, but at that moment he was swept out of his chair by a mountainous human presence, which enfolded him in a bear-hug. The young man who had been playing the fiddle with such furious energy a moment earlier was his friend Crazy Nikos, supposedly on permanent sentry duty or languishing in a military prison.

Nikos deposited Ruben back in his seat and drew up a chair for himself. He yelled an order in Greek and within seconds a full bottle of raki appeared on the table, accompanied by side-dishes of meatballs, feta cheese and cucumber.

Nikos lined up three glasses and splashed the bottle in their direction, raised his glass and said: – To freedom.

– Freedom, muttered Igbar, looking around the room nervously.

– What's up? Asked Ruben.

– Bandits at one o'clock.

– I can't see behind this pillar.

– Theodore, head of security police, and his ape.

Ruben peered around the column. Theodore was an occasional visitor to the Lyrakia, but not a welcome one. He sported a goatee beard and his clothes were studiously informal: white chinos and a short-sleeved navy shirt. At his side, leaning on the bar, was the lumbering shape of Sergeant Spiros.

– They follow you here Niko?

– Huh? No. What the fuck they care about me? I'm just crazy fucking Nikos. I'm a military concern, not civilian.

– Military nightmare, more like.

– Yeah? That's more or less what the Commander said. What is it in English? A *liability*? Petronakis, he said. You are a high risk sailor. A military liability. I could have you court marshalled for this.

– So why didn't he?

– He's my uncle. My second cousin's father. My second uncle. These things still count for something.

Crazy Nikos had spent four years in Montreal before deciding to accept the inevitable; return to Greece, and carry out his military service. But he was a reluctant conscript and his experience of three stints of military prison within the past twenty months had done nothing to chasten him.

– So what's the deal? You turned informer?

– What you saying, Ruben? This guy's my uncle. I give them all the information they need, they let me go with a truckload of sentry duty.

– *All* the information?

Nikos glanced up at Igbar, then said in a stage whisper: – He *safe*?

Ruben considered this for a moment. Igbar was an inveterate drunkard and a gossip.

– No. He's Igbar. You know that.

– Okay. Igbar. You close your ears. Any of this gets out I know you're responsible and I come break your face.

– I don't want to know, Niko. I've just spotted someone. See you guys.

Igbar picked up his drink and wandered over to a table where a blonde woman, who Ruben guessed must be Pascale, was talking in French.

Crazy Nikos pulled his chair closer, hunched over the table, a well-intentioned bear.

– You know the explosives I tell you about before they busted me?

– Sure.

– They make me tell them where I hidden them. The guy who runs the stores, what they call this in English?

– Not sure. Quartermaster?

– This guy, he's doing his head in. Truth is, he's a *malaka*. An idiot Greek jerk-off. He don't know what he got in his stores, what he's missing. He got *no idea* how much explosive I took. So, to make himself look less stupid, which is difficult, he decides to *minimize*. He tells the court he thinks I've stolen such and such a quantity. He's trying to save his face. I say yes sir; that is so. I come over humble peasant fisherman. I tell them I stole the stuff for dynamiting fish!

Ruben looked at Crazy Nikos with new respect.

– And they bought that?

– How I suppose to know? But it made the Quartermaster look not so much a prick, and me, it made my actions, well, *explainable*. My uncle says I always been a tearaway, but a Good Greek Kid at heart. He says I most likely tell the truth; that dynamiting fish was, unfortunately, still practised in my village. Patronised me, sure. The half-wit nephew. But I didn't mind. They say I have to tell them where I stash the explosives, so I do. I lead them there myself.

Nikos looked up, grinning. He was still talking in a low voice, but his glee was transparent and, like everything else about him, infectious. He poured a fresh round of drinks.

– *Sigia!* He said, clinking glasses, and they downed in one.

– But of course you didn't give it all back, huh?

– You read me, my *friendos*. *You* should have been on the investigating committee. I didn't give it all back because I plant it in two different places, and I only show them the stash with the amount the Quartermaster says was missing.

– Interesting. Very interesting. But Niko, why you

telling me this?

Nikos looked around the taverna this time, hushed his voice.

– I think maybe you like to help me make a big bang someplace. Someplace it counts. To show that Greece is not just, just some tourist venue waiting to be fucked over by McDonalds' cowboy culture. To fuck us in the ass with their nuclear warheads.

– *Hombre*, that is quite an assumption you are making.

– It has base on our friendship over these two years. I know what you feel about the bastards. You have your own Junta.

– That might be so. But we hardly have a tourist industry in Argentina. You talking about two separate types of invasion, or you think tourism and NATO bases come to the same thing?

– They're separate, sure, and they're the same. Keep the Reds at bay: feed the people chocolate brownies. It's all the same fucking shit. What is a tourist anyway? Someone who comes and craps all over someone else's country. They rob us of our culture, gradual, slow and clever. Because some Greeks are greedy, it's easy. They think that they are getting rich out of tourism. And, yes, they make some money. There are some very rich people on this island, thanks to tourism. They get rich in money but their souls get poor because along with the land they have sold to build apartment blocks and swimming pools, they have sold their birthright and their culture. Let me tell you, Ruben, something that happened to me when our Colonels' dictatorship was still in power. Yes, *those* bastards.

Nikos spat out a sunflower seed shell on the sawdust-sprinkled floor.

– I was just a kid, in Athens. Wanted to be where the action was. There was a big riot, er, *demonstration*, and the students barricaded themselves in the *Polyteknika* and the Junta ordered the tanks in. There were tanks stationed in front of the main gates, barrels pointing at us. The Cretan singer Nikos Xylouris stood up there and sang Ποτε θα κανει ξαστεριια – you know it, *When will the sky be clear?* And me and the other people, in our hearts we feel a great strength staring our enemy in the face and know that we will win our freedom, whatever we have lost in the years of fascism. When we stood there and the first voices join Xylouris in the chorus, then more voices, more voices until the ground is shaking. Our defiance. Our victory. Staring them in the face. And then, what I thought was the earth shaking from our song, I see that it really *is* shaking, that this tank is coming towards us, straight into the gates. So they won that round, but kids died and the dictatorship was disgraced. Their time was up. Even their buddies in the CIA knew that. So it goes. I'm there in the photograph, standing just below the great Xylouris.

Nikos took a wallet from the back pocket of his jeans and carefully unfolded an old newspaper clipping. He laid it gently on the table between them, firming out the creases with his thumb. On the right of the photograph, a tall, handsome man with long wavy hair and a Cretan moustache was poised in song, his eyes fixed mid distance, his arm extended, exhorting other voices to join him. He was standing on the pillar by the gates to a large building that could be dimly made out in the background. Below him swarmed a throng of young people following an already outmoded dress code based on bellbottoms and banned mini skirts. Nearest to the famous singer, with a toe-hold halfway up the gate, was a figure that could only have been Crazy Nikos, age eighteen, shock-haired, grinning, and making an obscene gesture with his free hand in the direction of an armoured military vehicle that occupied the left side of the picture.

– It makes me real proud to see that. And it reminds me who I am, and why I'm here. Xylouris is dead now, but our government is still selling us out. Every day they sell or give away a little more of what it means to be a Greek. They give the Americans freedom to install their weapons systems on *my* island, they give the go-ahead for a massive tourist programme so that not a stretch of beach in all of Greece is clean, the water clear. They fuck us two ways. Their bombs and our beaches. And us, we're friendly peasants with a donkey and everyone knows the Greek word for foreigner is the same as the word for stranger therefore all foreigners are our guests. Stick that myth in your pipe and smoke it Mister President. Or you get a Vietnam with *mezes*.

– So what exactly are you proposing? Do you have a plan?

Nikos looked startled, then unusually earnest.

– A plan? I have a hundred plans. I want to show the world that Greece is not for sale. But I want a plan that will work. One that will cause them to sit up and *notice*. One that will have the Greeks off their lazy asses about the way that tourists are tearing the flesh from our bodies, rather than, you know how it works, drink ouzo with the husband till he passes out then go off to shag his wife. Cos that's all they want to do, you follow me? But you, I know it, *you* can provide a plan that works.

– I wouldn't make such claims for myself. But thanks anyway.

– Think about it man! You know, you're in the land of heroes.

Nikos had been leaning forward in his seat, his face up close to Ruben's. Now he straightened himself and spat another shell onto the floor.

– It would take more than a well-placed crate of dynamite to force the tourist industry to back out of Greece. Or the Americans to abandon their biggest naval base in the eastern Med, said Ruben.

– Yeah. OK. But what the hell, it would be worth it just to see their faces, no?

Ruben thought: probably not.

– Doesn't it worry you that you might, no let me rephrase that, on your current record, you *would* be caught. And whoever you roped into this.

– No. I'm not gonna get caught. You know, last time, with the ordnance from the Navy, I *wanted* to be caught. So I could return some of the stuff and keep the rest. If someone hadn't made a confession they might have found the real amount of what I took, and discovered the Quartermaster was lying to save his ass. But if we *do* get caught? So what? We'd be national heroes. Come the revolution we'd be like gods!

– No.

– What's that?

– No. Get some other idiot to take part, or stick to dynamiting fish. Or else come up with a *real* plan; something that nobody, not anybody, would expect. But if any plot contains the line 'come the revolution' my answer is No. I'm not interested in rotting in a Greek jail. You're crazy, Crazy Nikos!

– Maybe. But that's not necessarily a disadvantage in my country.

9. *Alysa's Story*

The bus that carried Cosmo and Alysa back to Xania had first to descend the breakneck road between Anopolis and the coastal village of Chora Sfakion. The driver carried out this part of the trip with a recklessness that unsettled Cosmo's stomach. Each time the bus took a descending hairpin the passengers on his and Alysa's side of the bus were left with the sensation of being suspended in mid-air over a deep chasm, before the bus completed the corner and the mountains regrouped around them.

They had taken coffee in the kafeneion of the night before, the chill of the morning air relieved for the shepherds by shots of raki taken between hoarse greetings. Black-clad women waited on a bench outside for the bus to start, baskets at their feet. The driver, grey cap tilted back on his head, was enjoying a high-decibel argument with the bar-owner.

Having descended to Chora Sphakion and deposited several elderly ladies, the bus started to climb again, crossing the central spine of the island. Cosmo still had the machine-gun bullets in his coat pocket. He had been astonished by the absolute certainty of Alysa's intuition the night before: not that she had expressed it as such, far less attributed to it a precise explanation lodged in historical fact. But the bullets had taken care of that. Cosmo fingered the hard cones in his pocket.

– Open your hand, he said.

Alysa obliged, and Cosmo dropped four bullets into her palm. She stared at them for a long time.

– They were on the ground, in the place you didn't want to sleep.

– They're old bullets, right?

– They're machine-gun bullets. You don't use them for shooting rabbits.

– You think it was a killing ground? A place of execution?

– What do you think? Your reaction was, well, *weird.*

– I felt something bad there – a terrible, awful sadness. She held one of the bullets up against the window. – To think they've been lying there in the soil, undisturbed, all these years. She remained silent as the bus crossed an upland plateau: wind-battered trees, a flock of ragged sheep, a brigand shepherd. Parched in summer, snowbound in winter, this was a landscape scoured by the elements, of internecine conflicts and clan feuding, of rustling and of eking out a life from the severe constraints of soil and climate. Even the sheep look wild here, thought Cosmo.

Alysa started talking. No hint of tearfulness in her voice now.

– Cosmo. I want to tell you something I haven't told anyone before.

She paused, staring directly into Cosmo's eyes. He resisted flinching under her gaze.

– Three years ago, soon after I arrived in America, I was approached by a man who claimed to be a friend of my father. I know I haven't talked much about my father. He left us in 1967, when I was ten years old. He went to America, according to my mother, in order to find a job and a place to live: we were to follow once he had some money. That was the story. We heard that he ended up in Brooklyn. There were rumours, malicious I dare say, cooked up by some neighbours in Cardiff, that he was living with another woman. Then he died, quite suddenly, within a year of leaving. So I never really knew him. My mother didn't talk about him, once it was clear he wasn't coming back. That's the kind of woman she is.

– This man, the one who claimed to be my father's friend, was a Greek too. He told me a lot of things about my father. How he had joined the Greek resistance against the Nazis as a very young man, became a member of the Communist Party and continued to fight on their side during the civil war that followed the world war. My father, this man said, was quite a hero. He had fought the Greek Royalists and their British and American allies, gone to prison in 1947, where he was tortured; escaped and joined up again with the pro-communist army before its final defeat. Did you know that it was here in Greece, on Mount Zargos, that the US Air Force used Napalm for the first time, on our soldiers? Many of the dead were only boys, children. Girls, too. I am abbreviating here: the man told me a lot of things, but enough about my father to convince me that he was not making his story up. In any case, why should he?

– Go on.

– After the civil war and the rout of the communist resistance, ELAS, many of my father's comrades fled into

Albania, or Eastern Europe. Some went to Russia. Others were imprisoned for many years, or simply disappeared. Or they were shot. You see, Stalin never gave the Greek communists the support they asked for. He kept advising them to make deals with the Western Allies. Of course, this was partly because he had agreed with the Allies to leave Greece alone, but that wouldn't have been enough to stop Stalin from helping out if it had been in his interests to do so. *He* was more concerned that Yugoslavia had gone its own way and that Tito was encouraging ELAS to do the same in Greece. As it turned out, everyone turned their backs on ELAS: Stalin, Tito and eventually even the Albanians closed their border to ELAS refugees. And when British money dried up in 1948, the USA took over and Greece was primed as an American client state, which is how it's remained, with Souda home-porting the sixth fleet. But that's jumping ahead. What I'm getting at is that after seven years of war, fighting first the Germans, then assorted Right-Wing militias, supported by the Allies and made up of Nazi collaborators, thugs and other prison debris, then the Greek royalist army, my dad found himself a wanted man. Imagine it – you spend your life from age nineteen to twenty-six engaged in a life-and-death struggle, you think of yourself as a freedom fighter, and next thing is you're wanted for treason. My father, and all those people who had fought and suffered under the Germans were betrayed by their so-called allies. The Western powers were so paranoid about communism that they preferred to keep ultra-conservatives or even neo-fascists like the Colonels in power rather than concede any ground to the Red Menace. Anyhow, I discovered that my father was something of an escape artist. He got away. He got hold of false papers, found work as a merchant seaman, and eventually came to Britain, to Cardiff, which was still an important port in those days.

– The coal trade?

– Right. He settled down with my mother and we children were born. Then, eighteen years after the civil war in Greece had ended, he spotted a man in Butetown who he recognized as an informer, a Greek who had switched sides from the communists to the royalists. His alibi, his false identity, was gone. He would be found out, reported to the police, taken back to Greece, where the Colonels had just had their coup, imprisoned, who knows? This is what this guy told me, and I think he was telling the truth.

– Why? What evidence did he have?

– Nothing, like, *incontrovertible*. He showed me photos, some Communist Party bulletins and what he claimed were Commissariat memos. He also told me that, once in the USA, my father had taken the most menial jobs, lived a pretty solitary life, and – she paused here – he would have liked to be able to report that my father died of ill-health and a broken heart, which was the official version; but *he* believed my father had been murdered. 'Poisoned by United States intelligence operatives' were his words. Well, that was the gist of it. I had no way of knowing how much of his story was true. The photos he showed me of my father were mainly taken during the civil war, though there were a few recent ones from New York, including one of him with my father. They had their arms around each others' shoulders and were dancing. They were in a Greek restaurant somewhere in the Bronx, apparently. But as I say, many of the pictures were old, faded and stained, and in nearly all of them my father was carrying a gun. My new acquaintance was with him in two of them. That sealed it for me, that he was probably telling the truth.

– How do you know the photos weren't fakes?

Alysa looked across at him, irritated.

– What is it with you? Why would I expect them to be fakes? What earthly purpose would it serve?

– Well, knowing they were genuine or not might help to establish what this guy's purpose was in tracking you down.

– Would it? I mean, *really*, would it make any difference? The photos were good enough for me. I recognized my father. What is there to fake?

– So there was no agenda behind this guy? He didn't want you to do anything for him? I mean, why was he getting in touch with you?

– They were brothers in arms. He said that while he was fighting alongside my dad in the civil war, they had made a pact that if either of them were killed, the other would go out of their way to inform their family themselves, so that the information didn't come from some anonymous official. Of course my dad didn't have a family of his own then, they were talking about parents, sweethearts et cetera. But the guy reckoned that he was sticking to their agreement by finding me and telling me what he knew. So far as he is concerned, the war isn't over. The pact he made with Dad still applies: Dad was murdered, he said, because of his political beliefs and because he had links with agencies opposed to the United States Government. So he had come to find me, in line with their agreement.

– So is this guy a spy? He's working for the Soviets? Like your dad was?

– Fuck, Cosmo. Why do you have to make that sound so, so *dirty?* A person has a set of principles and he lives by them. He sees the world poised between the opposing forces of communism and rampant capitalism and he makes a stand for what he believes is best. What's wrong with that? In the Greek civil war people had to make a stand, be counted. You were either on one side or the other. There was very little space for the undecided. So you either worked for the Imperialists or the Reds. Simple. The Brits and the Americans understood that, at least. They didn't cut our people any slack. This guy told me he was with Dad when they were captured by the Royalists. There was another man with them, a young politico, rising star in the Party, a Central Committee man. Their train stopped at some station in Macedonia and the prisoners were bundled out, I mean the *kapetanos*, the leaders. Him, my Dad, and this young guy from Communist Party HQ. In the station waiting room were a group of Royalist officers and a foreigner. The foreigner didn't wear a uniform; he was from British Secret Services. One of the regular army guys begins to interrogate the Party man. The three other prisoners have to watch. The Party man gives nothing away. So they start on his eyes. They take out his fucking *eyes* in front of his comrades, who of course are under armed guard and can't do a thing. The British agent just watched the whole thing, impervious. They destroyed the guy's face, then, when he still wouldn't talk, they shot him. They dumped his body in the river that ran alongside the station.

Cosmo heard the emotion in Alsysa's telling of the story, and felt a twinge of shame at the belligerent skepticism he had just expressed.

– I didn't know about any of this. I mean, in Crete, I thought the Germans left and people got on with their lives. The civil war wasn't big here, was it?

– Much of the fighting took place in the north and the

Peleponnese. Crete avoided most of the unpleasantness of that, though divisions still ran deep within communities, still do for that matter. But, you know, it's very odd: no one in Britain or America talks about the Greek civil war. It was as much a prologue to the cold war as the Spanish war was to World War Two, yet it's not spoken of in the same hushed tones as the Spanish war, with a clear idea of good and evil, right and wrong. That's because the Brits and the Americans supported the reactionaries, the Royalists, and stabbed many of our people, their so-called allies, in the back. A lot of those partisans did not consider themselves communists at first, simply freedom fighters. The way that Churchill, Truman and Stalin carved up Eastern Europe meant that Greece went under the protection, if that's the word, of the Western Allies, and they set out systematically to destroy the very forces which had formed the bedrock of resistance to the Nazis. I'm telling you this so that maybe you can understand how I felt seeing these photos. My father, on horseback, a *kapetan* of partisans, somewhere in the north of Greece. Even behind the big beard I recognized my father. His eyes were quite unique. Cretan eyes. I see those eyes everywhere now that I'm in Crete. Tassos in the Unspeakable has those same eyes. Anyhow, I also learned that my father had remained loyal to his principles, and had never relinquished his dream of a just society based on the Marxist-Leninist ideal. So much for that.

Alysa was gazing out of the window at the distant sea. The bus took yet another hairpin and began its long descent to the coast. Cosmo knew that he had angered her. He felt naïve, because he knew so little of the history. But he was also stubborn, and by questioning the veracity of the story presented to her by a stranger, he realized he was, in some way, taking a swipe at her father and his beliefs, not merely compensating for his own ignorance of the political affiliations that seemed to preoccupy Alysa. He could grasp the emotional dimension of her anger: their experience in the olive grove had spooked her, and she had immediately related it to stories this spy had told her (as well as other fantasies that she had no doubt elaborated out of these stories) about her father and his years as a partisan. Cosmo had an innate distrust of political diehards of any description, and, as ever giving way to his intuitions, he felt that something about the story was not quite right, and he wasn't sure what it was.

– That must have been a shock to you, arriving in the States and inadvertently finding out about your father.

– I'm not so sure how inadvertent it was. I intended looking for some clues, anything, about my dad in America. I was twenty-one, and was living my own life.

– How was the States, other than you meeting this guy who knew your dad?

– Complicated. Princeton itself was a very protected community. Wasn't relevant at all to the stuff I was finding out about Greece and my father. I had arrived in the States with some trepidation. I guess that's the word. I was a black woman, and although Cardiff docks wasn't a such a bad place, I'd grown up in a racist society. When I was twelve some white kids beat me up. On the street, middle of Cardiff, place called Canton. I'd never even seen them before. I knew the score though: I wasn't going under. I enrolled for Martial Arts classes, and eventually got a black belt in Karate and then, later, in Aikido. Made sure, at least, that I could handle myself. Then I dabbled with a Trotskyist group at Oxford, but found it all a bit implausible. Middle-class white kids playing at revolution. I wished, I truly wished, I had the conviction of my father, or of what this guy said about my father. I couldn't really verify his story but it did add up. Like I say, I wished, in a way, that I had it within me to act out of conviction, and a sense of loyalty to Dad. I had always wanted a father, and having this idealized portrait of a dead father was even better than having a live father who wasn't a hero, and certainly better than no father at all. It was a difficult time for me, learning about this man I hardly knew. I had felt so angry towards my father; but after hearing about his past I felt I understood his behaviour better and I think that's why I came back, came here, to Crete. My father called me. I suppose these bullets are here to remind me that a part of me recognized what had happened in that place, that a part of you always remembers, guarding the things you think you have forgotten or have no way of remembering.

A few minutes later, when Cosmo turned to talk to her, Alysa was asleep.

Back home, Cosmo set to work with a new idea for a painting and continued straight through the afternoon and into the evening; and would have worked into the night had Ruben not called him down to eat. He embraced his friend, and sat down to table with the women while Ruben served up a stew of lamb, lentils and potato. He drank two glasses of wine straight down and ate his stew hungrily, refilling the bowl before speaking.

– Mountain air, he explained, gesturing at his bowl.

– We heard, said Jade, about your night of passion.

Cosmo looked up at Alysa and grunted, a mild admonition.

– Everything?

– Of course not, said Alysa. Just the pigs.

– The pigs were enough, hey, said Cosmo, dunking a crust of bread.

Ruben, elbows on the table, produced a mocking smile.

– Christ, I don't know how you can live with yourself, man. Why didn't you beat them with a stick, drive them out?

– *Hombre*, fuck off. These pigs were big. Immense.

– Sorry, mate. Ruben mimicked Cosmo's own inflections. – No way. You just didn't have the bottle.

– Yeah, yeah. Like you would've *head-butted* the fuckers. Got down to a bit of Turkish wrestling with the chief porker. I can see you there, rolling in the dirt, giving it a bit of hand to trotter combat. Bleeding Che Guevara. Then ripping them both to rashers with your fucking Kalashnikov.

– Why don't you big boys go and have a pint together? Said Alysa, with a sigh. – Do some bonding. Have a punch-up, whatever it is men do. Jade and I want a chat. Girl talk.

– I was going to suggest the same thing to Cosmo, said Ruben. But I'm working on some pictures right now. I need to spend an hour in the darkroom first.

– OK. I'll take a stroll down to the Lyrakia, and meet up with you there.

Cosmo fetched a sketch-book from his studio, and a couple of pencils. He felt like keeping up his momentum, making sure the flow of ideas did not atrophy.

10. Underground

At the end of the street he headed towards the harbour. Once inside the Lyrakia, he stretched out at his favourite table, under a large scale map of Newfoundland, with a saucer of nuts and a carafe of raki. He drew some luridly pornographic images as he daydreamed. Flying phalluses hovered over swollen vulvae. Various sexual conjugations were detailed with no concession to understatement.

– Excuse me. Can I sit here?

Cosmo looked up to see a young man, barely out of his teens, with an infectious smile and long untidy brown hair, dressed in blue jeans and a white granddad shirt.

– Help yourself, said Cosmo, folding his sketchbook and putting it to one side.

The young man, whose name was Lucas, said he was there to listen to the music. He was a student of composition and had a lot to say about lesser-known traditional forms of improvisation. Cosmo listened, though the words and their meaning largely passed him by. Lucas explained that the combination of lute and *lyra* was dying out in places other than the mountains of western Crete. Tonight there was a *lyra* player that Cosmo didn't recognise, apparently a star performer. He was not on yet, but was talking with Andreas the dancer at the end of the bar. The Lyrakia was more crowded than usual - it was not ten o'clock and the place was heaving. Word must have got out about this evening's performance.

– He's got an incredible rawness to his playing. I heard him in Rethymnon. He's very fast, but not showy. Fluffs plenty of notes, but it doesn't seem to matter because of the energy and the soul. Sometimes it sounds like a fusion of Indian and Irish music. Though different from either of them. Similar, but different.

– And geographically, I guess, halfway between India and Ireland.

– Geographically and mythically.

– Huh?

– There's this massive wave of stories that appear in various versions, in different ways, from the Ganges to the Shannon. Myths telling similar stories holding the same properties. Crete was the passing place, the crossing over place of these myths. Of course, a lot of the myths have to do with bulls. There's the Minotaur, obviously, and in Ireland there's the two bulls in the *Táin*: the White Bull of Connacht and the Brown Bull of Ulster. Bull culture must have spread westward, across the Mediterranean, into Gaul, then Iberia, home of the modern bullfight. May I have a look? He had his hand on Cosmo's sketchbook.

Cosmo shrugged, nodded.

Lucas flicked through a few pages, lingered on the last with a creased smile, and looked up from the sketchbook without comment. Cosmo took a keener interest in his new acquaintance.

– Know any bull stories, Lucas?

– Bull stories are the oldest stories around, said Lucas. He pulled himself upright in his seat. – Zeus wanting to shag in a bull's form. Women shagging bulls. Bulls shagging women dressed up as cows. Bulls shagging . . .

– Is that it? The bulls are nothing more than a potency symbol? Raw macho energy?

– No. There's a whole lot more. It gets quite complicated.

– You shitting me?

– No, honest. The bull is the key symbol of natural power to a herding culture. The tribes that moved down through the Balkans in the centuries before the Classical era were nomadic herders. Perhaps it's obvious our European myths should derive from theirs. Sumerian bull-culture, Cretan bull-culture. And sacrifice. Did you know that the Cretan kings are always represented in Minoan art as being young men, like, not much more than twenty years old? If I was a Cretan king I'd be approaching my sell-by date now, because the king would be sacrificed every cycle of the planet Venus. That is, every eight years. What do you make of that?

– Sounds like the women had the whole thing sorted. Hey, I want to know about bulls. I mean, I know the basic stuff about the Minotaur, how his father was a bull and his mother Queen to King Minos, and how Minos himself was supposed to have been sired by Zeus, also disguised as a bull. But where do these myths come from? Did someone sit down one day and make them up, or are they a part of some kind of collective imagining? And why am I asking you?

– Because you have a vague memory of meeting me before, perhaps? Crete is a stopping off place. All these people, on the way to somewhere else, stopping off and getting stuck here. Like stepping inside a labyrinth. It does something to the mind. You've seen me here, but we haven't spoken. And because Crete is that kind of place, where perceptions become blurred, you have forgotten me, that's all.

– A stopping off place, like a crossroads. A haven for itinerants. Do you think a place can change its defining role? I mean, that's precisely what it is now, still, has always been.

– A crossroads?

– Yeah. Like a *Zone*. Do you know what I mean? The gods still walk here. Bulls and stuff; wounding, sacrifice, bloodshed. Loss. It's woven into the history so tightly in Crete.

– Perhaps that's why we've come.

– You say that a lot.

– What?

– Perhaps.

Cosmo was feeling the effects of the raki quickly. This happened to him after working for a spell: it was as if his tolerance diminished and he became more sensitive to every influence, every slightest variation in the chemical or tactile or erotic ambience. As a rule, he allowed himself to be swept along benignly as his speech and motor faculties fell apart, but on this occasion he was not going to be left in peace. Crazy Nikos appeared, as unobtrusive as a freak typhoon, gesticulating and bellowing, and pulled up a seat at his side, along with a young Athenian woman, Loula, who enjoyed a local reputation as a *femme fatale*. Cosmo had slept with her once, during the winter, and although they had parted amicably, she had not returned to his house, rather to Cosmo's relief, although she had later tapped him for a thousand drachmae, which she never returned.

Nikos was beginning a scatological rant about tourism being a mafia racket, a variation which must have only recently occurred to him as he gave vent to his fury with the passion of a neophyte. He turned to Cosmo in order to press another point home.

– You know the movie *Midnight Express* was funded by the Greek tourist board? He demanded, indignant.

Cosmo, who had no idea what he was talking about, nodded solemnly. He could see Ruben beckoning to him from the doorway. He bade farewell to his company, and stepped outside.

– What's up? Cosmo asked, once they had rounded the harbour and were walking along the tarpaulined promenade that led away to the west of the city.

– I need to bring you up to date. Pig-nut man has procured me a magic key for the underground shelter.

– Whoah. You act fast. What did he want for it? Your soul?

– Score some charlie.

– Man, you're taking this way too seriously.

Ruben didn't answer, and Cosmo sensed the rebuke in his silence. They were approaching the turn in the road close to the Marco Polo Hotel. Past it, a thin line of trees followed the street towards Neachora under flickering orange street lights. A dilapidated house with a colonial façade stood in front of them, and to the left, the building site where they had seen the American officers emerge from the ground.

They pushed past the makeshift fence that marked the

building site off from the road. Two empty oil drums had been rolled over the hatchway, so they moved them aside, and saw the glint of new metal on the manhole. The street-lighting barely reached the building site. Ruben felt in his jacket pocket for the compact flashlight that he had brought, and handed it to Cosmo, then squatted on his haunches and found the keyhole. The key turned easily and he lifted the cover. He lowered himself down and called up to Cosmo.

– There's room to stand here. Pass me the torch and close the cover. I want to see if I can get out from this side without the key.

Evidently he could, because a few seconds later the cover rose and Ruben's head surfaced. He was grinning.

– You coming down?

Just then, the questing eye of the lighthouse swept over Cosmo and he watched the smooth passage of its beam as it sped across the bay. The alcohol Cosmo had consumed drained out of him on a gust of sea air.

Twenty metres away, in the shadow of a small cedar, eyes watched him slide into the vault.

Below them lay another trapdoor, with the digits 0 to 9 set into a luminous pad. Ruben tapped out the number he had memorized and pulled back the cover. This was a heavier and more sophisticated device than the one that led to ground level. When Cosmo peered down he saw a short ladder and then a tunnel, illuminated by small green lights set into the walls. He wondered if the lights had been switched on by opening the trapdoor. Ruben turned to him, smiling.

– Hey, *Gringo*. How about we do a line?

– Fine by me.

They sat on the floor near one of the embedded lights with their backs against the wall and Ruben produced a small plastic bag of white powder and a razor blade from his wallet. He carefully arranged two generous lines on the back of the small leather notebook he always carried with him and rolled a thousand drachma note into a tight tube.

He snorted his line in two sharp bursts and passed the notebook to Cosmo with both hands. Cosmo re-rolled the banknote and ingested in turn. A bitter taste hit the back of his throat and he felt the throb of hot blood in his veins as his pulse quickened. He swallowed deeply, wishing he had brought water with him.

– This part of the consignment to the US Navy?

– Si, señor.

– So you ripped them off?

– Now, *hombre*, that is harsh. I took commission is all.

– Commission. That's a posh term.

– A legitimate cut. You know – like sulphate from those Greek slimming pills you munch up when you're painting all night, plus baking powder, chalk, that kind of shit.

– Was that wise? I mean, you think you can handle pig-nut man? He's built like a brick shithouse.

Ruben laughed, too loud. Then, calming himself, he said, – as I've explained, the charlie isn't for pig-nut man, it's for an officer. Now the stuff we have just sampled is good, right? Class gear.

– It's pretty good.

– Right. Fucking good. Admit it's fucking good.

– It's OK.

– No, it's. Fucking. Good.

– It's passable.

– So if you were this officer, and you receive something

like seventy percent this good and thirty percent cake mixture, you gonna complain? Who to? Mr Shit Brickhouse Courtney?

– Brick shithouse.

– I rest my case. What's he gonna do? Court-marshal Courtney for selling him dodgy coke? Give me a break.

The invented scenario of the court-marshal seemed to amuse Ruben greatly. He started again, helpless with laughter, thumping the ground with the flat of his hand as tears trickled down his cheeks. Cosmo smiled, a little nervously.

The tunnel descended at a slight but noticeable decline, heading inland. Fairy lighting studded their passage and Ruben flicked off the torch. After a hundred metres, the passage forked. The way to the right, punctuated still with green lights, veered sharply, seeming to double back in the direction of the coast. To the left, the passageway was lit in red and it was this path that they took, Cosmo wondering what precisely his friend had in mind by coming here. Surely, he asked Ruben, it was not enough simply to have accomplished the entrance. He must have some plan, otherwise why go to the trouble and expense of procuring the key from Courtney?

– I want to see what's down here, then decide, Ruben answered, without slowing. And at once, the passage widened into a large circular space. Subsidiary paths led off from this nexus, and there were four doors set at intervals along the circumference. Ruben tried the first door. It was dark inside. He flashed his torch and found a switch on the wall. Strip-lighting revealed a row of bunks, and at the back of the dormitory was a washroom.

– For the guards? Ruben suggested. – I imagine the top guys don't sleep in bunk-rooms.

They tried the other doors in turn. One contained stores: carton after carton of tinned meat and fruit; dried noodles and pasta, chocolate and a truckload of coca-cola cans.

– Uncle Sam's pantry, sneered Ruben, picking up a monster jar of peanut butter. – Think this stuff will ever get used?

– How long does peanut butter last? Cosmo tried to read the label under the flashlight's beam. – I can't see a sell-by date.

Ruben was taking photos with a compact camera. When he'd finished shooting, he leaned against the doorway of the storeroom, arms folded.

– An anthropologist, staying with a group of isolated, very unfriendly Indians somewhere up the Orinoco, was relieved of all his provisions by the natives he had come to study. They stole the lot, first night he was there. Everything except the peanut butter. Know why? They thought it was monkey shit.

– No kidding.

– God's honest truth.

– But it doesn't answer the question. How long does peanut butter last?

– It lasts for ever. Let's have a look down here.

Ruben took the tunnel out of the concourse area, following a further set of red stud-lights. As the two descended further, complete silence settled about them. It was an impenetrable space down there, and its lack of occupation, its dereliction of human life, seemed to make it more oppressive than even the thousands of tonnes of rock and soil that lay above them could account for. Here they were locked inside the earth's unwelcoming gut. The town's busy tavernas and the night breeze blowing in from the sea seemed very distant from this aluminum and formica netherworld.

Jesus this place is uncanny like a science fiction movie that one by Tarkovksy I thought just for a second there I saw my dead granddad in his red waistcoat and slippers trying to open a can of fucking beans with a Sweet Afton poking out his gob and that's not the coke that's this place shit I'm sweating and I have the fear that disinfectant hospital fear that eats at the bowels just what is this place about and I can feel them around me as though they are the ghosts of the future well why not why do ghosts always have to be confined to the past clanking around in armour or descending stairs in Victorian gowns no these intimations these shadows that keep flitting by just out of my line of sight belong distinctly to the things that have not yet happened in our normal understanding of time passing time past time present time future in a line oh no in these places there is none of these time is one vast ocean and there isn't a backwards or a forwards we are fed a line about the forward movement of time because it corresponds with our fucked up ideas of progress and evolution of time going someplace just as you go on a journey somewhere but time goes nowhere time isn't anything we are scattered dropped deposited in this this lets call it time but really there is no time only space and in this space there is an awful sense of bad things going to happen

As they followed the tunnel, it became clear that the shelter was a far more labyrinthine construction than either of them could have imagined. Unlighted passageways led off from the main tunnel and Ruben stopped to inspect one such artery with his flashlight. They followed the subsidiary passage for twenty or thirty metres. Ruben flashed his torch over the surface, and grabbed Cosmo's arm.

– Look at that!

The walls of the tunnel were ancient. Massive blocks of square rock had been placed end on end and the ceiling of the tunnel was not arched but joined by huge stones serving as plinths across the width of the passageway.

– That would explain how they could build this thing without drawing too much attention, said Ruben.

– What do you mean?

– Piles of rock and debris at the surface. Lorries loaded with rubble. Perhaps the gringos didn't need to dig at all.

– You mean the tunnels were already here?

– Precisely. All they did was plaster and paint the tunnels near the entrance. The rest of the excavation had already been done for them.

– In Minoan times. Jesus.

– These big square stones. Where else do you get them? Knossos, Phaistos; Mycenae too, I think.

– They discovered a Minoan tunnel system and turned it into a nuclear shelter?

– Looks that way.

– Christ almighty. The effects of the cocaine were making it difficult for Cosmo to take this in, or express himself coherently. His brain was busy making connections at a frantic speed.

– Who knows where these tunnels might lead?

Ruben was examining the upper structure of the tunnel, and the beam from his torch lit up his face as he peered upwards. Cosmo watched him, his lips turned in a curious smile.

– Hey, Ruben. You think we might find a Minotaur?

Ruben looked at his friend quizzically.

– The Minotaur was a Mythical Creature, my friend.

– Granted. But we might find some spores. A little dung perhaps.

– Bullshit.

– That sort of thing.

– But it does raise questions of another nature.

– Enlighten me.

– The other night Igbar was sounding off about twin horns. How, from space, the west of Crete presents this weird, what was his word? Profile. I think he might have been saying that the island itself, by means of its shape, represents the symbol of the horns.

– How so?

– *Che*, Cosmo, get with it, man. The horns. The labyrinth. The peninsulas of Western Crete. Igbar reckons that Sir Arthur Evans, with his multi-coloured funhouse at Knossos, was looking in the wrong place. Ancient Crete, says Igbar, was a country with a hundred cities. According to someone. Homer? So Evans simply found one palace. One city, let's say. Where are all the rest?

– But the cities were not mazes.

– Perhaps not, but what do we know for sure? For all we know, every city was a labyrinth, or else the entire island is crisscrossed by an enormous labyrinth under the surface. Or a hundred mazes like this, unconnected.

– They called their mazes cities? And lived in labyrinths? Cosmo was taken with this idea. So what does Igbar say about the palace at Knossos?

– That it was like a metaphor, a religious metaphor: that finding your way through it symbolized the soul's passage through the world. The idea of the labyrinth, its practical application, extended into people's everyday lives, and – this is his theory not mine – their towns and cities followed the same metaphor.

Cosmo thought about this, to the best of his ability.

– But a labyrinth is only unintelligible to outsiders, right?

– Sure, otherwise how would you find your way home at night?

– So it could be a defensive system also.

– No artefacts of warfare seem to have survived.

– Even better. So they lived in mazes for purely aesthetic reasons. Maybe there was a night patrol, you know, of brickies, masons? They'd come around and change the arrangement of the maze, put up false walls, block off existent alleys, open new ones. They did this every lunar month. And maybe random re-arrangements to celebrate the passage of a planet, Venus say, or Mars. So their labyrinths were in a perpetual state of re-arrangement. To fit in with astrological considerations.

Ruben was looking at him, curious, waiting for him to continue, but Cosmo had already moved on. His paranoia had gone. Strangely, he felt far more at ease in the place knowing it was a Minoan construct than he had done ten minutes earlier.

They wandered back towards the lighted tunnel, and followed it a little way further as it veered to the left. Another small concourse area opened in front of them. This time there were two solid looking doors. One of them opened easily. It resembled the other store-rooms in its Spartan design, but this one was empty. The other door however, would not open. Ruben produced a screwdriver and a length of fine metal from inside his jacket, and began poking at the lock.

– You came prepared, I see, said Cosmo.

Ruben continued trying to work the lock.

– I'll need something stronger, he said, finally, wiping the sweat from his forehead with the sleeve of his jacket. – Something that offers leverage. Like a jimmy?

– Jemmy.

– A jimmy. OK. Or a shotgun.

– You really want to open this door, hey Ruben?

– Fucking sure I do. Something tells me this is the door that hides Montezuma's gold.

– I wouldn't be so certain.

– I need to check this room. Fuck it. Ruben had worked the screwdriver into the furrow between the door jamb and the lock, and was trying to wriggle it loose. He retrieved the screwdriver, twisted and useless.

– We'll have to come back and open the fucker.

– Not tonight. You're not going to find a jemmy tonight, Or a shotgun.

Cosmo realized, as he said this, that Ruben was the kind of person who could quite easily find either of those things in any number of Xania coffee-houses this same night if he put his mind to it.

– We'll come back, huh? Find out what the fuck these guys are up to down here.

– You're getting excited, *gaucho*. Your excessive use of the expletive 'fuck' and its derivatives gives you away. It's like a metre of your excitement quotient. It's clear what they're up to. They're building a shelter for long-term use in the event of nuclear war. What else do you need to know?

– There's always more to know. How can you be so fuckin' *disinterested*? We're in the belly of the Beast! Doesn't that mean anything? This is where US admirals and selected

VIP's will be entertained in the post-nuclear holocaust, while all around them, outside, people die horrible deaths. I wanna know what the fuck they expect to do down here while the rest of the world burns. He paused. – Plus, you know, you don't have to come back. But if you do, you might find some of those Minotaur droppings you're after. Fucking monster shit. Doesn't that tempt you?

On impulse, Cosmo put his arm around Ruben's shoulder and kissed him on the cheek, giving him a rough hug. Then the two of them returned up the tunnel, the way they had come.

11. *The World gets Weird*

Cosmo was painting bulls. Bull-men, startled out of sleep, surprised by sirens. Shores scattered with copulating couples; monsters with engorged phalluses poised in the shadowy entrances to caves; the ravished victims of the Minotaur's relentless lust. He piled the acrylic on thick, smearing the stuff in layers with his fingers. His bulls were blue and purple and black, bruised and bellowing combatants in a war against anaemia. He had found a copy of the Minotaur story and was tracking the pursuit of Theseus by the bull-man, weaving through endless tunnels of pitch, the scent of fresh blood in his nostrils. Confused by the carnivorousness of the creature's bloodlust. How could a bull be a carnivore? So much in this story was inverted. This was not a bull but a man with a bull's strength and virility, a man's lusts and hungers.

The Minotaur is conceived through the lust of Minos' queen, Pasiphae, for a white bull. The inventor Daedalus creates for her the likeness of a wooden cow, and she steps inside this unlikely contraption, squeezes in, arse first, and lets herself be fucked into dark oblivion by the white bull. Her lust is sated and she gives birth to the bull-boy, Minotaur. To hide his shame and hers, Minos orders Daedalus to build a labyrinth in which to confine the creature. He roams its endless tunnels roaring and groaning and ever-ravenous, ever-lustful. In a nice variation on his mother's bestiality, he can only be sated by the flesh of young Athenians; hence Theseus' decision to volunteer as one of the tribute of victims from Athens. And from the moment that she sets eyes on him, Ariadne, daughter of Minos, decides he is the one. She betrays her father by consulting Daedalus and finding out the secrets of the labyrinth. From Daedalus comes the idea of the thread that Theseus must trail behind him, unravelling as he roams deeper into the fantastic construction of earth and rock. When he hears the Minotaur's roar he quakes, but he overcomes his fear as heroes will. He has acquired this self-control through years of practice in his young life, against adversaries with greater guile than the Minotaur, if lacking its brute strength. Through his skill and agility he manages to overcome the beast and slays him. He follows the thread back to the waiting Ariadne and they escape in the night, back to Theseus' boat, taking the freed Athenians youths and maidens with them. Minos can either send his boats in pursuit, or else acknowledge the failure of his life and the loss of his daughter. The swift Cretan vessels would surely have caught the Athenian boat. But Theseus is protected by Poseidon, and no boat shall cross the sea-god's kingdom without his permission. If boats were sent out they would have been smashed against the rocks.

The levy of seven youths and seven maidens from Athens to satisfy the Minotaur was explicable in terms of allegory: how the Cretan empire was at some stage strong enough to impose such sanctions on the relatively young and weak state of Athens; but it was not merely a story of taxes and levies. It was a story of sacrifice on several levels. The obvious sacrifice of the Athenian tribute, which after years is thwarted by Theseus; the sacrifice of Ariadne by Theseus, later abandoned by him, after risking everything to help him escape the Minotaur. The notion of sacrifice, in this story, runs deep and bloody. It continues even after the Athenians' departure, with Daedalus, the labyrinth's creator, losing his son Icarus in his attempt to fly from the labyrinth that he created and in which King Minos has imprisoned him for helping Ariadne to rescue her thankless lover.

Cosmo became so involved in painting the story that he forgot himself. He had returned from the nuclear shelter that night and had begun at once, painting with the same lascivious absorption that he had lavished on his new lover over the preceding days.

Ariadne sacrifices her own elite position as King Minos' daughter in order to escape with Theseus, first by helping him with the famous thread that leads him out of the labyrinth then by leaving the island of her birth for an unknown future in faraway Athens where she could hardly be assured of a welcome – Minos' daughter? Pass me the cleaver! – Besides, they all said Theseus was promised to another . . .

Alysa acted cool at first, as Cosmo immersed himself in his work. When he started limiting his conversation to monosyllables she became put out, and when he extended his repertoire of drug use to mainlining, she became aloof. Cosmo had discovered that he was able to purchase a particular brand of amphetamine-based slimming tablet without prescription, which he ground into powder and injected when he was alone in the studio. The speed rush delivered both a pronounced sense of visual dislocation and a state of deceptively benign emotional grace. Unfortunately the comedown was a bastard, teeth-grindingly neurotic, unless sated with plenty of booze. He harassed Ruben for more cocaine and shot that up also. He worked through the first night and the following morning, crashing like a felled tree onto his bed in the early afternoon and resuming as soon as he awoke in the evening. He had smeared fragments of the map of Crete onto the canvass along with photographs, illustrations torn from a child's story book of Greek Myths that he found in a tourist shop, scratchings of dusty soil and sand, resin, seeds, his own blood.

She sacrifices her patrimony to be with him, and then he dumps her on the island of Naxos where she is discovered by followers of Dionysos, the god of drunkenness and madness and sundering, of mad celebration and tearing apart, and in the orgy that follows she is sacrificed to the god. Or else again (and it may amount to the same thing) she is joined with him, Dionysos, in a state of marriage, the wild god's only bride, accompanies him on his travels to the east, and on her death is added to the constellations of the sky.

He knew that soon Ruben would want him to return to the shelter as his accomplice but he needed to make his own preparations, to assimilate the old story beneath his skin, because once they had discovered that the shelter was built upon the skeleton of an ancient, forgotten labyrinth, it had ceased to become a nuclear shelter and had become a thing of myth, inadvertently appropriated by the late twentieth century, with its own jumbled legends of imprisonment, sacrifice and bloodshed. For him, the labyrinth held the secret to the implosive violence of Crete, the power of the chthonic humming in his ears above the eternal grind of tectonic plates; of an ancient voice that growled deep within the rock, and that thrilled and tantalized him with its whisperings of illicit sex and death.

The second evening after their reconnaissance visit to the shelter, Ruben had set off, armed with his wrench and an acetylene torch, to do some more exploring and to attempt to break into the locked room, but he had returned disappointed: a group of youths on mopeds were hanging around the small adjoining park and they had shown no sign of moving on. He did not try to get into the bunker alone and had gone to the beach with Jade for the whole of the next day.

Alysa had spent this fourth morning of Cosmo's manic work binge reading on the bed, and in the middle of the afternoon she informed Cosmo that he was an antisocial Frog dickhead, and went to eat at The Unspeakable. He said he might join her later, and that anyway he was only half-French, in which case did that mean he was only half a dickhead, and what part of his anatomy did his Irish half correspond to; but she was on her way already and, as soon as she had left, he grabbed a lemon and a spoon from the kitchen and cooked up some more of the speed cocktail. He jacked up in the studio and after the initial rush, spent a while pacing the studio, his mind following a line of thought that took him to Ariadne's desolation and abandonment on the island of Naxos. In between cigarettes and cups of coffee, he continued to smear paint onto a massive new canvas that was intended to represent the outcome of Ariadne's abandonment on Naxos. She had fallen into a sleep, and in the painting was being awakened by the ministrations of a group of Maenads, Dionysos's wine-frenzied harpies, female acolytes of the god who would rend and sunder, tear and destroy, but only after (or while) enjoying her, only after feasting on the delights of her body first. The sexual panic that alighted on Ariadne's face on awakening to this group of female lovers was ambiguous, contradicted as it was by the arching of her body. Other figures were piled together close by, in various acts of debauchery, male on female, male on male, female on female, all splayed and agonized and delirious. Cosmo stood back and looked at his work in its entirety for the first time. The Athenian maids and youths had turned into orgiastic revellers on a beach beside a blood-red sea. The night was black, penetrated only by an El Greco moon.

Cosmo thought the picture looked tacky, kitsch, so proceeded to smear copper dust and glue over the orgiastic scene. But painting the scene had made him horny and he returned to his senses, realizing Alysa had left the house. As he sat on the sofa and looked at his work, the erotic imagery startled him into full tumescence, something of a miracle considering the usual shrivelling consequences of amphetamines. His head was in a mess. Images of the cavorting Maenads, demented bull-men, ravished bodies, devils, white skin on black, black skin on white, the tangled thatch at Alysa's crotch concealing the red slit of her sex; all spun in his imagination, and he realized that by working in this way he was going to paint himself dry. He needed to find some kind of inner balance, but was now supercharged and could not slow down.

Scraping away all the surface shit in order to start digging, brushing away a few handfuls of topsoil and burning some weeds before pitching the shovel at the gravelly earth and spading in there yes that is satisfactory scoop that out and toss the remnants over your shoulder that is very good what is painting but a type of excavation and there is no point in stopping now DO something get a high or a low or a jolt of some kind what can I put in my mouth now what can I ingest inhale imbibe inject what can I get off on now for the moment for the explosive seconds that follow on from a hit a toke a blast a fix the rush the insane craving for a bigger hit a bigger blast a bigger fix and more and more and certainly more shattering than anything I can summon up here something to do battle with the senses rearing and roaring the need to combat all the forces of fucking tedium that lie waiting at every juncture in order to entrap and ensnare and enslave you into producing pap for the slowest and dullest felons of the soul and all that your vision requires a little placebo for your so-called creative requirements the idea that everything can be bought off yes the artist too in the service of mass entertainment and mass misery and mass addiction to pap and more pap yes I can yes I will have more so I can rise vengeful and terrible and paint into the soul of nothing the dark seething mess of nothing that inhabits my soul plaster it onto canvas for myself to stare at and praise but also to desecrate and abuse for this is the mirror of my fortune this is the animal source of all my dreaming this bull-man this rage this frenzy this thirst this need this craving this yearning . . .

Down in the kitchen, there was a five-litre flagon of raki by the fridge and he helped himself to a glassful, knocked it back in one gulp; poured another. He hadn't felt this way since Corfu and Alex. When the desire for blackout came up on him he was absolutely powerless.

But for the moment, with the first thrill of strong liquor and with the amphetamines and coke still raging in his blood, he decided to dance. He put *The Clash* on Ruben's sound system, the volume blasting around the interior of the room as he danced, hunched over at first, then stretching out, his feet kicking in mad carnival, arms gyrating, pogo-leaping and limb-thrashing, breathless, sweat-drenched.

After an hour of solitary drinking and furious dancing, Cosmo took a cold shower, *Rudie can't fail* still ringing in his ears, and was about to leave the bathroom when he spotted a plastic cylinder high on the cabinet above the sink. Light-years beyond rational thought, he reached up for it and found that it held a quantity of bright purple pills. Cosmo had a vague memory of what they were, but couldn't recall the name. They had been left there by a former girlfriend of Ruben's, a young woman with mental health problems. Well, he reckoned, with a cognitive hiccup that had him laughing out loud, that seemed to be a prerequisite for entering into intimate relations with Ruben; though he found it hard to identify any signs of flakiness or dementia in Jade, so perhaps she justified the adage of exception to the rule. She was certainly an enigma to Cosmo. With an effort, he steered a mental course away from Jade and back to the here and now. He guessed the pills were some sort of downer for psychos. He swallowed four, solemnly speaking the name of each member of the household as he did so – *Alysa,* swallow; *Ruben,* swallow; *Jade,* swallow; *Me, a name I call myself,* swallow – then replaced the cap and got dressed. Downstairs, he poured himself more raki and smoked a spliff, using the black hash that Ruben kept hidden in an old tea-pot.

By the time he left the house, his own sense of corporeal unity had almost disappeared, all sentient messages negated by the madly churning currents in his blood; and in place of flesh and bone he seemed made of something malleable, volatile; his limbs the consistency of vegetable mash, chest cavity a vat for hot molten substances that bubbled through him, exploding every now and then with electric shudders that in turn propelled small ecstatic elvers to swim frenetically through the system of arteries towards the breeding pool of his abdomen. As the chemicals raged inside him, he entered an entirely inaccessible zone in which all contact with other beings was conducted through some invisible intermediary, who bore the outward appearance of Cosmo, even looked and sounded like him – though decreasingly, as the hours went by – but whose actions and behaviour were akin to those of a primitive and exceedingly obtuse shaman in a state of religious trance.

He set off unsteadily, and decided, in the blur of perception that now reflected previously unknown colours off rooftops and drainpipes, and sprayed diaphanous light through the foliage of trees, that he was arriving at the threshold of a new life. He might have appeared to others to be in trance, but to his own way of seeing things he was just breaking out of one. He found his bearings and his balance in the bright early evening, walked quickly up Gerasimou, knowing, with the infallible logic of the utterly stoned that to slow his pace could be disastrous; crossed Splanzia square in front of the church of Aghios Nikolaos and headed for Skridlov Street and the Unspeakable.

There was a small party in progress on the pavement. Two tables had been pulled together and as he approached, eyes straining into the sun, Cosmo saw that Alysa was sitting next to a young man whom he vaguely recognized. Pascale was also there (without her Canadian boyfriend), as were Ruben and Jade.

In spite of his sterling attempts at motor coordination, Cosmo made the mistake of doing two things at once; dragging a seat up between Alysa and the unknown boy, and trying to sit on it in one movement, with the result that he toppled sideways and crashed into the table. He grabbed hold of the boy with one arm and Alysa with the other, and pulled himself up straight.

– Whoops, he said, and looked leerily around the table, resting his gaze for too long on each person, before settling on the stranger. – Who the fuck are you?

Lucas grinned, unfazed, and did not answer.

– *Jesus*, Cosmo. To what do we owe this honour? Asked Alysa, straightening herself. You look like a walking *disaster*.

– Priapus and his bloody hard-on.

– What is this? Asked Pascale, who, to Cosmo, in that instant, looked stunning, radiant, heavenly, in a practically transparent white dress; a Botticelli Venus, her dirty blonde hair tied back, revealing the tattoo of a scorpion on her shoulder.

– Fuck me, a goddess, he slurred.

Ruben was grinning at him across the table: a big Latino sort of smile, thought Cosmo. A bandit's smile.

– Answer the lady, Cosmo.

– The demi-god of stiffies, said Cosmo, turning towards Pascale. – The wine god's sidekick. Always at the ready. Member fully engorged. You can see him in the tourist shops showing off his wanger. His dick's as long as his arm.

– *Qu'est-ce qu'il dit?* Pascale asked Jade, who spoke French, as did Cosmo, fluently.

– She meant who are *you*, whispered Alysa, at his side.

– Oh fuck. Like they say. Cosmo shrugged. Expectant silence broken only by the yelling of a leather merchant in a shop across the street. Pascale tried again.

– I think you must be Cosmo. Stated not as a question.

Cosmo blinked, fish-mouthed, at Pascale, who giggled.

– Yeah, all the variations. Cosmic, cosmopolitan, cosmogonist. But actually I'm a, er, cosmonaut. Cosmo the cosmonaut. Tracking the invisible skyways. Skiddling through the warm wet void. Strange things to report. Build-up of dark matter right now. Black holes at every turning. Pleased that the sun is still on.

Cosmo smiled and lit a cigarette. He was in a state of almost perfect bliss. A stirring and a yearning in this hour of colours before the dusk, the night ahead a promised pantheon of erotic zeal and oozing pleasures. Then he remembered that his own question had remained unanswered. He gazed at the stranger. Cosmo was only interested in people, both men and women, to whom he could respond on an erotic level. The newcomer pleased him. Cosmo was conscious enough to know that he had been staring at him for too long. Lucas was beginning to look just a little uneasy.

– Don't worry, mate, Cosmo said. I'm not gonna *bite* ya.

Lucas put out his hand:

– Hi, he said. I'm Lucas. We met the other night.

Cosmo shook his hand.

– Any service at this bloody restaurant, Lucas? *– Igbar?* He yelled in the direction of the street door. Then, seeing that the waiter had not appeared immediately, dropped into a rich baritone and called out, in Tassos' voice, in Greek: *– Igbar; ela edo.*

– The very worst sort of customer, sighed Jade. Impersonating the restaurateur. Disturbing the peace. He'll be smashing crockery next.

– You consider Tassos a *restaurateur*? Asked Ruben, grinning.

– Technically, he is, replied Jade.

– It's just that it seems, well, a lowly establishment for such a grand term.

– Is this the prelude to one of your wind-ups, Ruben?

– No way, man. An innocent question.

– No good boyo, said Alysa.

– That's the one, said Jade. – Even his attempts at innocent discourse rattle with suspect qualities.

– Come out here you scabby ratbag. Come out of your rat-hole, Cosmo bellowed suddenly, causing a pair of window-shoppers across the street to turn in alarm. He pulled himself up, nearly knocking the table over again as he did so. He lumbered towards the door and disappeared inside.

– No good boyo, repeated Alysa, but it was unclear to whom this was directed: her own boyfriend, or her friend's.

Everything was dark in the Unspeakable after the muted sunlight on Skridlov Street. Cosmo saluted Tassos and ambled past the kitchen area into the back room, where Igbar was clearing a table.

– Hullo mate, Igbar said pleasantly.

– There you are. Can't see a fucking thing in this place. Too dark. Too much *black air*.

Igbar stared at Cosmo, curious.

– You all right?

– Too bloody right I'm all right. I'm fucking flying. Starving though.

– You can have *britzola*, replied Igbar.

– Flesh of the pig. Fine. Would prefer the bull, but the pig will do. Make sure it's not green. I've seen some dodgy items in Tassos's fridge before now. Cosmo stood there swaying for a moment. He was making a monumental effort to form coherent sentences. He stretched out an arm for what appeared to be a stationary wall. – I see the lovely Pascale is outside with the crewage. Where's the boyfriend?

Igbar's face lit up.

– Oh they've parted. It happened a couple of days ago. She decided to stay here. He left. I'm damned pleased, I must say.

Cosmo made a loud baying noise. It might conceivably have been a laugh, but sounded more like a hound giving birth inside a tin barrel. From his hideaway by the cooker, Tassos adopted a perplexed expression, unique to him, involving a lifted eyebrow and a dangerous smile.

– I think, alas, my charms are somewhat lost on Pascale. Besides, she seems to have taken a shine to that Lucas, the Welsh lad.

– Nice young Welshman, Cosmo muttered into his shirt. – Nice Welsh wench spotted also. Strange indeed.

– Quite so. But I was glad to see the back of the tall Canadian.

– Why's that?

– I don't think that he was right for her. Too hairy for a start. A very hairy man.

– You are reasonably hirsute yourself. The man with the big moustache.

Igbar grunted.

– They had a scene in here, but I missed most of it. She threw a glass of beer over his head. I believe it was at this point that he used the expression 'a crock of shit' for the last time and buggered off.

– So what stopped you, Igbar? You know, seizing the moment.

– Take advantage of a young lady in her moment of distress, you mean?

Cosmo's head nodded up and down as if jerked by

strings.

– That's the kind of thing I'd expect from Ruben. That would be the action of a cad.

– Oh, I see. Better to suffer in silence and see young Lucas with his hand in the honey-pot. The English way. Are you sure your proclivities are not almost always entirely vicarious?

Cosmo heard himself uttering quite convincing sounds, but found it difficult to connect what was going on inside his head with the words his mouth were forming. At the same time he had discovered the wall, rather like his use of language, to be insubstantial: it jellified under his palm and he was certain that if he leaned too hard his entire arm, and possibly his upper torso, neck and head, would sink right into the wobbly construct.

– Cosmo, is anything the matter?

– Motor co-ordination nothing serious I've got to pee.

When Cosmo emerged from the foul-smelling latrine, he swayed past Tassos, still busy at the stove, and returned to the table on the pavement. They were now the only customers in the quiet spell before dinner, and Igbar was taking time out for a cigarette, leaning far too obviously over Pascale's cleavage.

Alysa watched Cosmo carefully as he sat down. His hair was sticking up at all angles; his vest and army pants, which he had not bothered to change after showering, were splattered with paint of every hue, but predominantly purple and red. Nor had his shower been effective in removing the oil and acrylic from his skin. It was his eyes, though, that gave cause for greater alarm: wild, bloodshot and indecently dilated. He took a sip of wine and smacked his lips.

– A most peculiar beverage, Tassos's wine. Tastes like

prune juice laced with mud. Where does he get it, Igbar?

– Somewhere out by Kolimbari. It's about 15 degrees proof.

– Do you *need* wine, Cosmo? Asked Jade. – You look certifiably insane already.

– You can count on her for a flattering appraisal, said Alysa. Although personally I think she's being generous.

Cosmo turned to Lucas, on his other side. – So you've met my friends?

Lucas nodded.

– In the realm of the impious, the one-eyed trouser snake is king, Cosmo confided.

– Horny and brain-dead, said Alysa, eavesdropping. – Stop staring at her tits, will you? She nodded over at Pascale.

– Was I? asked Cosmo, disbelieving.

– No good boyo? Pascale offered, as though in delayed response to an earlier question.

Igbar had pulled up a seat alongside her. – Of course, he started, in ancient Greece, Cosmo would have been a High Priest of the Dionysian Mysteries.

– Quite so, concurred Cosmo.

– Explain yourself, said Ruben

– Well it's pretty straightforward. Ancient Greece had the perfect set-up for getting rid of its demons. Like anywhere else, they used shamans. Someone who has penetrated the otherworld, like Cosmo here. In mid-winter the women would leave Athens and get completely shitfaced up in the mountains, drinking and dancing themselves into a frenzy and then they'd tear a goat to pieces and eat it raw.

– Yuck, said Jade

– So the frenzy serves a purpose. All of society's rules

and norms are inverted for the duration. People delve into the unknown.

– Or the unknowable, in Cosmo's case, added Alysa, as Cosmo nodded sagely.

– Well, quite. What I mean to say is, this was perceived as a religious experience. People who ignored Dionysos, wouldn't let the god into their lives, were cast up and ripped apart by the frenzied maenads. By indulging freely of mind-altering substances, some would say, you can commune directly with the god. And have visions. Just ask Cosmo. But if you don't let Dionysos into your life at all, if you repress it, you're going to go insane. That's one reason why the Brits and other northern Europeans go barking mad in the sun. They abuse Dionysos. But Cosmo, I think, is different. He is on a mission. He's an adept of the Dionysian mysteries.

– My, the lengths you boys will go to justify getting wasted, said Jade.

– No, you misunderstand, argued Igbar. – I was being deadly serious.

Cosmo sat up sharply, and said to the company at large – The repression of Dionysos is the main cause of incremental insanity, you know, the slow creeping kind, in all countries that contain the letter N.

Igbar turned back to Pascale, nervously. – Let me bring you some prawns, he said. – On the house.

Ruben spluttered. – That's a first.

– Thank you, said Pascale. Prawns would be very nice.

– For you, replied Igbar, showing yellow rodent teeth and immaculate timing, – anything.

Tassos had taken up his customary sentinel on the far side of the entrance, his feet up on a second chair. Occasionally, when voices were raised, he turned in the direction of their group, a proprietary smirk on his lips, his eyes slits. The babble of lubricated conversation rose and fell and shadows had begun to lengthen in the narrow street when the tall, hunched figure of Kees the beggar approached the group. He stood behind Cosmo and asked for a cigarette.

Cosmo sighed and pushed his pack of unfiltered Papastratos towards the edge of the table.

– And one for my girlfriend.

Cosmo squinted up at him. – I wonder, he said, would you ever be fucking off?

Kees stayed put, puzzled, trying to work out if he had just been insulted. Meanwhile Ruben rose slowly from his seat. In his hand he held a lighted cigarette, half-smoked.

– You want a cigarette, asshole?

Before anybody had time to react, Ruben had stretched across the table and crushed his burning cigarette forcefully into the Dutchman's cheek. Kees leapt back, holding his hand against the wound.

– *Christ. Fuck,* he said, before launching himself at Ruben. Plates and bottles crashed to the ground as Kees' full weight landed across the table. Everyone else, except Cosmo, moved from their seats, as Ruben responded to the counter-attack with a couple of sharp punches to the Dutchman's head. Kees attempted to engage Ruben at close quarters, aiming to lock his hands around his assailant's throat, but Ruben was too quick for him and sidestepped, causing Kees to crash headfirst into the broad chest of the restaurant's proprietor. Tassos, angry at being disturbed from his afternoon nap, grabbed Kees by the scruff of the neck and, like Bad Eye George before him, steered him into the road, aiming a kick at his backside and delivering a parting spate of blasphemies.

– I say, Ruben, said Igbar, – that was a bit uncalled for.

Cosmo looked up from his seat, having not stirred a muscle during the whole brief performance.

– South American cigarette trick, he muttered. – Seen it before.

Igbar went inside and returned with a dustpan and brush. Ruben helped him pick up the broken crockery and glass from the pavement. Alysa, Jade and Pascale stood together, scanning the mess the two men had made.

– I think we'd better go, said Jade.

Tassos, who had been angrily surveying the smashed debris outside his restaurant, began to laugh, a quiet amused chortling, then clapped Ruben on the shoulder. Ruben stopped brushing underneath the table.

– *Bravo*, Rubaki, he said, using his own affectionate diminutive of Ruben's name. He drew an invisible pattern in the air, a circling of the hand followed by a sharp stabbing gesture, to indicate his appreciation of the cigarette moment. He grinned approvingly.

– He's congratulating him! exclaimed Jade, outraged.

– No good boyos, said Pascale. All of them.

– He doesn't like Kees at all, said Igbar, mopping up a pool of wine.

– Nobody likes Kees, added Cosmo.

– Poor Kees, said Pascale, sadly.

– Bloody men, said Jade. – Ruben, you're a dangerous bloody lunatic.

– *Es un hijo de puta*, explained Ruben.

– That's offensive, said Jade. – To his mother.

– Bloody men, echoed Pascale. – Bloody Patrick.

– Bloody blimey, said Cosmo, to nobody in particular.

– Someone had better offer to pay for this before the guv'nor docks my wages, said Igbar.

– Worth every penny, said Cosmo. – When can we have the action re-play?

– Idiots, said Alysa. – Come on, she said, linking arms with Pascale and Jade. – I'm sure these mighty hunters can make do without us for a while. Let's party.

– Party party party, mumbled Cosmo. He slumped back in his seat as the women set off down Skridlov, heading for another destination.

– You want a hand? asked Lucas, – getting up?

– Party party party. Cosmo's eyes were an impenetrable confusion now. Helped by Lucas, he stood, looked up and down the street. The day had ripened into darkness and a platinum moon was rising, full and ominously vast, beyond the rooftops. Everything was happening in slow motion, the gesticulating of the shopkeeper in the leather store across the way as he finalized a sale; the hand that young Lucas was offering to guide him onto the road; the passing dog that had stopped by their table and was scooping up a morsel of spilled meat from the ground with its long tongue: everything was happening very slow indeed.

12. *Polyrhythms and Microtones*

Cosmo awoke in his bed to see a pair of feet close to his head. His internal clock told him it was mid-morning, golden sunlight slanting through the terrace window. He sat up and inspected the room, amazed by the clarity of his own thought. Dust motes specked the beams, each minute particle suspended in its own slow trajectory across the galaxy of light. On these occasions he would normally have expected a throbbing head at the very least, but apart from an unfamiliar taste lingering inside his mouth, he felt remarkably spry. His first thought was of the painting he had been working on the day before, and he realized how thoroughly he had been dwelling inside the pictures of Dionysian excess, inhabiting this group of pictures more intimately than anything he had painted before. He suspected, in his solipsistic way, that he had incited some kind of fusion between the artefacts of his imagination and the conscious world of his environment.

Only then did he consider the human contents of his bed. Alysa's head lay on the pillow, beyond the feet. He lifted the sheet and identified Pascale, whose arms lay around Alysa's hips, her head lodged on the soft of Alysa's thigh. Immediately he began to feel a melting in his groin, and the determined twitchings of arousal. He let the sheet fall and attempted to reconstruct the events of the previous night.

He had emerged from blackout quite suddenly, to find himself in the kitchen of his own house. The room was full of people, the party in full flow. He had the vaguest recollection of his group gathering, and losing, several hangers-on at the Lyrakia – individuals, who for Cosmo, only provided extra strata of suspect and flawed reality. Even now, Cosmo didn't immediately register that he was conscious, and listening to the voices around the table on which he was slumped he tried to identify the separate voices while keeping his eyes shut.

– Apart from that, the music is often fast and syncopated.

– Diogenes lived in a barrel.

– The Bobby Sands saga will only make Thatcher more trenchant, more fascistic.

– He could only, *tu sais*, get aroused, if we do it doggy style. *Moi, je préfère un peu de variation.*

– There's no pleasing some people.

– She was on serious medication. Cosmo must have helped himself.

– He spoke only in metaphors.

– Fast and syncopated, not fast and loose.

– Kill all the bastards. Videla, Pinochet, Reagan, Thatcher. Rip their fucking lungs out and feed them to the dogs.

Cosmo opened his eyes and tried to focus on Crazy Nikos, whose gravelly voice had uttered the death sentence on four world leaders. He was declaiming to a group that included his friends from the earlier session at the Unspeakable.

– Because you know what's left of the world after these bastards have their fun? The new way of feeding opium to the people? They turn what's left into a fucking Tourist Resort! You know, we in Greece already have to make ourselves, how d'you say, *available*, to provide for the great god Tourism. It's Tourism, not enemy invasions, that will destroy my country, my culture. Tourism that brings in the Yankee dollar so we can play at being capitalists and make plenty money by ripping off our comrades. Tourism rips our villages apart, I've seen it in Aghios Nikolaos, in Ierapetra, everyone looking over their backs to see if their neighbour sold that piece of land for development yet, and if so how much did he get for it. Christ, man, I've got a plot where we grow tomatoes down by the beach and I want to be a millionaire too. Land that's been in the family since the time of Plato! It's tourism that will smash and destroy all the hidden quiet places of the world and flog off the pretty bits to a Theme Park consortium and cook the scrapings in a Big fuckin' Mac.

Cosmo continued to stare at Nikos, impressed by his oratory but totally confused as to his meaning.

– You know what I was trying to tell these guys, said Ruben, indicating Cosmo and Igbar with his hand, – just a couple weeks ago? That it's us, as well, *us*, the ones who leave our countries and set out to live in foreign places who have to carry some of the blame. The backpackers are ex-pats too. In fact it's backpackers who do the initial damage. Mass tourism will always follow on the heels of the backpackers. They're like the scouts for total tourist swamp. You wait and see. Everywhere a backpacker drops his pack and lights up his spliff of cheap local weed, on that very spot will grow a five star hotel. South-east Asia will be next, then South America, once we've got rid of our embarrassing dictators.

At least two other conversations were in progress at the same time. Lucas was again sitting close by. He seemed to be acquiring the characteristics of a shadow. Cosmo pulled a cigarette from a nearby pack and Lucas, smiling, lit it. He was talking music with Igbar and seemed to be an expert on polyrhythms and microtones, terms alien and tantalizing to Cosmo. He listened for a while, then, pulling himself to his feet, wandered over to the cooking area, where he filled a coffee pot with water, while the chatter around him continued to rise and ebb.

– How can you have oral sex with a man who does not wash his *bitte*?

– Ah no, that was not in the Oedipus story. Not in Freud. Not in Sophocles.

– And if the listener isn't used to hearing quartertones, then he doesn't *hear* them, and thinks the instrument is being played out of tune.

– Two minutes, maximum, *et c'est fini. Whoosh!*

– *Whoosh?*

Cosmo found cups and placed them on the table. He skirted the group and squatted in front of Alysa, putting his hands on her shoulders and kissing her on the side of the neck.

– You back from the dead, my lovely? She smiled at him. And in that instant, possibly for the first time in his life, Cosmo thought he understood what it meant to be in love.

Everything about her entranced him: her smile, her eyes, the lilt of her voice. He felt as though he had been emotionally disemboweled and was left only with this raw, grating ache for her.

– Was I a disgrace?

– Utter disgrace, man. You shamed yourself. Lucas had to mind you cos you got awful chopsy with some poor hippies in the Lyrakia. You were *very* bad. She looked at Pascale who was sitting opposite, her feet resting in Alysa's own lap. She had turned aside to speak to Jade, enhancing the strong line of neck and profile. – Isn't she gorgeous? whispered Alysa.

Cosmo nodded, confused, wondering why she had asked. He poured coffee for himself and Alysa, put the pot on the table, and left the kitchen, spectral, as though the transition to wakefulness were simply an organic extension to the deep trance into which he had slumped for the past few hours. He would have been content to stay and join the chaotic descent of the partying, but he had work to do upstairs. In the bathroom he took another long cold shower, dried himself roughly in a towel, and slipped on shorts and a sweatshirt. Casting a look around the bathroom, his eyes alighted on the plastic cylinder of pharmaceuticals. He picked them up and dropped them in the bin, then picked a foil wrapper from the cabinet above the sink and snorted the last of the coke that he had hassled off Ruben.

Inside his studio, Cosmo ferreted behind a crate and found a bottle of Yugoslav plum brandy. He added a slug to his coffee and lit a cigarette. By the time Alysa and Pascale slipped through the studio an hour later, he was entirely engrossed once more in a world of elusive colours and hypnotically gratifying forms. He heard some of the guests leave the house, making out the voices of Nikos and Igbar raised in laughter, and then there was relative quiet, the house taking on its old familiar night-time breathing, a feature of the internal architecture to which Cosmo was finely tuned. He mixed colours, now favouring an oil paint, a richer purple-blue for the bull that was twisting in mid-charge towards the onlooker, knowing that the picture was going to need a whole lot of messing and skilful distortion to stop it appearing too contrived, too artfully orgiastic. His thoughts raced ahead of his hand as he painted faster in an attempt to keep up with these projections. But despite its often frenzied appearance, the essence of Cosmo's painting was, and always had been, slowness; a measured concupiscence, a thrilled teasing of the erotic from the fusion of colour and texture. It occurred to him, pursuing a musical metaphor, that this was the first time he had moved onto the symphonic, after years of producing chamber music. This thought provoked another, and he rummaged through his music collection, looking for a favourite cassette of Stravinsky's *Rite of Spring* to put in his personal stereo. He normally preferred to have music booming through the studio while he worked but at this hour and with Alysa and Pascale's soft chatter fluttering from the adjoining bedroom, the Sony Walkman seemed a more sociable option. Returning to work, he applied more oil with a pallet knife in great tranches, smearing first black and magenta, then diagonally, and slightly overlapping, white with flecks of yellow and pink. He thought of Alysa and Pascale as he did so, smiling to himself at the way they had infiltrated his thought through colour. He felt very wide awake.

I should feel like shit but I've never felt better this is the way smear that over and down and bulk out that limb a shade it looks too pasty and flaccid these two figures are howling and that one is completely gone and that one what was the name of that movie Céline et Julie vont en bateau *mais oui perhaps we have a blueprint there and the god Dionysos will make his entrance and my black Ariadne will not be tricked or alone or cast out she stays on Naxos because Theseus was so fucking boring she wasn't dumped there because he was tired of her at all she was a sacred custodian of the night a king's daughter and a high priestess she* made *this choice and the waves heave great slabs of black sea in the background there black sea red sea black sea red sea the night is black and the sea is red no the sea is black and the sky is red shit what difference does it make I need more black more red more indigo and purple here yes here a streak of bright yellow where the sun has fallen into the ferns and the world is wailing and it will not be long not be long before the planet dies screaming carrying the bleeding sores of radiation and animals will run terrified through the forests . . .*

After an hour and a half he decided to stop. He was not tiring, but his visual reservoir was completely flooded by the night's work and he knew from experience that it was better to quit before exhausting the ideas that were crystallizing in his thought. Better to keep them in reserve for the morning, so he would know where he was starting from. He rubbed his hands in white spirit as the music reached its juddering climax, and washed them in the sink, before taking off his headphones.

His hearing took a moment to re-adjust after the orchestral onslaught, the last few bars still juddering in his ears as he poured himself a second brandy. He could make out low moans drifting from the bedroom. He would have left it there, and settled on the studio bed, but the door had been left ajar, and he was certain that Alysa would have closed it had she intended to shut him out.

Moonlight flooded the bedroom. From the doorway, he made out Pascale, kneeling, her long hair down, face buried between Alysa's thighs. Alysa lifted her head, between gasps, and beckoned to Cosmo. She grabbed his arm and pulled him towards her. She traced a finger slowly over his lip, and Cosmo tasted the body of an unfamiliar woman. Still holding him, she wriggled her tongue into the depths of his ear, then retracted, biting the lobe gently. Her hot breath filled his ear where only a minute before savage music had accompanied the imagined gyrations of a girl who danced herself to death. – I want you to fuck *her*, then me, she said, in a choking whisper. *– I want to watch you fuck her please Cosmo do this for me.* There was a desperate edge to her voice, and it might have been a trick of the light, but Cosmo could have sworn that her eyes were brimming. She repeated this demand, with much filthier language than before, muttering the obscenities as though they were an incantation or a prayer.

Now, in the daylight, Cosmo was concerned. Scarves and a leather belt were hanging loose from the bedposts, evidence of the night's curious conjunctions. He began to wonder what precisely Alysa wanted from him; let alone what she wanted from Pascale and him. He was not, by preference, a voyeur in sexual matters, and besides, a passive role was not what Alysa seemed to require from him. Nor did he know where this kind of sex was leading, which was exciting, but also worrying. He could understand the bondage and a bit of rough behaviour; but it would not be long, he intuited, before she was into laceration, fistfucking and strangulation, none of which were a turn-on for Cosmo, who took a dim view of plastic bags over the head on purely aesthetic grounds. Last night he had stolen a glance at Alysa as Pascale manoeuvred herself on him, and her face was incandescent with a kind of repressed fury, or lust, which one he could not be sure. In a way it made no difference: the two emotions, anger and desire, were seemingly fused in her to the point of coalescence. It worried him that she needed to put herself, and her sexual partners, through this trial of endurance in order to find release. He realized he had not been accessible these last few days and decided he would talk with Alysa, in earnest; see if he could help in any way. Maybe he was missing something.

Cosmo slipped quietly from the bed and lowered the canvas blind to block the sun's glare from the sleeping women. Downstairs, he found Jade and Ruben drinking tea. Jade was nursing a hangover. Ruben, as usual, seemed untouched by the excesses of the previous day.

– What you want, Cosmo informed Jade cheerily, is a hearty breakfast. Lots of minerals and vitamins.

Jade groaned. – Why are you so bright and breezy? You were the swamp monster last time I heard you speak.

– I have a quick recovery rate. In any case, I'm going to the market. Clear your liver and bowels with Doctor Flute.

Ruben looked up. – You going to cook?

– I'm going to shop, cook, everything. You take it easy Ruben. I have a *strategy*.

– A man with a plan. I might come along, if that's OK, said Jade.

– Sure thing.

– You're taking Jade? You are a drug addict and probable sex maniac. I'm not sure this is wise.

– Jade can look after herself, said Jade, aloof.

Carnivorous Cosmo had a penchant for beef, and if possible, bull-meat. In fact, what he would have liked to buy were bull's testicles, but realized that it was unlikely anyone else in the house, other than Ruben, would appreciate this delicacy. He ordered a huge hunk of meat, with the intention of cooking a *Daube*, learned from his French grandmother, and also bought eggs and vegetables, plenty of fresh fruit. On leaving the market, Jade asked to stop for a coffee, and they found a table in the shade of a plane tree at a nearby *kafeneion*.

– So, Cosmo, can you tell me what's going on with you and Ruben? What's the secret deal?

– Woah, Jade. You jump right in, don't you?

– What other way is there?

– You could ask Ruben, for starters.

– Ruben gives elusive answers. He blathers on about pre-military activity, but never actually says what he means by that term or what he's up to.

– Blathers on? Cosmo played for time.

– Yeah. Blathers on. He says he'll tell everything when he knows what there is to tell. But at the moment he doesn't. I was wondering if you might be more forthcoming. You see, it's not that I want to monitor his every action, or yours. But nor do I want you getting into some kind of trouble. We're mates, right?

– Right.

Cosmo's thoughts were drifting: why did she sound like an Australian? She was a chameleon, changing accents at will. He wondered why he hadn't clocked this facility of hers before.

– Well, you shouldn't have too many secrets between mates, should you?

Cosmo looked around the little square. A lizard was climbing the low wall behind the plane tree. He flicked a couple of flies away from the dark grains that stained his coffee cup and reached for his cigarettes.

– Keeping mum, hey?

– I can't very well tell you if Ruben hasn't.

– Have you told Alysa?

– She hasn't asked.

Jade nodded.

– That makes sense. Or does it? I don't know. She seems unreasonably disinterested when I've broached it with her. Almost as if she didn't need to ask, because she knows already.

Jade stretched out her hand and placed it on Cosmo's. He lit his cigarette, trembling slightly. Her touch unnerved him.

– I won't tell Ruben that you told me. I'm worried is all.

Cosmo remained silent, flicked ash.

– Okay. Let me help you. So as you don't end up telling me. You just have to hear my hypothesis.

Cosmo leaned back in his chair. – Fire away.

– During your absence Ruben makes a brief trip to Athens, withdraws a lot of cash – I checked in his bank-book – and I learn that he has been seen in the company of an American serviceman more than once, talking kind of secretive. Now I don't believe that Ruben really has much truck with the US military, so what the hell is that about? My theory is that the trip to Athens and the intimate meetings with sailor-boy are not unconnected. That a bargain was struck, an exchange offered, the handing on of money or goods took place, and that Ruben, or Ruben and you, have bought information that might, just might, put you both in serious danger. Am I a million miles away?

– Go on, said Cosmo, signifying nothing.

– My informant tells me Ruben has been eager for information regarding US 'pre-military' activity in the area. Ruben has been taking photos that could get him into trouble, I know. He does that when I'm around. So what am I saying?

Jade, who rarely smoked, paused and took one of Cosmo's cigarettes. – Can we have a beer? She asked. – Hair of the dog and all that. Besides it's getting bloody warm.

Cosmo called over to the waiter, who disappeared inside the bar and returned a few seconds later with a bottle of Amstel and two glasses.

– What I'm saying, what I'm asking is: Ruben seeks information about US military activities, for reasons best known to him. Yes, I've thought about Igbar's fascination with the suspect KGB agent but I don't buy that. Not with Ruben. He's an anarchist, not a commie. Why should he care? What drives Ruben is something else. His *research*. Deep Hanging Out. Or is it? Come to think of it, the whole Deep Hanging Out riff is a bit of a non-starter isn't it, with you two I mean. If you or Ruben think you're not driven, you are deluded. But maybe I'm missing the point. Maybe you are both nuts. You realise that the whole Deep Hanging Out thing is based on the idea that you are watching, that you are the observer? But hey, what if your sense that you are doing the watching is misplaced, completely misbegotten? What if you are the ones being watched? Has that not even occurred to either of you?

She glanced at Cosmo for any reaction, but Cosmo was playing poker.

– OK. Your obsession, painting, isn't likely to get you shot. Not yet anyway. But Ruben, he's got wind of some military data, that's the first thing. I'm certain you and Ruben went to your secret place, whatever it is, the other night, because I went to the Unspeakable with Alysa, briefly, and Lucas told me Ruben had come in briefly and gone out again with Courtney the sailor. So it can't be far away. My guess is – here she looked around as if to check they were not being overheard – that Ruben has found some military installation that he wants somehow to photograph or even, and this is the frightening bit, sabotage. I know he's friends with crazy Nikos and my informant tells me they were thick as thieves one night in the Lyrakia while you and Alysa were away. You know that crazy Nikos has only recently done time in military prison for stealing explosives?

Cosmo tried hard not to show any expression. This was an alarmingly clever woman.

– It's a fascinating theory, he said, finally.

Jade drained her beer.

– Thanks. She looked thoughtfully at Cosmo for several seconds, and appeared to have made up her mind about something, then stood and picked up one of the bags of food from the market. – Oh, and one last question; did Pascale end up having sex with you last night, or with Alysa?

Cosmo collected the two remaining bags and paid the waiter. He reflected that the partition walls in his house were not soundproof.

– Both of you? I thought as much. You should watch her.

Jade smiled, flicked her hair out of her eyes, put on her

dark glasses and set off towards home. After a few paces she stopped and turned, swinging the shopping bag in both hands and scowling into the sun.

– Hurry up Cosmo. You're going to cook, remember?

Cosmo caught up with her.

– What happened to young Lucas last night? I thought he was, like, with Pascale.

– I guess Pascale has her own peculiar needs. He went off by himself. He was cool.

13. Things become Complicated

When they arrived back at the house, Lucas was there, chatting with Ruben. Jade brewed coffee while Cosmo cracked eggs into a bowl for omelettes. After eating, Alysa, Pascale, Lucas, Ruben, Jade and Cosmo were all seated around the table, drinking coffee, when Igbar Zoff appeared in the doorway, breathless, shocked and red-faced. He leaned against the door-jamb, gasped, and took a melodramatic suck at his asthma inhaler. All eyes turned towards him.

– Give him a raki, Cosmo instructed Ruben, but Igbar waved his hand. He leaned there still, panting. Pascale got up and steered him into a seat. He leaned on her a little more than was probably necessary, then sat at the table, fumbling in his shirt pocket for cigarettes. He addressed Ruben.

– You know Courtney, the American sailor?

Cosmo glanced at Ruben, but not without Jade noticing.

Ruben nodded.

– He's dead.

Igbar let this announcement sink in while he lit his cigarette. He was shaking terribly, but this was normal for him before lunchtime. – Now give me a drink, would you?

Ruben reached over for a bottle of raki and poured a large shot into a tumbler. Igbar knocked this back and started again.

– Found with his throat slit. He'd been dead two days, the police reckon. Tassos has just told me. He said to stay away from the restaurant today; the police are bound to pay a visit and he doesn't want to answer too many questions. I don't have a work permit, obviously.

Everyone, including Pascale, knew who Courtney was, and there was a moment in which no one spoke. Jade was watching Ruben, who looked as shocked as everyone else.

– *Che*, that's terrible, he said. They cut his throat?

Igbar looked down.

– Yes. The story is that they had some fun with him first, but Tassos says these might just be rumours.

– Fun? Asked Jade.

– Tassos mentioned lacerations, cigarette burns. Bruises around the genitals.

– He'd been tortured?

Igbar shrugged.

– Jesus.

– You know his mate, Marvin? Here he looked over at Ruben, who nodded. He came in last night, after you had wrecked the place, looking for his buddy. He said Courtney was AWOL since Wednesday. Then some MPs came around, same intention.

– MPs? Pascale looked confused.

– Military Police. We never get MPs in the Unspeakable. They collect the debris from the bars around Souda, and the

Xania nightclubs. But they don't come to our place, as a rule.

Igbar helped himself to more raki, and drank noisily. His trembling had subsided a little after the first shot, and now he had an audience, he was keen to make the most of his role as Bearer of Bad News. The stunned reaction to his story spurred him on.

– He was a good guy, continued Igbar. He didn't have that brain-dead feel that so many of the Yankee military do. He paused. – And he loved his pig-nuts.

Alysa spluttered into poorly-restrained laughter.

– Could be his epitaph. *Here lies Courtney, who loved his pig-nuts*. Sorry. God, what am I saying! Sorry.

– How horrible! Pascale kicked Alysa in the shin. *Salope!*

– Sorry, sorry, sorry.

– What did Marvin tell you exactly? asked Ruben.

– Only that Courtney had been acting, 'real strange' for a couple of days. That he had had a run-in with some officer and was pretty jumpy. Mind you, he was pretty jumpy himself. But he did ask if I had seen you, Ruben. He seemed to think you might be able to help him.

– He asked for me by name?

– No, he was in a state. Couldn't remember your name. Just asked me if I knew where Courtney's Colombian friend was. Seems geography is not his strong point. I reckoned he must mean you.

– You didn't mention this last night.

– Sorry. Too pissed. By the time I got to the Lyrakia, I'd clean forgotten.

– Don't worry. If Courtney was found two days dead there wasn't much that could be done in any case.

There was an uneasy silence, broken by the miaowing of the cat, asking for food. Cosmo got up and cut some of the trimming from the round of beef he had bought at the market, and put it on a saucer. He began to prepare the meat in a large pan with the other ingredients.

– I'm going to put this on a low flame, he announced, – and then I'm going to take the *Nektar* out. Maybe find a quiet beach, maybe just drift. Anyone want to come?

They all assented (except for Igbar, who pleaded seasickness). A boat-trip seemed a good idea right now. Packing fruit and water, and collecting towels, they set off down towards the sea.

Once they had steered clear of the Venetian harbour, Ruben joined Cosmo at the stern of the boat, where they took turns at the tiller. Alysa, Jade and Pascale lay on the wooden deck up front. Lucas was perched at the prow, just beyond them. The sea was calm, and they chugged smoothly through the water. To their left, the White Mountains were shrouded in a heat haze. Cosmo was too preoccupied with thoughts of Courtney's torture and death to think about fishing, but Ruben was already threading shrimps on a line.

– I'm going to go back to the bunker tonight, said Ruben, breaking in on Cosmo's thoughts about the need for certain people to inflict pain on others; and of others to feel pain inflicted on themselves. – Will you come?

– You *what*? Are you *totally* crazy? Don't you think it's likely that Courtney's lieutenant has spilled the beans? About the key, the code. Jesus, why do you think that idiot Marvin was looking for you?

– There's no panic. If the place is guarded then we'll stay out of sight. If it's not, we're probably in the clear.

– You think that's beyond doubt?

– Beyond reasonable doubt.

– All the more reason to stay away. It's precisely the irrational, the unknown, that we're up against here. The situation stinks, man. Diabolical forces of unreason are being unleashed even as we speak.

– Don't you think you're like, over-reacting? Besides, I need to get some pictures. And I need to get into that room. Why is it locked? Why is it the only locked room down there, in a place already code-locked and with infra-red about to be installed? Can't you see, man? I don't get in now, I never get the chance. Will you come?

Cosmo looked ahead. Alysa was rubbing sun lotion onto Pascale's back and shoulders, massaging the oil in with a look of easy concentration. Cosmo could make out a nasty swelling beneath one eye and purple bruising on one of Pascale's upper arms. He didn't want to think about how she got those. But he remembered the crash of her cheekbone on the cast-iron bed-head as she thrashed naked above him, head gyrating like a voodoo priestess in the full thrall of spirit possession.

That was it she was sweet at first then she was a hurricane and she must have woken the whole street and then later Alysa was on her and she tied her arms and Pascale was moaning I think she liked it the tying up part and Alysa lay full stretch on her with her hand between Pascale's legs she was pushing hard I couldn't see what she was doing or what she was holding in her hand but she was forcing Pascale's arms down and she must have bruised them then I don't think it was malicious but Jesus who knows what goes on inside her head she simply needs to get off on this stuff for whatever reason and how did she know *that Pascale was going to go along with all this shit is there some kind of scanning system that they use like the freemasons secret handshake I mean did they* discuss *it beforehand did she say hey Pascale how about some high octane kinky sex avec mon mec seems unlikely so how does she know it beats me we were all hyper by then we were all so wrapped up in it so fucking liquidized I didn't give it a thought at the time Pascale wasn't complaining or anything in fact quite the contrary she was really gone she was pleading but Alysa kept her tied up while her and me had a good long fuck so Pascale had to watch but couldn't touch I think that* really *blew Alysa's fuse that being watched she just kept on coming like forever but later I was dozing and I woke up and she was licking Alysa again which turned me on like crazy and I took Pascale from behind she grabbed my cock and moved it wanted it in the arse and she made Alysa come again and when we'd tried out most of the permutations and variations that can be achieved without the use of pulleys or traction or other contrivances I guess we must have slept though come to think about it I can't have slept for long at all cos it was light outside long before the two of them were asleep it was a heck of a night.*

The women were talking, but Cosmo could not hear their words against the sound of the boat's engine. Alysa turned her head as Cosmo watched her, watching him.

– They know something's up, he said.

– I know. I've had the questions.

– Me too, this morning, with Jade.

– And?

– She's practically worked it out already. Even knowing, guessing, that you got the key to some place off Courtney. Everything except what's actually down there – which, when you think about it, we don't know either.

– Shit. How she do that?

– Natural intelligence, plus a bit of help from Igbar Zoff. I didn't give her any clues. She put it to me as a ready-formed theory. Uncanny. But she's done her research.

– Something's got into her. She goes on to me about not telling her anything, but all the time I get the feeling that really it's her who's not telling me stuff. Now, why should that be?

– Because you're paranoid?

– I don't think so. Ruben reached in his pocket for cigarettes and offered one to Cosmo. He leaned over, cradling a match from the wind. When his head was up close to Cosmo's, he whispered:

– Courtney was a spy.

Cosmo sat, absorbing this, while he smoked.

– Have you any evidence for that statement? Or is it just another cold war hypothesis?

He noticed Ruben's sly, questioning smile.

– You're taking the piss, Ruben.

– Maybe yes, maybe no.

– Oh come on. Don't fuck about. Courtney was too low-ranking to be worth the Russians investing in. But even if he was spying for the Russians, the US military wouldn't have had him murdered up a back alley. They would have tried him for treason.

– Wrong on both counts, answered Ruben, serious now. – Sure, as you say, he was a lowly seaman. He would only have been of limited interest to the Russians. But he could have led them to someone else, just like he did with me. Plus they do take on strong-arm guys too: cold war espionage is not all about Cambridge queens. Second, if he was a spy, the Americans could not afford the scandal of a trial, all that negative publicity, not at this stage, after the boycott of the Moscow Olympic games, and now the face-off with Brezhnev. It would make sense to have him disappear and make it look like something else. A local issue. You know, screwing a Cretan girl, getting her pregnant. Angry father, brothers. And by the way, who said it was the Yanks that had him killed? If he was working for the Russians, and cocked up some way, then they wouldn't hesitate to silence him. Don't assume, as you probably do, that if Courtney was their man in Xania, they'd airlift him to Moscow and parade him as a convert to the Soviet cause.

– Dead, he can't win either way.

– Dead, he's less of a liability. But I'm not sure of any of this. The shelter isn't going to be of major interest to the Russians. They're interested in ordnance, stock, warheads.

– Ruben, don't take this personal. But aren't you just trying to make yourself feel better about Courtney's death? Aren't you just a teeny bit anxious that you might be implicated?

If Ruben was aggrieved by this suggestion he did not show it.

– No. I liked Courtney. I liked his company. I spent some time with him before the issue of the shelter came up. We'd have a few drinks together. He had his feet on the ground. He was no fool, in spite of the company he kept. Sure, I'm sorry he's dead. But I can't get worked up. In the scale of things, one death more or less counts for very little.

Cosmo looked at his friend, astonished. This last utterance sounded like the kind of platitude made by somebody entirely persuaded by political conviction. Or else by a psychopath. He hadn't thought of Ruben as fitting into either of these categories. And Alysa had shown a similar aloofness from the murder with her joke about pig-nuts back at the house. What was going on? Was this callousness a front of some kind, perhaps devised to keep at bay the true horror of what had been done to Courtney? Or did the two of them believe, as Ruben seemed to be suggesting, that in the broader context of bringing about political objectives the lives of individuals were expendable? Cosmo was puzzled. He shifted his seat and trailed his feet in the water, while staring at the boat's wake. Ruben handed him the tiller and moved down to the prow to sit with Lucas.

That evening there was a big Communist Party rally in town. Charilaos Florakis, the KKE leader, was due to give a speech and it was common knowledge that his prime target would be the continuing US Naval presence (or *occupation*, as Nikos would have it) at Souda. The house in the Splanzia had been listless – almost deathly, since the boat trip that afternoon. Jade had gone upstairs to sleep. Cosmo, unable to paint, was feeling fractious. Alysa was reading a book (*ELAS, Greek Resistance Army*) on the sofa in his studio. Ruben seemed the least distracted and had spent several hours in his darkroom. After eating, Cosmo suggested to Alysa that they might take a wander up to see what was going on in the market square, where the rally was taking place.

– What for? she responded, briskly.

– I'm not sure exactly. I thought you might be interested. Florakis was in ELAS too, during the Resistance. Like your dad. And, er, he's a communist, right?

Alysa clicked her tongue.

– Oh for God's sake, Cosmo. You sound like an imbecile.

Cosmo grinned like one.

– Tell me why you want to go, she said.

– I thought *you'd* like to go.

– So you're thinking of me?

– Yeah. That's me all over.

– Creep.

Alysa pretended to read.

– Hey! This isn't fair. What's bugging you?

– You are. She sat up. – I suppose trotting along to the rally constitutes Deep Hanging Out, does it? Or is it just voyeurism? Because, face it Cosmo, you really don't give a shit whether they're communists or fascists. It's all the same to you, isn't it. You want to go and have a nose around, give yourself a sense of being an insider, while remaining on the outside. You want to count the other people but don't want to be counted yourself. Isn't that it? You have no idea of the arrogance of such an attitude. Most people simply have lives to lead. They get on with them. Why do you think working people in Greece support the Communist Party – for some kind of a thrill like those kids at Oxford playing at revolution? No, they support the KKE because they believe it will deliver them a better quality of life, and because they believe that it would be a more just system. But then you wouldn't understand that either, because your dad is a rich French Professor and you've never really wanted for anything in your life.

– Ouch! said Cosmo. He had not encountered Alysa in this mood before and was trying to take what she said lightly. But for the second time in a day he realized that he didn't know how to read her. Was she being serious now, or playing with him? The mocking tone seemed genuine enough, alerting him to another element of cruelty in her. Whatever the case, he determined to ignore the insults because something about her demeanour and her attitude troubled him more than he was prepared to admit. She seemed somehow diminished since the news of Courtney's death that midday. But Cosmo too possessed reserves of cruelty, and did not like the notion that he was about to storm out of the room while she held the high ground on the moral front.

– And you do give a shit, right? You stand alongside the poor and the oppressed? If you oppose the deployment of US missiles in Europe, then why aren't you at Greenham Common, eating greasy pea samosas and smoking soggy roll-ups and getting beaten up by police? I don't see much action on your part. You align yourself with your father's outdated political beliefs because it's your way to feel his love, even now he's dead.

– Oh leave the amateur psychology out, please, said Alysa, getting up from the sofa and dragging a vacuum cleaner from the cupboard by the washstand.

– OK then. Try this for size. When Igbar was around today, you made that joke about pig-nuts. Courtney's epitaph. Was that meant to be *funny*? Did you seriously consider Courtney to be an enemy of the people? I was under the impression that he was an ordinary working-class black guy from Detroit who'd signed up for the Navy, most likely to get away from grinding poverty or, at best, a job with General Motors turning a bolt on a conveyor belt for 10 hours a day. Was he an imperialist? Did he deserve to die? Was that the subtext to your little joke?

Alysa had dumped the vacuum cleaner in the middle of the studio with a clatter and was now beginning to clean things, almost frenetically. She was re-arranging cushions, dusting shelves, then was on all fours trying to remove spillages of oil paint (of which there were many) from the floor with a pallet knife, scraping noisily at the floorboards.

– Fuck off, she said.

– Don't worry. I will. He stood there for a few seconds, watching her scratch at the floor, wielding the tool like a dagger in both hands.

– What exactly are you doing? he asked her.

She did not reply.

– What are you doing? This is *my* studio. These are *my* things. I like it the way it is. If I want to clean them I'll clean them. Or I'll pay someone else to clean. But I'm not having you doing this crap simply to exorcise your neuroses and to try and make me feel bad.

Alysa looked up at him briefly, eyes livid, then returned to her cleaning.

Cosmo decided to leave before she switched the vacuum on, but he lacked the self-restraint to resist slamming the door behind him. He went down and called on Ruben in his darkroom, just beyond the kitchen. Ruben emerged, scowling.

– I was going to take a stroll up through town. Have a look at the KKE rally. And then . . .

Ruben raised an eyebrow.

– And then?

– Sod it, I'll come with you to the bloody bunker, OK?

– *Che!* You sure? No, don't answer that. I'll be with you in a minute.

The town was packed. A huge crowd had assembled in front of the market, and many of the activists were chanting and carrying red banners after their march through the centre. The chants were repetitive and, to Cosmo's mind, faintly idiotic. They contained variations but were all on the 'Americans Out' theme. Cosmo wondered briefly why he found the chants embarrassing, and decided that it was the hopelessness of the cause that prompted his reaction. There was absolutely no way that the Americans were going to relinquish their bases in the Eastern Mediterranean, nor was there any great likelihood of the Greeks electing a government that would be able to insist upon it. He was oddly moved by the sense of solidarity and the passion of resistance, however ineffectual it might be, an emotion that sent ripples up his spine when the chanting grew louder and more insistent. But essentially he regarded the rally as an exercise in the unattainable.

Ruben was taking pictures of Florakis, the communist leader, as he began his speech. They were at quite a distance from the platform, and Ruben was using a powerful zoom. After twenty minutes or so, when it was evident that Florakis was in for the long haul (he was pontificating on the phenomenon of Eurocommunism in such a way that Cosmo could not work out whether he was vehemently opposed to it or actively supportive of it) Ruben gave Cosmo a nudge and began edging his way out of the crowd. It was slow progress, since people were bunched tightly together and their attention was directed towards the leader's speechmaking, but eventually they found their way out of the crowd and wound up in a side street near the market. It was getting dark now, and hundreds of small birds had settled in a nearby tree, embellishing the dusk air with a cascade of chirruping sound. Random groups of demonstrators and latecomers to the rally sauntered past them, heading for the Square. Further down the street, in the doorway of a kafeneion, Cosmo spotted an unmistakeable figure.

– Hey, isn't that Nikos? I'll give him a shout.

– No, wait, said Ruben, hand on his shoulder, dragging him behind the tree. – Wait. The guy he's with. Courtney mentioned someone had been following him, gave me a bit of a description. Said the guy wore a Yale sweatshirt, baseball cap, had a Mediterranean appearance. Take a look at him.

Next to Nikos, the man looked diminutive, wiry. He was standing thirty metres away, but facing them, and in the light from the coffee-shop, Cosmo could make out the lettering on his sweatshirt: YALE. He was a small man with olive complexion and sharp features, and he wore a faded baseball cap.

– Why don't we just go up and say hullo? asked Cosmo. We've got nothing to lose.

– You crazy Irishman. You don't find out what's going on by, like, waltzing up and introducing yourself. You *case* the situation. You keep one step ahead. You don't let them know you're onto anything. Elementary espionage.

– Yeah, but by going up and saying Hi, you stand the chance of wrong-footing them.

– Only if you know what it is you mean to find out. And have some way of corroborating what you already know. We're in the dark with this guy.

– You just told me he was shadowing Courtney, just before he got murdered. We know that much.

– We might. But that could have been Courtney's paranoia. We can't go making big assumptions. The guy might be working for the US secret services, on a tip off. We just don't know and can't go fucking things up.

He pulled himself short: – Hey, look! Isn't that Alysa?

The two men had been joined by a woman. She was tall, and looked dark, but the lack of street-lighting and the woman's headscarf prohibited a clear view. Alysa often wore a headscarf, but so did many other women. Cosmo could not be sure. He hadn't seen her approach, though evidently Ruben had. If only she would move, make some characteristic gesture, or even start walking, Cosmo would be better able to judge if it was her or not, but at that moment a large group of stragglers filled the street directly in their line of sight, and when they had passed into the Square, there was no sign of the three figures in the doorway, or anywhere else in the street.

– Let's go, said Ruben, and headed down the side street.

They walked quickly, and as they approached the windows of the coffee-shop, Ruben again pulled Cosmo back.

– We'd better not walk past together, peering in. I'll cross over and signal to you.

Ruben walked slowly past the café on the opposite sidewalk, nonchalantly scanning the interior of the place. Once he was past he turned and walked back to Cosmo.

– They're not in there. And if they had been, it would have been dumb to let them know that we were onto them. Any idea what this is all about?

– Search me. Decidedly suspicious. Do you really think that was Alysa? I'm not so sure. I didn't get a proper look at her.

– It was her.

– What now then? Plan A?

Ruben looked thoughtful.

– If we go back to the house now, we could check for sure whether or not that was Alysa, said Cosmo.

– She could be almost back there already. Plus if we go

home and then go straight out again, they're going to follow us, aren't they? At least, Jade will, bearing in mind what she said to you this morning.

– We could lose them. Take some false turnings. Slip through restaurants that have two doors.

– Forget it, man. Let's go. But the long way around, down Daskhalogias Street, in case we can catch sight of them. They must have gone that way. They can't have vanished.

But evidently, they had done just that.

14. Return to the Labyrinth

Half an hour later Cosmo stood over the trapdoor of the bunker while Ruben knelt to tap in the security code. All was quiet on the street behind them. Cosmo reflected how different was this raid on the labyrinth compared with their first visit, when Ruben had entered the place in a mood of high excitement, snorting coke, laughing and joking. Now a man was dead; someone they had known as a friend. It was likely that the security code had been changed: and if it hadn't, didn't that indicate something worse? Cosmo had voiced these doubts as they approached the end of the harbour walk, but Ruben was obsessed, and Cosmo decided to hold onto his fears and stick by his friend. Now he watched, as Ruben lowered himself through the trap onto the ladder. Cosmo took a last look around, scanning the immediate area beyond the building site towards the sea, and followed him down. They both had flashlights, and in his small rucksack Ruben carried acetylene torch, wrench and screwdriver.

They followed the sloping tunnel with its studs of

coloured light down to the lobby area of the bunker where they had found the supply stores and bunk-rooms, and then continued through the older tunnelling to the second wider space with the two doors. The door of the empty room hung open, while the other was still firmly and securely locked. Ruben set to work with the screwdriver, first trying to loosen the handle in order to get leverage on the steel door where lock met jamb. Cosmo sat on the ground and was about to light a cigarette when he noticed a nozzle protruding from the arched ceiling and thought better of it.

– Smoke alarms? Spray system? He wondered out loud. – Where would they run to if there was a fire? Out into the post-nuclear holocaust?

Ruben continued working at the door. He had taken a small acetylene torch from his rucksack and was trying to burn a trench around the door-handle. He slipped on a pair of shades as sparks flew from the end of the torch.

– In any case, how long would they have to stay down here before it was safe to venture forth? And would the supplies of peanut butter and Coca Cola hold out? How much peanut butter would be required to keep the numbers of men down here in good spirits? Or men and women. Presumably there would be women down here. And if they were here for a matter of years, what measures would be in place to guarantee the maximum decorum in matters of sexual conduct? Would there be facilities for small children? Or would steps be taken to prevent any pregnancies from coming to term? Who would have the final say in these matters? Wouldn't the conditions down here lead to constant power struggles between opposing factions, on whatever grounds? There would be mutinies, no doubt. Plots, murders: probably the invention of a new religion. The practice of witchcraft, other new-fangled sorceries. And of course a number of people would go barking mad. Doollally.

– Should have brought a fucking shotgun, Ruben said. – No one's going to hear us down here. What is *doollally*?

– Loco. How long is this going to take? Cosmo asked.

– I've no idea. As long as it takes. You impatient? Anxious to get back to your women?

– Hey, that was uncalled for. I'm your loyal assistant here.

– Ruben turned an eerily-lit grin towards Cosmo. – Cosmo's women. What you do then? What is the, er, *architecture* of your ménage a trois?

– I beg your pardon?

– What's the logistics man? Who gets to put what where and when and in whom and in what combination?

– Christ Ruben, you have a vulgar way with words. Even without naming body parts.

– Can't help it man. I was brought up . . .

– Quiet, hissed Cosmo. I heard something.

– An echo, said Ruben and continued trying to force the door. – Stop trying to change the subject.

– No: something else. Stop that a minute.

Ruben sighed and stepped back from the door, waited.

– See. Nothing. Just your nerves.

In response, as if from a long way off, or else hidden behind thick walls, came a deep guttural noise. Cosmo would later describe it as a pained lowing, though it was a human sound, containing the barest outline of language, the rolling of the tongue on palate, the upward screech of vowels. As the sound grew louder, its voice becoming more distinct, Cosmo thought, preposterously, that he could detect the stern melody of *When will the sky be clear*, an old revolutionary song from the days of the Ottoman Empire. The words were somehow muted, mangled, a grotesque and carnival rendition; but the modulations of the droning hymn were unmistakable and the Greek words, known as the unofficial anthem of Crete, told of fire and blood and vengeance: *When will the sky be clear, when will it be February: to take my rifle, my lovely mistress, to come down to Omalos, on the road to Mousoure, to make mothers sonless, and wives widows.*

– What the hell is that? Cosmo was on his feet, peering down the tunnel.

– Is it coming this way?

– I don't know but I don't think I'm going to hang around to find out.

– Oh come on, man. I've almost got through this thing.

– You aren't being serious. Oh, you *are*.

Ruben was pulling at the wrench with all his strength, foot pressed against the door-frame. Cosmo stared at his friend, disbelieving. Ruben's determination to break into this one locked room had taken on an obsessive significance, and he was not going to be distracted. Meanwhile, the demented chanting was getting louder, and as it did so, Cosmo detected pauses in the song, pauses filled with muffled and improbable Greek curses, yelled at full volume. He took another step into the dimly-lighted inner tunnel and almost collided with the huge form of a man striding purposefully towards him. The man's shoulders were topped by a vast black bull's-head and his hands were unspooling a length of fuse. Over one shoulder swung an assault rifle.

In response to Cosmo's strangled cry, the Minotaur turned its great head, peering closely, first at Cosmo, then at Ruben. The mythical creature gave the appearance of being overjoyed. It enacted a hop and a shin-slapping vault typical of traditional Cretan dance, grabbing Cosmo by the hand as it swayed on landing, before attempting to lead its bewildered partner on a balletic circuit of the little concourse area. Its singing resembled a prolonged roar, its movements a burlesque of exaggerated poise and gesture. Trailing Cosmo limply across the corridor, the Minotaur executed a final leap before turning again towards Ruben and tilting its head to examine his activity at the door with apparent interest, still holding the length of fuse in one hand. Ruben returned its blind gaze.

– Nikos!

There was no doubting it: the huge body, the enormous feet, and now the manic laughter that spilled from inside the bull-mask.

The Minotaur took a deep bow.

Ruben had put the acetylene torch away and begun kicking at the door, but realizing that greater force needed to be applied, stood back to shoulder-charge it. He heaved himself into the door, but still it would not budge. Nikos stepped forward and brushed him aside.

– I do this, he growled, the sound muffled by the mask. – But you must leave, understand? No time. Let me tell you something quick. Soon this place gonna blow sky-high, and take that fuckin Marco Polo with it. You know where we are?

His voice was hoarse, thick. He gestured at the roof of the tunnel.

– The hotel right above us now. What you say about killing two birds with one bang? Tourist terrorism.

He stood back a few paces, took vague aim from waist level, and let off a double salvo from the rifle: then he launched himself against the door, and this time there was a loud crack as it disengaged from the lock. Ruben stepped up and delivered the decisive kick. The door sprung open and a brilliant golden light spilled out. Nikos stepped inside the portal, the black bull's head silhouetted against the extraordinary radiance that flooded the doorway.

The first explosion, from far down the inner tunnel, rocked the floor and walls. The second, which followed after a few seconds, caused all the lights to go out and an avalanche of rock and dust to fall around the doorway, isolating Ruben, who had backed away in the direction of the exit with the first detonation, and leaving Cosmo and Nikos stranded behind a wall of debris. Cosmo, guessing that Nikos must have set a trail of explosives at intervals further inside the labyrinth, flashed his light around him, catching Nikos in the beam. He was jumping up and down, screaming *Ela, ela!* Any sane person would have removed it, but it seemed to Cosmo entirely in keeping with the unfolding events that Nikos continued to wear the bull's-head mask. The Minotaur was screaming at Cosmo now, something urgent; that he must run, that the sealed room was full of explosives and other ordnance. That he had set a fuse to blow the whole place apart. Dust was raining from the ceiling and there was the ominous sound of falling debris, the grinding of rock on rock from the deep interior of the labyrinth.

Nikos had stopped dancing and was now attempting to pull the oversize bull's-head mask from his head, bending forward and tugging the monstrous carapace from his shoulders. Cosmo stepped forward to help him just as a rumbling crescendo began to echo down the corridors and another section of the roof caved in. He levered himself against the wall of the tunnel and pulled with both hands on the Minotaur's head. Nikos gurgled loudly from inside his dark shell, screamed an obscenity, and pulled free, the bull's-mask still on his head, but now tilted jauntily to one side. Before Cosmo could stop him, Nikos began to run blindly down the tunnel, away from the exit. He wobbled away into the falling dust, broad shoulders supporting the black horned head.

Cosmo called after him; but another detonation made his words redundant and knocked him to the ground. He pulled himself up and, turning his flashlight back up the tunnel, began to scramble through the dust and rock fall that had fallen between himself and Ruben after the first explosion. He clambered up the heap of debris and pointed the torch into the thick grey dust that churned around him, in the direction he believed the tunnel followed back towards the trapdoor. He knew he had to leave the tunnel before the store-room blew. There did not seem to be a way through, and he edged around the summit of the rock fall on all fours, seeking out a gap. Sliding and crawling belly-down through sharp rock fragments, the filthy air dense around him, he choked and spluttered his way across the rubble. His eyes were stinging and he could see nothing. Eventually he found a tiny area that gave out onto open space and began picking away at rocks and casting them aside in an attempt to widen the gap. Pausing for a moment to catch his breath between a fit of choking, he heard the bellowing of the Minotaur, deep within the cave. It sounded like laughter.

Cosmo squeezed through the gap he had made and rolled down the scree on the other side, collecting cuts and bruises to every part of the body. Dazed, but with no serious injury, he staggered onto solid ground and limped back up the tunnel. The air was impregnable around him though, and when he tried to breathe, his mouth and lungs filled with the taste of rock-dust and cordite. He took off his shirt and held a section of it over his mouth and nostrils. Leaning against the wall of the tunnel he tried to get his breath back, inhaling slowly through the cotton fabric, but he could not muster enough oxygen to gratify his lungs, and he slumped to the ground, with the horrifying intimation that he would die if he did not breathe fresh air. He started taking small fast breaths, and experienced a stab of panic. He had no idea how long it would be before the explosion that Nikos had warned him of would bring the whole structure down.

Someone was approaching. A torch shone dimly through the black dust and he raked his own light to the sides of the tunnel. The figure was blurred and moving slowly along the tunnel, and he tried to call out, but began to choke instead. The figure stopped in its tracks for a second and then came running towards him. It was Alysa. She removed the headscarf that she had tied around her face, bandit-style, and knelt down beside him. She made as if to embrace him, then, on seeing the state that he was in, covered in cuts, with lips and face plastered with dust, she cried out.

– What *happened* to you?

Cosmo could not speak. The inside of his mouth was stuffed with cotton wool and his tongue was a dead weight. He gawped at her.

– Ah, I see, said Alysa, pointing her flashlight in his face. You're a bit dry.

Kneeling in front of him, she moistened her finger with saliva and rubbed it gently along Cosmo's lips, then leaned forward and kissed him, very long and very deep. Cosmo's tongue stirred in recovery.

– Christ, he said, coughing up a lungful of dust, – you are a resourceful woman. No time to explain. Talk as we walk. The whole place is going to go up in a minute. Have you seen Ruben?

– Yeah, he got out ten minutes ago. Gave me his flashlight. I told him to make himself scarce. The cops are on their way.

– Shit. That's all I need.

– Ruben mentioned Crazy Nikos. Kept going on about him. I thought he was delirious. Said Nikos was dressed up as the Minotaur. He down here too?

– Yes. He disappeared back into the labyrinth. Off his trolley, that one. Singing, dancing. *Laughing*. Fuck, can we get out of here?

Alysa grabbed him by the arm and they began to run, or limp, up the tunnel. Cosmo's throat was sore, his eyes were streaming, and he was grateful for the guidance. He doubted that he would have found his way without her. He began to ask her how she had known he was here. Alysa was unflustered, but keen to return to ground level.

– Simple. I followed you. Now, save your breath, she told him. – When I get you out of here, you can explain everything. *If* we get out before the friggin' cavalry arrives.

He stopped walking for a moment.

– Hey, by the way. I'm sorry. About the things I said.

– Me too. She stroked his cheek with her fingertips. Forget it.

It did not take long to reach the trapdoor opening and climb the steel ladder, but emerging from the hole in the ground, they found a reception committee of a dozen Greek police had encircled the building site. A strong searchlight shone in Cosmo's face as he raised his arms above his head in response to a barked directive by an officer with a megaphone. There was no sign of Ruben, but Jade was there. After speaking briefly to a second officer, she approached Alysa and the two women were taken to one side. Cosmo was to be questioned separately by a Greek officer. He immediately told the policeman, in Greek, that they would have to move, that there were explosives in the bunker; that there had already been three detonations and might well be a fourth, at any time. Rather than act on his advice, the officer threw more questions at him, and as Cosmo struggled to make his initial answers as opaque as possible, a screeching of tyres announced the arrival of a US Military Police jeep. Three MPs and an official dressed in suit and tie got out of the car at the precise moment that an explosion shook the ground beneath them. It was all Cosmo could do to keep his footing. The American official, caught off balance by the blast, was not so fortunate, and suffered the indignity of making a poor entrance. Worse was to follow. Just as the reverberations of that blast died away, another, massive explosion threw most of those present off their feet. Cosmo stayed standing, swaying, and felt a strange thrill as he watched, two hundred metres away, the lower floors of the brand new Hotel Marco Polo concertina in on themselves and crash to the ground in an almighty cloud of dust, followed by the upper floors, which collapsed as if in slow motion, each storey colliding in sequence into the vast pile of broken cement, steel and glass that was all that remained of the Marco Polo. A ghostly cloud had formed, and it hovered, vast and ominous, above them. The lighthouse continued to sweep the bay, and whenever it passed the dust-cloud, millions of tiny particles were reflected in its beam. The total destruction that Nikos sought had been efficiently realized. Tourist Terrorism was on the map.

Cosmo wondered if Nikos had survived the explosions. Would he be able to witness the results of his handiwork? Was there another entrance to the labyrinth that Nikos, with his local knowledge, had found out about, and where he was now perched, his bull's head nodding enthusiastically at the destruction before his eyes? There was no way he would be coming out through *this* exit: the tunnel would be utterly demolished now.

A young policeman guarding Cosmo looked around nervously, as though expecting any further blasts from underground to be signalled by a clue in the movement of the nearby trees.

The Greek officer sent four men to go and seal off the hotel area and organize a search for casualties. Fortunately there were not any residential properties in the immediate vicinity of the hotel and the Marco Polo had not yet opened: all it had lacked were some soft furnishings and a final lick of paint. But there may have been a caretaker or night-watchman on site.

When the American official at last came forward, brushing dust from his jacket, a polite but strained conversation ensued, in which the Greek attempted to convey that this was an issue for the Greek Police, not the American Military. His English was fastidious but extremely limited in vocabulary, and Cosmo restrained himself from the beautiful irony of offering to interpret for them.

The American official was clearly frustrated and angry.

– What the hell were you doing down there, buddy?

Cosmo sighed. – I'm not your buddy. And I don't believe I have to answer that. He looked toward the Greek officer for confirmation.

– This is Greek prisoner. Greek matter. No questions.

Cosmo stared the American in the eye.

– See. I'd hate to interfere with protocol.

Jade and Alysa had edged closer during this exchange. The American spoke in a hushed voice with his Greek counterpart, and the policeman gestured to Jade, who stepped forward, calmly, and addressed the officer in her best American.

– It is exactly as I reported to the police when I called them twenty minutes ago. The three of us – that is, me, my girlfriend and her fiancé, Mr Flute – were walking along the seafront when we heard this huge explosion. I imagine everyone in Xania must have heard it. When we saw the entrance here, with all the dust around it, Mr Flute told us to find a telephone and call the police; that he was going to see if there was anyone down there. In case there were any injured people. Anyone who needed help.

– Is this true? The officer asked Cosmo, doubtful.

– Just as she says.

– And is there anyone down there?

Cosmo hesitated, wondering again whether Nikos knew of another exit to the labyrinth, to which he had been heading when he ran off.

– Isn't that what you guys are here to find out?

– OK, OK, interrupted the Greek officer, aggrieved that he could not follow the conversation at all well. – This is a matter for Greek Police. We go now.

Cosmo was bundled into the back of a police Landrover. Alysa and Jade were led towards another waiting car. They would be questioned separately, Cosmo realized. But he had gathered enough from Jade's explanation to the American officer what their story was meant to be. He would have to confirm their version and hope that nothing had happened to Ruben that would contradict it.

15. Stratis' Nasty Tale

At the police station Cosmo received a summary medical inspection and his wounds, which were all deemed superficial, were daubed with iodine. The police doctor clicked his tongue and muttered under his breath when he saw the track marks on Cosmo's arm but asked no questions and pronounced him fit enough to be imprisoned. His captors led him to a large cell below ground level, and he was told that he would attend court the following morning. The cell was already occupied by a rather dazed New Zealander who was being held for possession of cannabis, and a small, muscular Moroccan named Ahmed, who had deserted from the French Foreign Legion and been arrested after attempting to hold up a jeweller's with his service revolver. Losing his nerve at the crucial moment of emptying the shopkeeper's till, he had fled the jewellery store and thrown his pistol into Xania harbour, from which it had not been retrieved, in spite of the efforts of police divers flown in from Piraeus. Ahmed spoke neither Greek nor English, and was extremely cheerful, considering his circumstances, which were bleak, chatting to

Cosmo throughout the night in bad French, delighted to find someone with whom he could communicate. Cosmo tried to relax beneath the coarse blanket he had been provided with, but the constant good-natured banter from Ahmed and the gloomy prospect of an indefinite period of incarceration in a Greek jail prevented him from sleeping. A visit to the adjoining toilet brought him face to face with a very large rat, which, after surveying Cosmo with contempt, slid horribly down the pit into unfathomable darkness. The encounter unsettled Cosmo disproportionately and the image of the rat disappearing nose-first into the abyss haunted the snatches of sleep he managed between Ahmed's incomprehensible religious monologues. The dual themes of crucifixion and resurrection apparently held a particular fascination to the Moroccan. Somewhere in the folds of his sleep, Cosmo's unconscious constellated a muddled scenario of rats, sewers and crucifixion, which on waking he construed as a nightmarish metaphor for what was about to happen to him.

As it transpired, the court appearance was not too stressful, as no clear charges were raised against Cosmo, other than unlawful trespass. But he felt abandoned: although it was clear that the court session was not open to the public, he had certainly expected to catch sight of his friends at some point, or at least receive word from them. If Ruben had managed to escape identification then that was well and good, but he found it ironic that he, and not his housemate, should end up in the dock.

The police prosecutor said that more time was needed to gather evidence and applied for Cosmo to be held without bail until charges could be brought. In order to do this he needed to persuade the judge that Cosmo was a possible terrorist. The judge appeared skeptical, but conceded that the prisoner could be sentenced for fifteen days on the grounds of criminal trespass and would be held in Xania jail. That, Cosmo realised bleakly, would give the prosecutor sufficient time to collect evidence. As soon as the sentence was delivered, Cosmo was led out into a police van for the short trip to prison. He asked if he could be allowed to get a message to Alysa, but since they had no telephone at the house, and the police were not willing to run errands, his request was denied. He could have asked to call the Unspeakable, but knew that Tassos would be concerned enough with the investigation into the death of Courtney, and would not want to be implicated, however obliquely, in any new disaster.

News and rumour trickled through to prisoners in Xania jail far more speedily and efficiently than the authorities would have liked. So it was that Cosmo came to learn that there had, miraculously, been no civilian casualties as a result of the Marco Polo explosion. The night-watchman had been comfortably ensconced in a nearby coffee-house when the building came down. But it was also rumoured that a body had been found in the ruins of the nuclear shelter. He could only surmise that if this were true, then Nikos had been caught in a rockfall. However, the other inmates of the jail made no such supposition and so Cosmo, fraudulently perhaps, but with no intention to deceive, arrived with a readymade reputation as a hard case, a suspected murderer, to be granted the ritual respect accorded to the most notorious felons. Cosmo chose not to correct this advantageous if improbable identity.

He received a prestigious corner bed in a long dormitory that was home to a dozen prisoners of very mixed degrees of criminality. Seven were Greeks, ranging from a (genuine) murderer to dynamiters of fish and hashish smokers: there was also a young Brit (car theft while drunk) a French Swiss (robbing a church of alms), soon joined by the New Zealander from the cells beneath the courthouse. Ahmed the would-be jewel thief, who appeared in front of the judge shortly after Cosmo, was lodged in a separate four-bed cell.

The jail also accommodated an eminent member of the recently deposed Military Junta. It was on account of this aging Fascist's alleged presence – no one ever saw him since he was taken out for exercise at times when he would not be at risk of public dismemberment by his fellow convicts – that the prison tower above the yard contained a machine gun post and, it was claimed by the more excitable, an anti-aircraft gun. The yard was the only part of the prison that Cosmo got to see other than his dormitory, the bathrooms and the refectory.

It was a drab existence, and Cosmo learned that he would not be permitted to receive visitors until he had been in for two weeks, which was the length of his current sentence. He had no materials to paint with and no place to paint in, and since, for as long as he could remember, painting had been the defining activity of his life, he felt especially aggrieved. However, he was nothing if not adaptable, and his fellow-prisoners were an eclectic bunch. There were plenty of English books and a range of magazines to read, left behind by former residents, ranging from Herodotus to seriously bad pornography.

For the first couple of days Cosmo was in a somber and reflective mood as he got to know his new surroundings and the peculiar by-laws of prison life. 'If you go in the shower,' Pierre, the French Swiss told him, 'take, you know, a fork from the dining room with you.' He got to know the private alliances, enmities and grudges that the prisoners concocted and nurtured; he learned that a single bottle of beer was served twice a year, at Christmas and on *Okie* day, a national holiday commemorating General Metaxas' famous repudiation of Mussolini, and, most importantly, he learned whom to avoid. He also met Stratis.

Stratis was a lifer who ignored the other foreigners, and most of the Greeks, but he would sometimes sit with Cosmo at exercise time. He was a placid man accustomed to the tedium of prison life. Time, he told Cosmo, was something he had plenty of. He was in his sixties, but he was fit; slight and clever, light of foot. He was not from Crete and spoke Greek with an Athenian accent. They said he was a double murderer.

In the yard, he would sit polishing a smooth black pebble, the size of a large olive. One day, towards the end of his first week, Cosmo asked him about the stone, why he polished it like that. Stratis considered this question for a long time, and then launched into a most bizarre story.

– Many years ago I was in another prison, on the mainland, before they sent me here. It was not an ordinary nick like this, more a concentration camp for political prisoners. One particular night, I was playing dice by candlelight with my cellmates, Giorgos and Michalis. We had been playing for so long, the three of us, that whatever stakes were bid appeared of no consequence and the game had lost all sense of excitement or risk. At the end of a long silence, Michalis suggested that we should play for our eyes.

'How?' asked Giorgos.

'Two of us play, and the loser has one eye removed

by the non-player. The non-player then throws against the winner, and the one-eyed man must remove the eye of the one who loses that second game. And so on.'

'And so on . . . until?'

'Until there is one person left with one eye, when the game finishes. It is obvious that two blind men would not be able to extract his one remaining eye, should the one-eyed survivor lose the last game. Here are five black olives.'

He produced some olives from his pocket, cleaned them with a handkerchief, and placed them on a saucer between us.

'For each eye removed,' Michalis went on, 'an olive must be inserted into the vacant hole. If the situation arises that one player remains with both his eyes intact, and the other two have lost both of theirs, the sighted player must remove one of his own eyes by way of compensation, as a sign of good faith, and because we have five olives. The sighted one does not have the option to terminate the game.'

'And' I asked, 'if a person continues to lose after forfeiting both eyes, while the other two still have at least one eye intact, what then?'

'Why,' answered Michalis, poker-faced, 'then we start on the ears.'

At this point Giorgos, who had been listening with strained concentration, laughed unpleasantly. Giorgos was a man of action, and he had a reputation for ruthlessness. But he was a comrade, and we had all been through a lot together. At times though, he looked and acted like a murderous child. By contrast Michalis was an intellectual, a propagandist and agitator. Michalis thought he could control Giorgos. In fact he did seem to manage him well enough, until that day. However, we had all been drinking heavily, and that distorted things, I guess. We had a demijohn of home-distilled hooch, real firewater, smuggled in by Aleko, the rat-faced screw, at great expense.

Michalis was grinning and Giorgos shook with laughter. I had a certain knowledge that something ugly would come of this, but seeing as we were on death row and all due to be shot dead in the morning, what difference could it make?

'And what,' spluttered Giorgos between attacks of hoarse cackling, 'what becomes of a player if he bleeds to death?'

'Quite simple,' came Michalis' answer. 'The contestant is prohibited from further play.'

If Giorgos had found the earlier rules of the game amusing, this he obviously thought uproarious. An inane joy lit up his face as he reached over for the liquor.

'To our health,' he said, with forced solemnity, as we touched glasses. There was a brief moment of quiet, broken by the shouting of a screw from across the yard. We drank down in one and prepared to throw.

The first to lose a game was Michalis. I, as the non-player, had to carry out the surgery. It was a revolting operation. Having no other instruments I had to use my thumbs. Michalis passed out twice, but Giorgos and I managed to revive him on each occasion. Within an hour the small cell looked like an abattoir.

The fighting started when Michalis had lost both his eyes and Giorgos and I had one each remaining. The floor was strewn with tendrils, muck and blood, and on the saucer were four upturned staring orbs – two of the same blue, which were Michalis', and two dissimilar brown ones. There was only one olive remaining on the saucer. The others had been inserted in place of eyes after washing the wounds in alcohol.

Michalis was throwing dice against Giorgos. He threw a four and a one. Nothing. Giorgos threw a double four, which loses, but my nerves made me hesitate in calling out the score, which was my job, and Giorgos, thinking I was preoccupied nursing the hole in my head, quickly flipped one of the fours to make a four and a three. I was about to protest, but Michalis had already taken the dice and thrown, and Giorgos stamped heavily on my toes with the heel of his boot. Through a mist of tears I saw Michalis throw a three and a one. I called: *nothing*. Giorgos took the dice and threw a double three. I called: *a win*. Giorgos turned grimly towards Michalis, the blood trickling from his face.

'You lose, my friend.'

Michalis said nothing. In the face of death, in the certainty of his execution the next morning, he had contrived to find a kind of balance, or redress: an abuse of his own body that would have made dying little more than a detail. By presenting himself the next day as a hideous human spectacle with holes for eyes he would confound his executioners. I believe it had only now occurred to him that he would not be able to see the faces of his killers, and the thought maddened him. His whole body began to convulse and jerk in a strange way. His mutilated face, soaked by rivers of blood and tears, became contorted, and he gibbered and chattered like a monkey, at the same time bobbing up and down with those spasms.

Giorgos had no time for him.

'This stupid game was your idea,' he said, 'and you made the rules.'

Giorgos was extremely drunk, on top of being mad

with pain. He kept wiping the back of his hand across his forehead to stop the sweat from running over his eyebrows. He lurched forward on his seat and repeated himself, this time his voice louder, and more unsteady.

'You made the rules so don't start playing donkey brains. It was your jerk-off idea, your little game, you sick bastard.'

He towered over Michalis, swaying on his feet, one hand making a fist, the other repeatedly wiping his face. He then covered his good eye with this hand, in the belief, I suppose, that he would be able to focus on his intended victim. Instead, he stumbled into his chair, crashed against the table, and ended on the ground, swearing loudly.

Michalis did not react. He continued to twitch and gibber, neglecting the blood that now flowed freely over his cheeks and chin, dripping down his shirt and into his glass. Lost in his own hell, he was.

Giorgos stood up and with one movement grabbed Michalis by the shirt-collar and pulled him to his feet.

'Hey you skinny bastard,' he yelled. 'You owe me one ear. You've got a debt to pay. Is there no good in you?'

This curious demand, and the uncontrollable direction of events led me, I must admit, to let out a short, nervous laugh. Giorgos shut me up with shrill venom, saying bad things about my mother and much else besides. I'm ashamed to say it, but I kept quiet. Giorgos had never liked me much and I was afraid of provoking him. Now Michalis hung limp in his massive hand. It was obvious he was losing too much blood. Giorgos pulled the smaller man's head back with a vicious jerk, and sank his teeth into his left ear, tearing with his canines, then turned his head towards me and spat out the fleshy remnants onto the dirt floor. Michalis let out a ghastly scream, but with it, with the shock that accompanied this new pain, fresh life seemed to flow into him, as though having his ear bitten in half had given him second wind. His convulsions stopped, he remained rigid for a moment, and, with a force I would not have believed him capable of, clamped both hands around Giorgos' throat, his thumbs crushing against the larynx. A long sliver of mangled ear was hanging loose from the side of his head but he maintained his clasp around Giorgos' neck, whose turn it was now to jerk, choke and dribble. I was startled by the sight of a broad grin of sadistic pleasure that began to spread across Michalis' sightless face. His horrible metamorphosis from twitching wreck to bloodied psychopath had me rigid in my seat, and even if I had been capable of preventing what was to come, I simply could not move.

Slowly, as though part of a deranged dance, the two bodies sank to the ground, the one entwined around the other, until, prostrate on the floor, Giorgos made a loud gargling sound, kicked his feet interminably, then at last was still.

Michalis kept his hands locked firmly in place for a full minute after Giorgos' last kick, and then let out a long low yell before rolling onto his back. He seemed sated, like a lover spent of his passion.

I sat there for a long time trying to take in all that had happened to us. Then I stood up and walked over to the bodies.

Stratis finished talking, and looked up, his lips creased in amusement at Cosmo's horrified expression.

– And the execution? Cosmo asked, incredulous. – What happened when the screws came to take you out?

– Ah, smiled Stratis, stroking his moustache. – That,

kid, is what we're getting to. I was in a kind of daze, locked in the cell with those two stiffs. Remember, we'd been drinking like pigs, and even the sight of my two comrades killing one another hadn't sobered me up completely. I felt completely numb, about the death sentence, about everything. It wasn't long though, before I heard footsteps coming down the passage. The door opened and there was the governor, the chief screw, and Aleko, the rat-faced guard who'd got us the booze. Rat-face came in first, and stood to one side, holding the door for the governor and the chief screw. The three of them just stood there like imbeciles. The chief screw was the first to recover his wits. The governor, a young fellow, turned green and spewed up on the spot. The chief ignored this and walked over to Michalis and Giorgos. He turned Michalis' head over with his foot, like he was concerned about dirtying his boot. He looked at Michalis and Giorgos the way you'd look at a dog mess on the seat of your favourite chair. Then he looked at me.

'Pseftopoulos, you surprise me,' he said. 'I would never have thought you had it in you. Mind,' he added, pointing to my bloody face – 'it looks as though they put up a hell of a fight. What a pity. It would have been so much easier just to shoot you. Or to let you go.'

He paused for effect.

'What . . ?' I could barely bring myself to speak. 'Would have been . . . ?' I felt sick.

'That's what we came to tell you,' continued the chief. 'You all right sir?'

The governor, who had been finishing in the corridor what he had begun inside the doorway, returned, wiping his face with a handkerchief. He cast a filthy look at the chief screw, and turned, speaking directly to me.

'Yes, Pseftopoulos. A general amnesty was declared for all prisoners of your category as from midnight last night. It would seem that your two comrades will not be taking advantage of His Majesty's clemency. And as for you, seeing as you have two bodies to explain away since the announcement of the amnesty, I hardly think the offer stands.'

– I was charged with double murder. I didn't even get a proper trial. I tried to explain that I had no part in the deaths, but no one believed my story. They didn't send me back to the same nick. They sent me here instead. And that was thirty years ago. – But to return to your question, kid: how did I get this stone?

He lowered his head, and with a twist of the thumb extracted the black oval pebble from his eye-socket. He held it out in his palm.

– This is a special sort of stone, that can't be found just anywhere. It's a kind of memento for me. A reminder of how low the human soul can sink.

He spat onto the little stone, polished it carefully in his handkerchief, and then slipped it back inside the hole in his head.

The sun was dropping out of sight beyond the yard walls now, and Cosmo imagined the mountains beyond the walls of the prison, beyond the rooftops of the town and the villages in between, pictured them reflecting the last embers of the day. Cosmo remembered the times he had spent in those mountains, especially his recent trip there with Alysa, and he felt a great loneliness, stuck in this miserable jail for god knows how much longer. He had no confidence that he would be released before a considerable amount of time had passed.

The bell clanged out for the evening meal, and Stratis stood up from the bench where they were sitting. The other prisoners started to file out of the yard towards the canteen and the smell of bean soup.

– Come on kid, said Stratis, clapping Cosmo on the shoulder, – let's go eat.

Cosmo found that Stratis was a good person to be around. People avoided him just as he avoided them. He enjoyed the older man's company, and liked hearing his strange stories and enigmatic asides.

– You see that one, he whispered to Cosmo over supper. – Odysseus, he was a baker. He baked his wife in the oven when he discovered she was sleeping with his brother. And him, the tall one, Stavros? He was a hero of the resistance against the Nazis. But after the war he was accused of being a communist. He was sent down on trumped up charges of sheep rustling. He got so mad he attacked a screw, paralysed him. So he's still here. Didn't have friends in the right places.

But despite his willingness to put up with a limited incarceration in the interests of worldly experience, Cosmo found the restrictions and petty rivalries of prison maddening. Every day he waited on news from his friends outside. He was certain that the girls and Ruben would be trying everything possible to secure his release, but why was it not possible for them to get word to him? Surely there was somebody the combative Ruben could convince (or bribe) to pass on a message.

After four days his patience was stretched and he had begun to develop a simmering resentment towards Ruben for involving him in the investigation of the shelter in the first place. While he knew that he was fully responsible for accompanying his friend, the injustice of his being locked up while Ruben, as far as he knew, was at liberty, seemed pernicious. It was in this disenchanted mood that one of the screws found him on the morning of the fifth day, sitting on his bed and reading a Robert Ludlum novel with complete indifference.

– Special delivery, said the screw, with a sly smile, and handed over a plastic carrier bag. It contained fruit, pastries, tobacco, a sketchbook, pencils, pens, ink and pastels. There was also a single red rose and a short letter from Alysa. In it she told Cosmo how she and Ruben were doing everything they could to secure his release, claiming, as he had in court, that he was an innocent passer-by who had heard an explosion and gone to see if there were any injured. The US Military were trying to block his release and were demanding the right to interview him, which the Greek police were, for some reason, keen to resist. She put it down to sovereignty. She had been up to Iraklion to visit the British honorary consul, a Mr Daedalus – an irony not of Cosmo's making provided him with a surfeit of national identities: growing up in London, with an Irish nurse for a mother and a French professor for a father – and he had promised to look into the case with all urgency. Alysa felt that this Daedalus might be as good as his word, and besides, there was no Irish representative and the French consul was reputed to be a dipsomaniac. She was certain Cosmo would be free before the rose wilted (as long as he kept it in water). In the meantime, she told him, her loins ached for him, and that she and Pascale were keeping his bed warm.

This last piece of information brought on an attack of sexual anxiety that lasted Cosmo for the rest of the day. It was only when he searched the bag again, looking for something to eat late that evening that he discovered Alysa had included a change of clothes. He slipped off the bed, showered (without a fork) and changed rapidly, remembering to plant the red rose in water, in the standard plastic beaker supplied by the prison authorities. Then he walked down the corridor to the long-sentence cells to call on his friends Ahmed and Stratis and to share out his pastries and tobacco.

16. The Honorary Consul

The evenings were a bad time for Cosmo. He would stare around the sordid dormitory and consider each of his fellow-inmates in turn, trying to assess the quality of their despair or their potential for outbreaks of sudden and unprovoked violence, before sighing and turning towards the wall. The truth was, there was very little violence or overt tension between the cons. People, by and large, tried to avoid confrontation unless they were very bored. It was, paradoxically, only when unutterable tedium set in that things began to get lively. Cosmo witnessed a couple of face-offs in the first week, and one ragged fist-fight, which drew in half the occupants of his room before spontaneously folding at the approach of a guard.

Other than his friendship with Stratis, Cosmo had a special place in the affections of Ahmed, the Foreign Legion deserter. For the first few days Ahmed followed Cosmo around and turned to him for explanations or interpretation whenever he found himself in difficulty, which was often.

He was prone to overreaction, as when, on the second day, he misinterpreted a thumbs-up gesture made towards Cosmo by one of the British long-term residents, placing himself belligerently between the two of them. Cosmo explained to him that no threat was imminent, but Ahmed was always on the lookout for possible slights or affronts, both towards himself and Cosmo.

Early in the second week of his incarceration Cosmo was summoned by a guard and told he had an important visitor. He was led down the corridor that held special category prisoners (including the Former Minister, from whose cell Cosmo could discern the tip-tap of a typewriter) into a large office with air conditioning. Three men in suits, tokens of a superior caste, stood in the room. Cosmo felt underdressed in his jeans and vest: he was beginning to understand the many ways in which a person might be made to feel insignificant by the process of imprisonment. And he had only been there for a week. He dreaded to think what might happen to his head if he stayed there for a number of years, or decades, like Stratis.

The governor of the prison did not offer to shake Cosmo's hand, but told him that one of the other men was the honorary consul, Mr Constantinos Daedalus. He had come to interview Cosmo, and see how, as the representative of Her Majesty's Britannic Government, he could assist him. Cosmo assumed that this was intended as an ironic remark. The third man's presence was not explained to him.

The governor showed Cosmo and Mr Daedalus into a second office that led off from his own and closed the door. Daedalus was a small, elderly man with long white hair, and an alert, upright posture. He had a face that exuded both gravitas and a subtle native playfulness. His broad forehead and deep jowls furnished him with the looks of a judge or senior politician, while his eyes moved restlessly and with a restrained amusement over whatever held his attention; in this instance, Cosmo. He gestured to a seat and took one himself. His first comment, delivered in precise but heavily accented English, took Cosmo by surprise.

– I'm sorry, Mister Cosmo, for all this bloody nonsense. He smiled apologetically.

Cosmo shrugged.

– Your situation is most unfortunate, and if I had been informed earlier, I would have come here sooner.

– That's alright mate, said Cosmo, warming to the consul immediately. – There might even be compensations in being locked up against one's will. A broadening of the mind.

– I'm glad you see it that way.

– I didn't say I did. I put it as a hypothesis.

– Oh, I see. You make a joke. That is good.

– Thank you. But right now, Mister Daedalus, I need your help in getting me out of this shithole, pronto.

– That is why I am here. But I need to ask you a few questions. You see, you have become an object of delicate negotiations between the Greek authorities and the American Military.

Cosmo nodded. This was hardly news.

– You were discovered in an American naval installation without permission. Somebody broke into that installation by using an entry code limited to United States Navy personnel. The Americans want to know if it was you or not. They *need* to know.

– It wasn't, Cosmo answered truthfully, since it had been Ruben who had tapped in the security code and lifted the trapdoor. He remained silent for a moment then asked, as innocently as he could:

– Is this linked to the death of an American serviceman?

– You know about this?

– Everybody in Xania knows about this. It was in the newspapers. Cosmo knew this for a fact, having read the short article in a guard's copy of the local daily. It had been reported just as Ruben had predicted, as though it were a minor embarrassment. The American sailor was thought to have been the victim of a blood feud, after *interfering* with a Cretan girl. All presented as speculatively as possible so as to preclude a full investigation.

– What I mean, replied Daedalus, – is: did you know the serviceman was suspected of stealing the key and code to the installation and passing it on to an unknown person?

– No. I didn't.

– Let me clarify. It would seem that the Americans took a couple of days to link the murder of their sailor to the disappearance of a key. They had no reason to connect his death with any kind of subversive activity. Until, that is, they carried out an autopsy and found the key in the sailor's belly. What do you make of that?

– Huh? That he was hungry? What am I supposed to make of that? I have no idea what all this has to do with me.

– The dead sailor was known to be an acquaintance of yours. And of your housemate.

– So why don't they speak to my housemate? Cosmo was beginning to feel angry again.

– They have. The police, that is. He says he knew the dead man but he has provided a secure alibi for his whereabouts on the night of the incident.

That was nifty, thought Cosmo. Who had he roped in? It couldn't have been Jade.

– I knew the sailor. His name was Courtney. He seemed a nice man. But I didn't kill him and I don't know who did. He didn't seem the kind of person you'd want to mess with, if you follow me.

– Quite so. But I am curious, as are the police, why a man whom the Americans claim to be the victim of a Cretan feud over a pregnant daughter, sister, should at the same time be accused of giving or selling a key to persons unknown and subsequently be found with said key in his stomach. The stuff of spy thrillers, no?

– It's an interesting question, true. But, as I have said, one which has nothing to do with me. Has the combined intelligence of the American navy and the Greek Police considered the possibility that there was more than one key? Privately, Cosmo thought that the finding of a second key might have been clumsily cooked up after the event. Heroic patriot swallows key rather than pass it on to the enemy. Retrospective action. But he said nothing to the consul.

– I see you are cynical. I can hardly blame you. As I'm sure you are aware, the Americans are sensitive about any exposure of Soviet espionage in the region. You understand what I'm saying?

– That if Courtney was a Soviet spy, the Americans would not want to flaunt the fact?

– Precisely.

– So why are you telling me this? Why am I being made privy to these affairs of state? As you probably know, I'm an artist. I have no interest in politics.

– I fully appreciate that. I was trying to give some

background, some context to your arrest. Not to justify it, so much as to explain it. I realise you have been wrongly imprisoned and will make a complaint to the authorities on your behalf in Athens. My purpose in coming here was to effect your release immediately. The man you saw in the governor's office was the regional attorney. He can have a court order made out as soon as we are finished.

– I'm pleased to hear it. However, I can hardly believe the British consular service ever does anything for individuals like me, only forwards the interests of financial, governmental and military agencies. Please prove me wrong.

– Bear with me for just one minute. I can secure your release only if I convince the Greek authorities that you are entirely innocent. While I may believe this, I also need *them* to. So can you tell me anything at all about the installation that you are charged with trespassing on?

Cosmo sighed nosily.

– It was full of tunnels. A labyrinth.

– And did you see anyone down there? Did you find anybody?

– Of course I did. This is Crete. I was in the labyrinth. What would you expect me to find?

– I'm sorry, I don't follow you.

– You are a Cretan, Mister Daedalus?

– Yes.

– Well, who lived in the labyrinth your namesake created?

– The Minotaur?

– Spot on, Mister Daedalus. The Minotaur. A great big bloody bull-man.

The consul shook with laughter, gently, with minor

convulsions. When the spasms had subsided, he took a handkerchief from his top pocket, shook it theatrically, and daubed his face and forehead.

– And you expect me to report this?

– Why not? This is the land of Myth, no? Since when was Myth ever separate from everyday reality in Crete?

– A fascinating perspective.

– One that interests me very much. Coincidentally, I have been painting a series of pictures relating the story of Theseus, Ariadne and the Minotaur. So I consider it highly fortuitous, in the best possible way, that I should have stumbled across this underground labyrinth. It confirms my belief that whatever goes on in the interior world will somehow manifest in the exterior one also.

– I don't think I follow you.

– Sometimes artistic creation, like dreaming, pre-empts reality; that is all I'm saying. I don't expect you to agree or even understand. I'm thinking out loud here.

– I see. You are *playing* with me, Mister Flute. In any case, it would be considerably easier if, in my report, we make no mention of the Minotaur.

– As you wish.

– Although, on a personal level, I happen to share your belief about the nature of myth.

– Oh? Cosmo sat up in his chair.

– Denying the reality of Myth is as dangerous as denying the myth of Reality, or rather, the mythical dimension of everyday life. It is something that the world is losing, I feel, if it has not already been lost. You see, having a name like mine has lent me towards many speculations of this nature. I do not say this has been entirely advantageous to me, but the name has certainly provided me with a need to question the routes that a person takes through the world. You see, Daedalus, the original Daedalus, apart from being an inventor of genius, was also a philosopher.

Here the consul paused, extracting a silver cigarette case from his inside pocket. He flicked open the latch and offered the contents to Cosmo, who took one, noting that it was a Senior Service. He deduced from this that Daedalus was an Anglophile, of the Old School.

– He would have had to be a philosopher, one might say, since every myth that comes down to us is a story aimed at telling us how to live, and if one is a part of the myth, then one is a part of the story of how to live. Daedalus shows us a way of living, of creating one's own myth while living it. You know the story of the animated statues in Plato's *Menon*? No? Well, of course such statues did not exist, yet Daedalus would encourage the belief that they did, because it attributes to him powers beyond the ordinary, powers which he would not dare to claim himself, for fear of committing *hubris*. Don't forget that hubris does not translate easily, certainly not as 'blasphemy'. It is a challenge to the gods, an attempt to make oneself god-like. This is a man who was on the brink of committing hubris throughout his life. And yet he avoids retribution by always making the hubris indirect. What is this myth of escape from the labyrinth, after all?

– Remind me.

– Daedalus helped Ariadne to save Theseus from the Minotaur, by suggesting the trick with the ball of thread. After Ariadne and Theseus escape the island, Minos discovers how Daedalus has betrayed him and shuts him away in the labyrinth as a prisoner, along with his son Icarus. There Daedalus makes wings, attaching them to their bodies with hot wax. The rest is well-known. They fly away from Crete, but it is the son, Icarus, who commits the hubris of flying too close to the sun. The heat melts the wax and the wings fall from his body, and he falls from the sky. So in a sense you could say that Icarus lives out his father's hubris.

– Would the ancient Greeks apply so much psychology to their stories?

– Psychology? Psyche, as you know, is the Greek word for soul. The whole pantheon of gods and titans and fates and so on are an account, or, if you prefer, a map, of the human soul. We Greeks were all Freudians long before Freud came along and took the fun out of Myth.

Cosmo reflected on the turn the conversation had taken. The consul seemed far more interested in the topic of myth than he did in the details of the American nuclear bunker.

– Freud recognised the importance of Myth, of course, but he took it as an explanatory device, you see? He took Myth to be a way of learning, even a way of moralising about the world, about love, about incest most particularly. And this obsession with the phallus and phallic power! What kind of reduction of Myth is that? He suffered from too much Jewish guilt, that man. I'm sure he didn't have the first idea of how the Greeks thought about their myths, of how they evolved out of the land and the sea, of how integrally they are lodged within the local geography. You talk of the external world following on, being in some kind of symbiotic relation to the internal, and there you have it: our myths evolved from the land and the sea and they evolved from the Greek mind or soul. Which came first? I don't think it is a real question because it supposes a division between what a person is and where they come from. For a Greek, this is an impossible distinction. So I do understand what you are telling me. It might mean that Crete has worked its way under your skin.

If that is so, you will never be the same again. Perhaps this place will pursue you always, like Cavafy's Alexandria.

Constantinos Daedalus whacked the table top with his sheaf of papers, as if to kill a fly, or else to signal the end of the interview. Cosmo looked up in surprise. He had been listening closely to what the older man was saying. He looked at Daedalus: the mane of white hair swept back off his forehead, the eager, intelligent grey eyes. Cosmo was shaken too by the dramatic tone of the consul's last utterance: he did not know whether to take it as a compliment or a kind of warning.

– Whatever you decide, the consul continued after a pause, it might do you good to get away from Crete for a while. Visit the Cycladic islands, you'll like it there. Amorgos, try that. Just give things a chance to cool down a while. Let the Americans blow off steam, as they seem to need to do. Take a holiday. Crete will still be here when you return. Nothing will have changed.

From the moment Cosmo left the Prison Governor's office, things moved rapidly. He returned to the dormitory for his few belongings and went to bid his farewells to Ahmed and to Stratis and one or two others with whom he had been on speaking terms. Ahmed was practically in tears, Stratis stoical and tight-lipped. The comings and goings of more temporary residents made little effect on him and in any case, his days passed to the ticking of a different clock from that of other inmates.

Cosmo didn't know whether Alysa, or anyone else, had been informed of his impending release. The Governor had signed his discharge papers, after the county judge had commuted the original sentence on the admission of new evidence (there had, of course, been no new evidence, only Cosmo's insistence on the veracity of his original statement).

At six o'clock in the evening Cosmo stepped outside the gates of Xania jail, and finding no one there to meet him, decided to walk home rather than seek out a taxi.

17. *Back in Circulation*

Cosmo might justifiably have felt piqued by his friends' abandonment of him while he was in jail. Other than the single parcel and letter from Alysa, which must have been accompanied by a bribe, they had been incommunicado. But as he set off towards town, he did not think for a moment that they had neglected him on purpose. He understood that they were not permitted to visit him, and he also recognised that it was dangerous for Ruben to be too visible in the aftermath of the assault on the bunker. There was, however, an edge of paranoia to Cosmo's thinking. By remaining out of touch, were his friends somehow distancing themselves from him for reasons he did not know? Was there another, more nefarious agenda to Ruben' fascination with the labyrinth and what had lain behind its single locked door? And did Ruben know something more about the alleged existence of a Russian spy than he had been willing to share? Cosmo doubted it; he felt as though he knew Ruben well enough to deduce if he were concealing something important. There was nothing definite about Cosmo's discomfort; no serious sense of betrayal, but he was certain that during his nine days in prison things had come to light that the others knew about and he did not. For this reason he was outside the loop, and he resented it.

Cosmo resisted the sentiment: he didn't want to return home angry, but the nearer he drew towards the centre of town, the more he felt like delaying his return to the Splanzia quarter, and home. More emphatically, the nearer he drew towards the centre of town the more he felt like getting pretty drunk before even considering going home, a characteristic trait when confronted by any conflict of emotions. On the one hand he would have liked to go home and take up his life where he left it before the disastrous visit to the labyrinth; on the other, he wanted to make a fuss, to draw attention to the inconvenience he had had to endure by going to jail, as he might put it, on Ruben's behalf. Going to jail *because of* Ruben; that was how he saw it. Ruben had wanted to investigate the labyrinth; Ruben had brought the blowtorch and jemmy; Ruben had insisted on breaking down the locked door even when it was apparent that Nikos was intent on mischief; and Ruben (damn him) had got away before the police arrived and enjoyed a life of liberty while Cosmo languished (he said the word out loud to himself, enjoying the sound of it) in Xania jail, surrounded by psychopaths, murderers and would-be arse-rapists.

By the time he reached the market square, Cosmo had worked himself up into such a state of querulous resentment that he was muttering out loud as he walked along. Instead of heading down Daliani Street towards home, he took a left into Skridlov and the Unspeakable. Igbar called out a greeting when he saw Cosmo in the doorway, while Tassos, from the recesses of his stove, held up crossed wrists to indicate cuffs or manacles, and chuckled loudly. The restaurant was almost empty. Cosmo ordered prawns and fresh sardines and a litre of wine.

– When did you get out? asked Igbar, setting the table and pulling up a chair.

– Just now. The food was shit. You're my first port of call.

– Have you seen the others yet? Then, before waiting for an answer, he added, – Alysa's been turning the world inside out for you.

– Oh yeah?

Cosmo chewed on a hunk of bread and grabbed a handful of olives from the saucer in front of him. He knocked back his second glass of wine and poured a third. It was murky and tasted of soil and electrodes.

– What's up? You don't seem your usual cheery self.

– Being locked up doesn't *do* much for the cheery self. Nor sleeping in a dormitory of felons wondering which of them is content with a wank and which might prefer some anal banditry, while out in the real world your so-called mates hang about for a week before sending for the cavalry.

– Sorry. I didn't realise.

– Why should you? Nobody else fucking did.

Cosmo relented, seeing how perplexed his friend's expression had become. – Not to worry, Igbar. I'll be all right. Just need to get it off my chest before I meet Ruben Fortuna and let off some more.

– Ruben's been lying low.

Cosmo grunted, then lowered his voice. – Any more news about Courtney's murder?

– Only a brief mention; that he was thought to be

the victim of some feuding over a local woman. Nothing concrete and no names. On the bush radio nobody seems to have a notion who might have been involved and in a place like this *everyone* would know if there was a scandal of that kind. You know how the Cretans are about family honour. So we can safely assume it isn't true. I don't think *anyone* believes that story. No mention of any arrests. The papers said 'A man was being held for questioning by police.' But they didn't say what he was being questioned about or where he was being held. Nobody thinks you killed Courtney.

Then he added, hurriedly, – I don't *think* anyone does, at least.

Jesus, it gets worse, thought Cosmo. Being a murder suspect had its advantages where he had just come from, but outside it was pure social handicap.

– What you mean is, the two things, the explosion in the underground shelter, and the murder of Courtney, are being linked?

– Well, sure. But not publicly. It wasn't the intention of the police or the US authorities to let it come out that way, that's just how it's being seen by some of the locals. It's not what the newspapers print either, of course.

– What *do* the newspapers say? The Greek papers. Access was limited in the nick. I just saw one report in *To Vhradi.*

– That someone broke into a US military installation and caused an explosion. No life was lost, a man is helping police with enquiries. That is, you.

– No life was lost? I heard in prison that a body had been found.

– There was a rumour. But it hasn't been confirmed.

Cosmo thought it best not to pursue this line of

conversation, since Igbar hadn't indicated that he knew of Nikos' hallucinatory appearance in the labyrinth. Igbar confirmed this by his next question.

– Why, was there someone else down there?

Cosmo rolled his eyes dismissively, gave a Greek shrug.

Igbar smiled and poured himself a glass of Cosmo's wine. – The police have cordoned off the whole area around the Marco Polo. Bloody great screens around a building site next to it too. I don't know what the hell you and Ruben were up to, but, you know, there's been a lot of speculation among my customers.

– Speculation which no doubt you have been fanning.

– Well, it's a good story. I like to flex my creative muscles. It has the makings of an even better story. He lowered his voice. – But no one knows that Ruben was involved: and he has threatened to castrate me if anyone finds out.

Cosmo wondered how Igbar knew of Ruben's involvement, but resisted the impulse to ask. Ruben would not have volunteered the information.

– Doesn't surprise me. So what version is most popular among your clientele?

Igbar looked around, checked that Tassos's back was turned to them and knocked back Cosmo's wine, refilling his glass from the carafe.

– That Courtney was doing a little work on the side and got in deeper than he could afford to go.

– What kind of work?

– Drugs. Cocaine, to be precise. There was a rumour that he had cocaine on him when he was murdered.

– Nothing linking him to a Soviet spy network then?

Wasn't he your man in Xania?

Igbar smiled indulgently. – Well, I have my theories on that front.

– And have been sharing them with all and sundry. So shoot.

Igbar cleared this throat.

– Courtney was a minor player in a Soviet operation to gain intelligence on military activities in the zone. As an ordinary seaman he wouldn't have had a lot of responsibilities, but might have been instructed to keep an eye open. He would have been asked to report on ordnance and so on, and he certainly mingled more with the local population than most of his buddies. But I don't think he was *the* spy, no. A supplementary player, maybe. My guess is that he got greedy, began to ask for more cash; maybe he had a cocaine habit, or was supplying someone who didn't want the world to know about it.

– You think Courtney was a coke-head?

– So the second option then.

– But that doesn't help explain anything. We have drugs; we have a possible spy, but what is the connecting link? Why have Courtney killed?

– If the person he was supplying drugs to was someone who had access to information of a kind that would be of interest to the Russians, then there's your connection.

And if you've worked that out, thought Cosmo, how many others will have done the same?

– I don't buy that, he said, dismissively. – Sounds too convoluted. There's my food, Igbar, he added, as Tassos slid the plates of seafood onto the counter. He necked another glass of wine while Igbar brought the meal over.

Less hungry than he had thought, Cosmo picked at

his prawns and fish. The restaurant began to fill with the usual suspects; Iannis the pimp with fat Maria, a clutch of enthusiastic Greek sailors out on the town, sunburnt German tourists. He was sitting back, finishing his wine, when Alysa appeared in the doorway, and, spotting Cosmo, hurried towards him.

– My darling boy. You're here, all alone! Why didn't you come home?

Cosmo stood up and they embraced. Simply seeing Alysa swept away at least two thirds of his resentment at having to walk out of the prison gates without a reception committee. Her hair had been plaited and she wore a knee-length skirt of black cotton and a black V-necked sweater. Cosmo suspected that she wore nothing underneath either. She looked an unconvincing widow, and as she crossed the room there was an almost tactile aura of erotic wellbeing about her.

– We went up to the jailhouse, started Alysa, as if reciting the first line of a song, and they told us you had left already, so of course we went home but you weren't there. So I thought I'd come looking for you.

– Well, here I am, said Cosmo.

– And how did they treat you? Oh my sweet, you look so forlorn. Were you beaten and buggered and made to sew mail bags?

– Not exactly. The company was alright for a short visit, but I wouldn't have wanted to stay any longer. By the way, thanks for sending Daedalus. He's quite a character. Talked to me about mythology and the psyche. And he got me out.

– I tried to get him to see you last week, said Alysa, pre-empting Cosmo's next question, but he was in Athens for two days, and I only got to explain things to him fully yesterday.

– So he worked quick.

– He seems an OK person.

Cosmo didn't want to talk about Daedalus. He was pleased to see Alysa, but still felt truculent. There was a strained edge to their conversation. It felt to Cosmo as if they had spent nine months apart, rather than nine days.

– Want some prawns? Cosmo gestured at the half-eaten crustaceans on his plate.

– Think I'll pass. But I'll have some wine.

Cosmo took the carafe and stepped up to the counter. Tassos, busy frying eggs, a task he detested, indicated that Cosmo should help himself from the large barrel propped up behind the fridge.

– When you say 'we', who came to meet me from prison? Cosmo asked, returning to the table.

– Me and Ruben and Jade, of course.

– Pascale still around?

Cosmo glimpsed the shadow of a confused expression on Alysa's face. He wondered if she was jealous.

– You keen to see her?

– I could be.

He was teasing, but did not know whether this was wise.

– But I'm not. You see, I'm a monogamist at heart, he said, all smiles.

Alysa made a face.

– Is that meant to make you noble?

– Noble? No. It just means I know when I've got something good going. With just one person.

– You make me blush. I have been a wanton woman,

exploring the miracles of the female orgasm with Pascale. And you have been locked away in chokey, condemned to hear the sounds of sweaty felons masturbating the night away.

– Well, precisely. I had a wank or two myself.

– You did? And did you fantasize about anyone in particular.

– Yes, as it happens.

– Anyone I know?

– Lassie the dog.

– Oh dear. Fancy that. Plus you were innocent of the charges.

– Everyone is innocent in the nick.

– So I've heard.

– I met one who really was. I think. And he told her the story of Stratis, who had a pebble for an eye, and who had survived a bloodbath only to spend the rest of his life in jail.

– That's a very scary story, Alysa commented, looking serious. – Do you think he was telling the truth?

– I have no idea. But I'm pretty certain that after all these years of hearing himself tell the story, *he* believes it.

Alysa nodded and drained her wine. While listening to his rendition of Stratis' tale, she had watched Cosmo closely, as though tracking his every word, every gesture. The story appeared to enthral her.

Cosmo was preoccupied, tapping out a rhythm on the table top with his fork.

– How did you find out where we were, Alysa? When you came to the labyrinth?

– I told you when we were down there. I followed you.

– Yeah, I know. But me and Ruben went to the rally

first, remember? And when we left, we thought we saw you with Nikos and a man who might have something to do with Courtney's death.

Alysa took this blunt accusation calmly.

– Oh, not this again. I've had Ruben on my case about the doppelgänger sighting all week.

– Huh?

– Like I said to *him*, you're both crazy. Must be seeing things. A woman with a headscarf, at night-time, half a street away? Jesus! Not that I need to justify anything to you or Ruben, but I was still fuming after you and me had our little spat, then I softened a bit and went to wake Jade. I wanted to go and find you. It was quite by luck that we did. Jade spotted you as you were walking along the harbour front. Now can we please just change the record? The person you think you saw was not me.

Cosmo could concede that her explanation was feasible. He hadn't been able to identify her in the side street, and he was a pretty observant individual, quite apart from being her lover. He was feeling magnanimous. In gratitude to her for rescuing him from the labyrinth, he could at least show her some loyalty, or at the very least not assume the worst of her when there was no other witness apart from Ruben. He decided to drop the subject.

Cosmo was beginning to feel good as the reality of his freedom came home to him; the small details that a life at liberty takes for granted – of being free to choose his own food and knowing that if he didn't want to eat it he wouldn't wake hungry in the night. Living among men had, even for a week, alerted him to the awfulness of a way of life that excludes the female, and how quickly these men without women begin to act out the most arcane and flimsy roles in a way that only denigrated and humiliated: *If you go to the shower, be sure to take a fork.*

– I missed you, he told her, and he meant it.

Alysa stretched out a brown leg and settled her bare foot lightly against his thigh, curling her toes against the cloth of his jeans then flexing and unflexing them so that they rubbed against his crotch.

– Will you do me a favour?

Cosmo looked up.

– Follow me.

Alysa led him into the back room, which was empty, and opened the door that led to the toilet, on the left, and a small storeroom to the right, a place filled with cardboard boxes and crates. She locked the door behind her and turning to Cosmo, loosened his belt and unzipped his fly, wedging herself between him and the wall of the dingy room. Cosmo slid his hand up her thigh and lodged his thumb in the warm delta of her sex. She trembled, bit her lip, and pulled him towards her. There was nothing remotely romantic about the venue, but the repressed energy of the past ten days coursed through Cosmo's limbs, and Alysa took him to the limit, squeezing with her hand between his legs as though milking him, and holding on just tight enough to ensure that when he came a series of small explosions were triggered in his brain.

Alysa recovered first, still standing, and brushed herself down.

– Good. Everything in working order, she said. – That was just in case you intended getting too drunk to fuck. Oh, and to make sure I got to you before I have to share you with Pascale.

– You don't have to. You *choose* to. Why is that?

Alysa shrugged. – We're always being told of things we can't have, but no-one ever gives an explanation of *why*. I like Pascale, she likes me. She also likes you. I like you. You like her. And I think you quite like me. So what's the problem?

Cosmo didn't actually believe things came as simply as this, nor did he believe Alysa believed it, but he was content for the two of them to behave as if they did.

– You leave first, said Alysa. I don't want Tassos leering at us.

18. *Unwelcome Visitors*

There was a homecoming party held in Cosmo's honour at the house on Gerasimou Street. Cosmo, his truculence undiminished, hugged Ruben warmly when he first came home but as the evening progressed his mood became volatile and accusatory. When he had drunk so much as to find standing problematic he decided to punch Ruben in the face, which was ill-advised, since he failed to make contact, spun around and lost his balance, bumping his head on the edge of the kitchen table on his way to the floor. Ruben hadn't even bothered to defend himself, guessing correctly that Cosmo's pugilistic skills were not to be taken seriously. Cosmo heaved himself off the ground and took another swing at Ruben, this time connecting with his friend's jaw. Ruben was knocked off balance, staggered, then rubbed his chin and looked thoughtfully at Cosmo, who stood swaying, directly in front of him.

– Sit down, you dickhead. I don't want to fight you. But don't try that again.

Cosmo, although drunk, was able to see that Ruben was serious. He slumped into a chair and smiled uneasily at the company. – Just *expressin'* meself, he said, sounding more like his mother's son than usual. But the fracas had the effect of upsetting Pascale, who had a shouting match with Cosmo in gutter French which no one else could follow, and then left the party with Lucas. The romance that had been slowly blossoming between the two of them finally took off that night, and the prospect of Cosmo developing his ménage à trois with Alysa and Pascale evaporated.

In the morning, peace was re-established between Ruben and Cosmo, and the two of them continued as though nothing had happened. Cosmo returned to his painting for the best part of a week, while Ruben spent extended spells in his darkroom. The house became a zone of sober industry. When Cosmo wasn't working, he spent his time with Alysa, walking and swimming and, at night, dining out at different restaurants along the seafront. The relationship remained passionate and occasionally volatile, notably when it was stretched by Alysa's demands for borderline activities in the bedroom. But while there were tense moments, and times when he felt like pressing her further about her time in America, especially her secret meetings with the spy, he exercised restraint, if only because he wanted to avoid conflict with someone as strong-headed and resistant to criticism as she was.

One afternoon, when Alysa and Jade had taken themselves off for a swim, Ruben walked into Cosmo's studio with a pile of photographs.

– Take a look at this guy.

He slid a photo into Cosmo's line of vision. The man was standing in a doorway, talking to crazy Nikos.

– It's the geezer we saw the other night. You took pictures!

– Yeah. But the light was really bad and I couldn't get one of the woman. I didn't want to use a flash, obviously.

They had discussed Alysa's denial that she had been the third conspirator in the side street. Ruben remained sceptical, but was prepared to keep his own counsel and not raise the topic with Alysa again.

– And then, this morning, I took this.

He showed Cosmo another picture. This time the quality was good, the light strong. The man was sitting outside a café, head turned away in profile. He wore a short-sleeved shirt and was hatless, but it was definitely him.

– Where was this taken?

– Kafeneion in Splanzia square. In front of the church, Aghios Nikolaos. Just at the top of our street. Take a close look.

Cosmo perused the photo slowly.

– Jesus! His ear.

– Quite, said Ruben. His ear is half an ear. Hardly an ear at all. He's a, what's the word, a *mutant*. See?

He held out another photo, a blow-up of the side of the man's face. The ear was mangled, the shape of a small sea-shell.

Cosmo let out a small exclamation.

– That is bizarre. Remember the story I told you, about the guy in jail, Stratis?

– Yeah, sure. Not easy to forget. The two other prisoners died, right?

– Right.

– And now The Mutant turns up in the square at the top of our street.

Cosmo was perplexed. To him, whose life at this moment was a clutter of conflicting stories, a rare species of internal logic insisted this man should be Michalis, the character in Stratis' tale. He also knew that this could not be so, but once the idea had established itself in his head, he hung onto this illusion with a rare tenacity.

– And anyhow, continued Ruben, you surely don't believe that your mate Stratis was telling the truth, do you?

– I don't know. Weirder things have happened. But I'm not suggesting this guy has returned from the dead. It just occurs to me that Stratis' story might have been some kind of allegory.

– Huh?

– Maybe his cell-mates didn't die, although something pretty sinister happened. Maybe he has spent so many years telling his story that he's chosen to forget the way things actually happened. Maybe he even believes whatever version he is relating at the time.

Preoccupied as he was with his paintings, Cosmo paid no heed to the consul's advice to leave the island for a spell. He had taken up the Minotaur canvasses with a renewed vigour. There was a different slant to his pictures now, as he drew upon elements from the night below ground with crazy Nikos. He had also introduced a new character to the series, modelled on the prisoner Stratis, who appeared on the outskirts of two paintings; a shadowy emaciated Christ, with a hint of the androgynous Tiresias. Working quickly, Cosmo realised the sequence had reached a point where it must either be terminated or else developed further, but with an added element that was as yet missing. He read more and more around the mythology of the Labyrinth and the

Minotaur, and learned of the bizarre psychological dramas played out repeatedly in the bull-cultures of the ancient Mediterranean. He wanted to paint in a way that suggested both the terrifying physicality and the ancient mystery of the encounter between man and bull. This was developing into the biggest project of his career, and he was pursuing it with a furious energy: but still something was lacking and he was not sure where to look for it.

Midsummer's day had passed and the long evenings now suffused the seaboard of the town in a golden light. Behind, the mountains peaked with a luminous sheen. From the roofs of the old Venetian houses swifts dived and banked, skimming the waters of the harbour.

One evening Cosmo, Alysa, Ruben and Jade ate out at a supposedly upmarket restaurant on the old harbour-front, a concession to Cosmo's new hobby of becoming an authority on Xania's eating-places. There was not a lot to choose between these establishments. They offered a stock-in-trade of badly-presented sea-food and stodgy moussaka, with a smattering of bad international cuisine. They also broke the cardinal rule about Greek wine, attempting to palm customers off with over-priced and antiseptic bottled produce when the local barrelled wine was invariably better. Cosmo and his friends had spent an hour over wine and cigarettes before ambling back towards the house, for once avoiding the allure of the Lyrakia. Cosmo, in fact, was worn out, having spent long hours at his painting. He was basking in the creative blaze of knowing that his work was going well, enjoying the heady mix of exhilaration and fatigue, and he wanted to rest before continuing the next day.

However, when they returned home, the door pushed

open easily before Ruben could engage the key in the lock. Entering the main downstairs room, they could see at once that the place had been raided, and by a person or persons who had made no attempt to conceal their visit. Drawers had been pulled from the kitchen chest, and their contents distributed messily across the breadth of the room. Cutlery, kitchen utensils, pots and pans, paper towels; all things that might be considered harmless. Several plates were smashed, though nothing, it seemed, was broken in a way that suggested a systematic search.

The trail of wanton upheaval and destructiveness proceeded upstairs. In the bedroom, covers had been pulled back, mattresses overturned, cupboards evacuated. The bathroom cabinet had been emptied and its random contents; toothpaste, eye-liner, aspirins, tampons, were cast about the floor.

Cosmo rushed up to his studio. There, among the scattered brushes and paint, the plants that he liked to have around him while he worked, the assortment of ornate driftwood collected from Xania's beaches and the pots of shells and rocks and seeds, lay the remains of his recent canvasses, slashed to shreds. Against the studio wall, two of his earlier paintings, describing the myth of the Minotaur and its encounter with Theseus, lay face upwards. They had had the contents of a pot of bright red gloss poured over them. Cosmo stood there in a state of shock, before sinking slowly to the ground. There he sat, on the floor, without speaking, gazing at the remains of the summer's work. Tears had begun to flood his eyes, and when he brushed them from his cheeks, he did not register sadness so much as fury. Alysa knelt beside him, unable to offer any comfort: Cosmo was inconsolable. Ruben followed up the stairs shortly afterwards and like the others, stood there in dismay, staring at the devastation in the studio.

– *Che*, Cosmo, I'm so sorry man.

Cosmo got to his feet.

– It's all gone badly fucking wrong, somewhere down the line, hey? He heaved himself onto the dilapidated sofa and closed his eyes. – Very badly wrong.

By the time Cosmo had cleaned up his studio the next morning and taken his canvasses down to the narrow pebble beach at Akti Miaoulis for a ritual bonfire, he had reached a decision. He would take Daedalus' advice and leave the island for a while. Ruben had helped him take the six ruined paintings down to the sea, and then had left Cosmo alone. It was an overcast morning. Cosmo poured lighter fuel over the stack and watched his pictures go up in smoke; dirty brown smoke drifting out over grey waves. The smell of burning paint filled his nostrils and he felt nauseous. He sat down and watched his work being carried off in ashy flakes across the water.

First thing that morning he had phoned Daedalus, whose initial reaction was strangely emotional, but consistent with his argument of a week before.

– I blame myself, Mister Cosmo. I should have foreseen something like this happening. I am sickened that you have lost your paintings, and only wish I had had the presence of mind to offer to look after them for you. And to insist that you left the island immediately on your release. Your continuing to be here has angered somebody.

– Angered who, Mister Daedalus? The Greek police? The American military police? Who, for Christ's sake?

– I suspect that your visitors were in the employ of

the American security services, though it would be hard to prove. Have you reported the break-in to the local police?

– No. I thought I would call you first.

– Good. I will call the chief of security police in Xania myself. You would be wasting your time if you went there, answering stupid questions, filling out bloody forms. I am deeply sorry, Mister Cosmo. Although I did not know your work I am aware of your reputation as a young artist of considerable talent. This brings shame on Greece. I will, of course make the necessary complaints, but the Americans will deny any involvement and nothing will retrieve your paintings.

– I know. You don't have to tell me that. But *why*? Why me? Surely they don't think I am a spy. I'm not competent to be a spy. I have no political convictions to speak of. Or rather, I didn't used to.

– Who knows? Perhaps they do think you are involved in espionage. Or you know someone who is. It's impossible to say quite what their motives are, but clearly they want to scare you, and although I appreciate that you might not want to leave Crete, let me suggest again that a break of a couple of weeks will give this thing a chance to die down. I will do my best, along with my friends in the Greek police to, um, quieten things a little. But as long as you and your friend Ruben Fortuna – yes, I know all about him and so do the Greek police – as long as the two of you are in Xania, the Americans see red. No, perhaps that is too precise an analogy: they see you as a provocation.

– Perhaps they should consider whether or not the Greek people regard *their* presence here as a provocation.

– Now is not the time for such thoughts, Mr Cosmo. You may have been startled into a strong reaction, even be inclined to acquire certain political beliefs, but I do not think they will do anything at this moment except make things worse. Let's be pragmatic. I'll be blunt: leave Crete while you are still alive. I would hate to have to send you back to your mother in a box.

– May I join you?

Cosmo looked up to see Igbar standing awkwardly on the edge of the beach, a few metres away. His face swollen and grazed, he had a black eye, and was clutching a plastic carrier bag. Cosmo watched him as he moved carefully over the rocks towards him, and heard the clink of glass on glass.

– Is that all that's left?

The frame of one of the larger pictures poked out from the pebbles, a gloomy charred triangle.

Cosmo shook his head.

– No. There are two unharmed. Perhaps you can find a home for them. I'm going away for a while.

– I'm sorry. Igbar looked at the ground and shuffled his feet. – I'm sure Tassos will look after them for you.

– Thanks.

Cosmo patted the rock at his side.

– Take a pew, Igbar. You don't have to stand there like a wet rag.

– Quite. Yes.

Igbar moved a strand of seaweed from the rock next to Cosmo and lowered himself onto it. He pushed a hand through his long greying hair and settled his plastic bag carefully at his feet.

– Not working today, Ig?

Igbar made the Greek negative; a clicking of the tongue

and a brief backward jerk of the head.

– I had an accident. Fell off a wall. Tassos told me to come back when I looked a little more wholesome. Said I'd scare away the customers with a face like this. Yannis the gypsy is standing in.

– Your erstwhile colleague and rival? The beauteous one?

– The same.

A year earlier, much to his alarm, Igbar's ex-wife, a plump, blonde terrier of a woman, had paid a surprise visit to Xania, and had embarked on a systematic bedding of suitable Greek youths, her favourite being a handsome gypsy who lived in a lean-to tin shack two doors down from Igbar. This was Yannis, Igbar's understudy in the theatre of the Unspeakable.

– You know I used to paint, Cosmo?

Of course Cosmo knew this. Strange to say, they had rarely talked Art together, but then Cosmo was, in general, averse to talking Art with anyone.

– They said I had a Beautiful Talent. He sighed and flicked ash from his cigarette.

– What? Who said you had a beautiful talent?

– Well, Felicity did, actually.

– Felicity?

– My ex-wife. A terrifying person.

– Oh yes. I met her. Anyone else?

– My tutor at The Slade said I had the potential to be the new David Hockney.

– Potential, huh? That's the word they use to cover themselves.

– Quite so. It remains with you to *fulfil* your potential. Which, of course will also fulfil their predictions about you.

And if you don't get anywhere, if you don't hit the jackpot like *you* have, then you remain a case of unfulfilled potential. That's what I am. A case of unfulfilled potential.

Cosmo put his arm around Igbar's shoulders.

– What you got in your placcy bag, Igbar?

– The usual. Proto raki. Want a snort?

Igbar pulled a long thin bottle from his carrier bag and two shot glasses. He poured, trembling, and they downed their drinks in silence. Cosmo refilled the glasses.

– Think you'll paint again? Cosmo asked eventually.

– Maybe, if my circumstances change. In fact I have a couple of ideas. Well, to be honest, I've been inspired by you. No, seriously, old chap. You're a bloody phenomenon. All that energy. Your work just *glows* with it.

– Thanks, said Cosmo, a little embarrassed by this sudden accolade. – Funnily enough, I think you'll start painting again too. But you'll have to get rid of those shakes. You're a bloody state, man.

Igbar nodded.

– I can do a few hours in the mornings, so long as I have a good breakfast. A small bottle of raki, orange juice for vitamin C. But then I'm too knackered to go to work. Have to walk bloody miles as a waiter. Half the way to Iraklion in one direction and half the way to Kastelli in the other.

This was an exaggeration, of course, but Cosmo let it pass.

– Where are you going to go? asked Igbar, after a long pause.

– I don't know. Anywhere but here, I guess.

– No ideas?

Cosmo shrugged.

– I don't know. I'd thought last night that I wouldn't

want to work on those paintings, that theme, any more. But this morning I got up with the opposite feeling. Why should these bastards stop my work? It would be a way of giving in to all the forces of fascist shite that corrupt this world. You know, Yankee Imperialism and all that, it doesn't affect me in a material way, not like I'm a Caribbean banana farmer or work in a Filipino sweat-shop. I like the States. I have good friends in New York, San Francisco, Chicago, all over. But you know, this murder of art, of soul, this dumbing down of everything to a moronic TV show passivity, well, what happened yesterday kind of put it in perspective for me. They know the best way to get to me is through my work, so they destroy it. Easy. They want to silence everything that does not blindly follow their Way of Life. They bullshit on about freedom and the rights of the individual; but the call to individuality is actually a demand that we conform to some other fantasy, like the Hollywood stereotype of the rugged individual. Step outside those limits and you're a fucking anarchist or a terrorist. So anyhow, I thought, look, maybe it's just a temporary setback. Pick up and start again. Jean Genet wrote the whole of *Notre dame des fleurs* again after a prison guard found the first version and threw it in the incinerator. Maybe I can do these paintings better. I started them in such a rush, without knowing where I was heading. If anything, after all that happened in the bomb shelter and in jail, I'm deeper into that material now, and it's even been strengthened as a consequence of their trashing my house, my studio. It's helped me put things into some kind of perspective.

– So you want to carry on with the same series of pictures?

– Carry on, innovate, take a different angle maybe. Essetially though, yes. Theseus didn't give up, did he? He was a man of singular intent. Though probably a bloody bore.

Igbar sat there, smoking. He looked up at the grey horizon.

– Where do you think you'll go, then? he repeated.

– Wherever I can pursue *this*. He gestured at the burnt remains of his paintings.

– The story that's behind your paintings is such a powerful thing. Perhaps it'll drive you where it needs to go, not you.

– Don't get mystical on me, Igbar.

– I'm not. I'm just saying that a narrative like that has its own momentum. The momentum that carried the sacred image of the bull across Mediterranean cultures for five thousand years or more.

– Leading where?

– Where is the one place in the modern world where the mythic power of the bull causes everything to stop for nine days?

– No idea.

– Spain, of course. And more specifically, Pamplona. The fiesta of San Fermín. The running of the bulls. You must have read Ernest Hemingway?

– Nope. But I've heard of the running of the bulls.

– I've got a copy somewhere. *The Sun Also Rises*. A group of young people who drink too much go along to the fiesta and Brett Ashley, the female protagonist, falls in love with a bullfighter. But that's a side issue. The important thing is, this is a place where the pagan cult of the bull is still celebrated, albeit under the weird auspices of a Christian saint.

– When's this fiesta begin?

– Sixth of July. Next week. You could make it with time to spare.

19. Confession, confession!

In the event, Cosmo did not make it to Pamplona with time to spare, but arrived instead when the fiesta was already underway.

He had discussed his plan with the others the same afternoon that Igbar had suggested Spain as a destination. Originally, he had intended to travel alone, but was soon convinced, first by Alysa, then by Ruben, that the four of them should make the trip together. While he would have been happy to spend time on his own, Cosmo didn't argue. He knew that Ruben was short of cash and suspected the same was true of Alysa; and, grateful for his friends' support, he insisted on paying the way for the four of them. Besides, as Ruben insisted, a fiesta was a celebration, and celebrations should be done in company, not in miserable solitude. The cost, along with Cosmo's aversion to flying, determined the method of travel: the chosen route was a ferry to Piraeus, then another boat, and a train up Italy and across southern France into Spain.

They had all been subdued on the voyage to Italy, Cosmo sleeping for much of the trip. At times it was as though the others were nursing a convalescent. When the ferry stopped off at Corfu, en route to Brindisi, Cosmo was ambushed by the memory of his brief affair with Alex, which seemed a very long time ago. He winced at his hazy recollections of that chaotic interlude: but the memory also made him reflect on the events of the past few weeks from a different perspective, as though all that had occurred to him in Crete were framed by these two boat journeys, one heading east, the other west; the vessel, however, remaining the same. That night, as the ship scattered phosphorescence in its path across a pitch-black sea, Cosmo dreamed that he met the man with one ear. In his dream, the man he had seen outside the coffee-shop with Nikos was the same Michalis who had shared a cell with Stratis. He stood before Cosmo, head down, eyes closed, and dark blood seeped over his temples and cheeks like molasses. 'Hey,' Cosmo said to him, 'you're supposed to be dead.' Michalis raised his head and opened his eyes. Two large black olives had been rammed in the sockets and now gazed blindly at him from the slits. 'Sometimes,' said Michalis, in a voice like rust, 'a person has to die in one story in order to get a life in another.'

The final leg of the journey took them on a night-train from Barcelona. While in that city, Ruben made telephone enquiries and had the good fortune of finding a hotel in Pamplona that took his reservation – normally every room in the city was booked up months in advance. A party of four was due to leave after the first days of the fiesta, allowing them to book into the Hotel Eslava, a little way from the epicentre, the Plaza del Castillo. They bought food and wine for the trip, and had a compartment to themselves. Cosmo stretched out on the long, comfortable seat and watched the evening sky silhouetting the dry landscape of Lleida as the train pulled across the wide plains.

Cosmo was not comfortable with the role of wounded artist that he had been designated: he drank little, wary of his own emotional turbulence, and his anger became muted as the distance from the house in the Splanzia lengthened. Now, nearer their destination, his spirits began to lift as he enjoyed a growing anticipation about the fiesta of San Fermín.

Igbar had pressed a worn copy of *The Sun Also Rises* into his hands when he came on board to see them off on the ferry from Xania to Piraeus.

– I don't know how much it's changed since the nineteen twenties, but do enjoy yourself. And take good care of Alysa; I think the poor girl's a bit confused.

Cosmo had glanced over at Alysa, who leaned on the boat's railings, gazing back at the White Mountains.

– Seems like I'm not the only one who's come to see you off.

Down on the quay, making no attempt to look other than what they were, two crop-haired men in lightweight suits leaned against a white Honda and from time to time glanced up at Cosmo and his friends at the stern of the ferry. Cosmo bent his elbow and smacked his upper arm, thrusting his fist in the direction of the spooks. One of them looked agitated, remonstrated with the other, who kicked the ground.

– Those people make me sick, said Cosmo, turning. – Let's go in and get a drink from the bar before you have to go ashore.

Now, in the dim light of the carriage, Cosmo remembered the image of the small Englishman, shuffling slowly down the gangway to the quay. The spooks had left, and as the ship's whistle blew to signal its departure, Igbar was, for a moment, a solitary figure on the quayside, ambling with his wheezing gait towards a blue bus that would take him back into Xania town centre. He had always been so much a part of the social landscape that Cosmo had never seriously questioned what strange turnings had led him to settle here in such obscurity. He was jolted, stung by the thought that there are certain lost souls, lost perhaps from birth, for whom every twist of fortune inspires nothing more than a sigh of resignation, for whom no mishap constitutes more than a minor but necessary adjustment in their personal litany of failure. And yet Igbar gave no sign of being dissatisfied with his lot: his admission that he would like to return to painting was the first time he had indicated to Cosmo any sense of larger purpose. He remained somehow buoyant, content with the limited role he had to play as celebrity waiter in the Unspeakable.

Cosmo looked up at Alysa, but addressed the question to the company at large.

– Why do you think Igbar settled in Xania?

Alysa shrugged, re-arranged her legs on the facing seat.

– Maybe because he's a spy, said Jade.

– Hell, not that again, said Ruben. – The guy's a complete waster, a major security risk.

– He's mashed, man. Ruben's right, said Alysa.

– Weren't Burgess and Maclean and Philby drunkards?

– Who or what are they? asked Jade.

– Eminent British double agents. But I take your point. Discretion is not Igbar's *forte*, Cosmo conceded.

Jade giggled. – If he was the spy, would he be so keen on playing 'spot the spy'?

– Why not? said Alysa. – It would, like, deflect from his own nefarious activities.

– Come off it. The little guy's completely *tonto*, said Ruben, – or rather, he isn't stupid, but he acts stupid, which is much the same thing.

– It's not the same thing at all, Jade contested. – If he's clever, and a spy, he might just act stupid.

– Let me re-phrase, said Ruben. – He is not stupid, but he is a drunk, and doesn't know when to keep his mouth shut.

– Could be part of his cover, being chopsy, said Alysa.

– Exactly, agreed Cosmo. – I know he gives it a lot of lip, but I've never heard him say anything or seen him do anything that could incriminate him. He stays out of trouble, in spite of working there illegally for years.

– That doesn't prove anything. It certainly doesn't mean that he's a spy, said Ruben.

With that, the conversation fizzled out, and the train toiled westward across Aragon. Cosmo had nodded off with his face pressed to the window, and when he next awoke, the main compartment light was off and both the women were asleep. Ruben was reading by lamplight in the seat opposite. He wore reading glasses, which transformed his looks from Bucaneer to Latin intellectual.

– Hi, he said quietly, as Cosmo stirred.

– All right?

Ruben nodded, closing the book and folding his hands on his lap. Cosmo sat up.

– Hey. I never said sorry for taking a sock at you when I got out of nick.

– Forget it. You were useless anyway.

– No, that's not the point. You judge a person by their intentions, right? My intention was to rearrange your face.

Ruben laughed softly. – I never said sorry for leaving you down in the shelter. All that noise and dust, man. Couldn't see my way back to you when the roof fell in. He paused and reached for an opened bottle of wine at his feet. – And I am gutted about your paintings. I do want to put that on record. I loved those pictures.

– Me too, I'm sorry about the paintings. Cosmo reached out and took the bottle. – But I'll do more. He paused for a moment, then continued. – By the way, I never asked. What did you see in that room down there. The one you bust into.

– Shit, I couldn't say. There was this weird light. Then the explosion. Man, I been trying to figure it out for myself, but I give up. I have no idea.

– Well, let me know if you remember anything more specific.

– Think you'll go back to Crete. I mean, long-term?

– Don't know. I'm more thinking about getting through the next few days. Do some deep hanging out. What about you?

– I guess I'm just along for the ride. But if everything I've heard is true, this fiesta is a killer.

They had breakfast in the dining room of the Hotel Eslava, which was a friendly, efficient place, and which like all other hotels and restaurants in town was set to make its annual profit that week, when the population of visitors far outnumbered local residents. They were given adjoining rooms on the first floor, and in the distance the Pyrenees rose from the plain, girdled in wispy cloud. Cosmo sat on the veranda in bright sunshine while Alysa bathed. He felt glad that he had come. He took a long shower and when he emerged Alysa was sitting on the edge of the bed, her hair wet, drinking from a bottle of cold white wine she had ordered from room service. To Cosmo, she seemed lost in pained contemplation of some matter to which he, as an individual, was not relevant. But when he approached the bed, she stood up and took his hand, pulling it to her breast, and said:

– Here. I want to feel your hand here: and she covered his hand with her own and he felt the hard nipple against the skin of his palm.

– You sad? Cosmo asked, feeling her heart beat.

Alysa shook her head. – No. Just a bit emotional. Then she laughed, and brushed what might have been a tear from her cheek. – I need to get dressed.

They collected Ruben and Jade from their room and walked towards the Plaza del Castillo. The streets were packed with people dressed in the traditional white and red of San Fermín. All the bars were bustling, with customers sitting, standing, or lying on the sawdust-covered floors. A cheerfully inept brass band had taken up residence outside one bar, and the musicians continued to play as various of their number filed in to buy rounds of drinks. Each new tune was greeted with applause and shouts from the revellers inside the bar, who offered special encouragement to an astonishingly incompetent tuba-player, capable of playing only a single note on his instrument, but who played his one note with such zeal as to temporarily deafen anyone within close range. Cosmo, who had been taking everything in, was impressed by the sheer scale of anarchic revelry. He led the way into the bar and ordered beers, a man on a mission.

– In a situation like this, he informed the others, as he passed them frothing plastic cups, a chap has to pace himself.

– Yeah, like you should know, said Jade.

– As I was saying, you start off gently, a few beers. Let the world glide by. Otherwise, otherwise, you end up like that poor fellow over there.

On the floor, belly up, arms akimbo, a young man lay snoring loudly. His trousers and shirt were stained a lurid mauve.

– He's spoiled his nice whites, said Alysa.

– And it's only day four, said Jade, with a sigh.

– My guess is he looked like that by day two.

– By day one, even.

– He didn't pace himself, said Ruben.

They moved on from bar to bar until the middle of the afternoon, and found a likely place to eat. When they emerged from the restaurant, the crowds were beginning to disperse with the start of the evening *corrida*.

– Let's get one thing straight, said Jade, as they settled at a table outside the Café Iruña, made famous in Hemingway's novel. – If we do this fiesta thing, can we do it without the bulls?

– It's possible to do it without the bulls, said Cosmo. But something of a cop-out, wouldn't you say?

– There's two ways of looking at this, said Ruben.

– At least two ways, Cosmo added.

– At least two ways then. You can do it with bulls. Or without bulls. And? He looked over at Cosmo.

– You can see the bulls as a part of it, but not all of it. The bulls are the rationale; Dionysian frenzy is the objective.

– Oh, I can manage Dionysian frenzy, said Jade,

with a smile, but I want to do it without the bulls, if that's possible.

– I'd say it was do-able, said Cosmo, though not entirely in the spirit of the thing. You are contravening a basic premise of the fiesta, and I'm not sure that's allowed.

– Hey, I'm not talking animal rights here! I don't want to spoil anyone's fun. I'm not going to parade down the streets of Pamplona with a placard that says 'Be Nice To Bulls' or 'Killing Bulls Makes Widows Out Of Cows' or any crap like that. I realize where we are, and why we've come here, because Cosmo is having a bull thing. That Cosmo *was* having a Minotaur thing, but got traumatized by Nikos and his funny hat, and then went to prison because the Minotaur, or rather Nikos, blew up the bunker and the hotel and himself, and Cosmo tried to blame Ruben for their getting caught but Ruben wasn't wearing it, Cosmo was just mad at Ruben for getting out of the bunker faster than him and not spending a week in Sing Sing; so Cosmo's Minotaur obsession became Cosmo's bull obsession, if it wasn't that already, only known by another name; I just want to do the fiesta, me that is, myself, want to do the fiesta, but am not crazy for the bulls.

Jade looked around, sipping from a cocktail glass, through a straw, something long and green.

The other three were all staring at her.

– Did I say something wrong?

Cosmo reacted first.

– Well, I can hardly deny that most of your allegations have a kernel of truth to them, but I can't accept your description of Nikos' Minotaur head as a 'funny hat'. Christ, Jade, you didn't see the thing. It was magnificent, a work of art. I should know. I made it.

– What? – Now all heads turned towards Cosmo. He enjoyed their surprise.

– Nikos came to see me when I first started working on the Minotaur pictures, a couple of days after Alysa and me got back from our hike. He asked me if I could do this mask. I set to work and finished it in one night. I didn't show it to anyone because he asked me not to. I used card, plaster of Paris and paint. And he never paid me for it, the bastard.

Ruben was staring at him strangely. His lips finally settled in a smile.

– You never let on about that when we were down in the bunker. You looked scared shitless!

– I was. I had the initial shock of seeing him with it on his head, of course, but that passed. What scared me, really scared me, was the realization of what he must have been up to; what he'd planned all along. What he was actually *doing* down there.

– Yes, well. I should admit some prior warning about that too, conceded Ruben.

– Say, boys, is this confession time? I love it, said Jade, stretching her legs. – I love it when you talk dirty too, mind, but secret confessions is better still.

– You're tight, Jade, said Alysa.

– I am not tight, dammit!

– You are. Pissed as a fiddler's bitch.

– *Confession, confession!* chanted Jade, banging the table.

Ruben launched his most arch, revelatory grin.

– Nikos told me all about the secret stash of explosives, while you two were away in the mountains. He offered me a partnership: if there was anything I thought might be worth blowing up, he was your man to do it. Together we would make history! I guess he must have found out what we were up to, somehow. Must have followed us the first night we went down the shelter, while he was still attempting to pass himself off to the Russians as a legitimate informant.

Whereas Ruben and Jade seemed prepared to rationalize the existence of a Xania spy ring and to examine its permutations – and upon which topic Alysa had little to say – Cosmo's concerns were centred almost entirely on his sense of personal loss and violation, and led him irrevocably towards conclusions that could only result in further loss and violation. He remembered his dream about Michalis, and wondered what fantastic slippage in the machinery of the universe had reassembled the dead man from Stratis' story in the character that Ruben had referred to as The Mutant. And although Cosmo had already given Alysa the benefit of the doubt regarding her whereabouts on the night of the rally, he now sensed the insidious return of those same suspicions that his lover had so vehemently contradicted. He knew he would not be satisfied until he had dug into this tissue of suggestion, and gone beyond the closed circuit of accusation and denial. Never one to place much faith in rational processes, Cosmo strayed open-eyed under the thrall and sway of the fiesta in all its Dionysian disorder. In this meandering and increasingly drunken obsession with uncovering The Truth, he allowed himself to be led only by his instinct, believing it to be the only sure guide.

20. *An Unseemly Altercation*

The white-clad *aficionados* of the bullfight were returning from the ring in raucous voice, crossing the Plaza del Castillo and crowding into the bars that surrounded it. Daylight was leaving and the atmosphere warmed towards another night of celebration. For the visitors from Crete, accustomed to small-town festivities and the relative predictability of a night out in the Lyrakia, it was like being caught up on a tide of collective delirium. Fire-eaters, jugglers, musicians, panhandlers, human statues; all these began to set up their positions around the city's various open spaces and the bandstand in the centre of the Plaza de Castillo was taken over by a medley of winos, dope-heads and beggars, who passed around their spliffs and bottles of *vino tinto* or *kalimucho*, calling out to random passers-by, telling tall stories, spinning lines, running life thin. The hippy mongrel dogs, forming an impromptu parallel pack of down and out canines, paced the square, tails erect, ruffs bristling, sniffing bins and lamp-posts and occasionally letting loose a chain reaction of frenzied barking. Kids set off firecrackers, which detonated with painful frequency against the backdrop of pure noise, noise on a scale that Cosmo and the others were simply not used to.

At the next table, a group of half a dozen Americans had settled in for the night. They wore variations of the local costume and talked excitedly about the corrida they had just attended. One of them, a long-term aficionado and visitor to the fiesta of San Fermín was giving a loud résumé of the skill and enterprise shown by one particular matador. The others hung onto his words, repeating key terms and phrases, adding to their repertoire of exotic-sounding names for the passes and turns and tactics enunciated so convincingly by the speaker. The expert on tauromachy went on to expand on the best technique for running with the bulls, the *encierro*, when the six bulls that are destined to fight that evening are set loose through the streets of the city with the whistle of a rocket at 8.00 a.m. It seemed that this man; lean, lank, bearded, with the wild-eyed look of the frontiersman, had twenty years' experience participating in the running, and had imparted his knowledge to groups of students and travelers with little variation over the years. No doubt it was good advice to avoid the bulls' horns, thought Cosmo as he eavesdropped, and not to provoke the bulls by whacking them with rolled-up newspapers, and seriously bad news when a single bull was isolated from the rest of the group and looking for trouble, but really, honestly, how can you prepare or protect yourself against the unforeseeable when you've signed up for a breakneck sprint along cobbled streets in the company of angry bulls? Cosmo had already seen that morning's *encierro* on television in the Hotel Eslava's breakfast lounge. He had been impressed by the beauty of the bulls, their stunning elegance and strength, and the running appealed to him greatly as a spectacle, and fed his eagerness to consume all and everything to do with the project he was still navigating in his head – his obsession with the *myth* of the bull – but he wasn't sure that he wanted to run the *encierro* himself. It broke away from myth and into the carnivalesque. And these would-be Hemingways put him right off. He felt, listening to the group at his back, that they had somehow *colonized* the experience of San Fermín, and whatever it had represented before this long invasion, it would never be the same again. In the account given by the American, it had become a touristic version of a fiesta, a simulacrum. Fortunately, though, there was enough of the real thing around for it not to matter too much. You could ignore these types; they only represented a fraction of the participants. *Don't let it spoil your time. Don't let them get to you.* There was something, though, about this particular group that would not leave Cosmo quiet. The moment he realized what they were, he acknowledged his aversion. He had left Xania because of the spooks who had trashed his house and his work; and now here he was in another enclave of Yankee Empire. These were servicemen, American military personnel on leave from some air base in Italy. He heard one of them address the waiter in broken Italian, reckoning that one Latin language was pretty much interchangeable with another. The veteran of a hundred *encierros* came to the rescue with his gravelly Midwestern Spanish. Cosmo glanced over at Alysa, beside him, who also appeared to be eavesdropping (it was impossible not to), while chewing on a portion of the crusty bread and Serrano ham that Ruben had ordered.

You come all this way to get shot of wankers like this and walk straight into a bloody commando unit of them sweet Jesus their faces when I told the others about the mask I made for Nikos wonder if the lunatic is still alive I dunno I can't believe he hadn't planned a getaway in spite of being crazy he had known what he was doing when he laid those wires it must have taken planning in which case he would have planned an exit strategy unless of course he wanted to die but that I cannot see that in Nikos no not at all the suicidal type not that I would know what a suicidal was supposed to look like Mark Rothko I guess and if you want to count up all the people who had killed themselves in all of history and lined them up head to toe how many times would it go around the world there were probably entire civilizations that we know nothing about because they developed a suicide cult and disappeared without a trace but hey how can these men sit there and be so fucking ignorant *that's what beats me as though they each had a customized brain extractor issued with the service handgun*

Cosmo's ruminations were interrupted by a voice behind him that, in his present combative mood, he could not ignore.

– What I can't take, what really sucks, is that these countries have *communist* parties and people damn nearly vote them into power! At least here they had Franco sort out that kind of shit.

– Until now, man. Who knows what's gonna happen now? They might vote in the commies here, huh?

– Or Italy, man. Half the eye-ties are reds.

Cosmo spun around in his chair, cheeks flushed.

– You guys approve of democracy?

Half a dozen faces scrutinized him closely. The older man, taking control, answered.

– Sure we do, buddy. What's your problem?

– Don't the people you're talking about have the right to vote for who the fuck they want to vote for?

– Steady on, buddy. We're having a private conversation here and I don't recall you being invited to participate. But since you mention it, and raise the subject, why don't we talk about your problem in an open and civilized manner, share a drink, and carry on enjoying the fiesta?

– I don't have a problem, other than you. I'm a European, living in Europe. What the hell are you doing here?

Cosmo felt Alysa's hand on his arm. He also noticed Ruben turn around to face the neighbouring table.

One of the other Americans, a man with a blonde crew-cut and attempted moustache answered this time. He was pretty angry, and globs of spit flew from his mouth as he spoke.

– What we're doing here is protecting you guys from our common enemy, not that we get any thanks for it.

– You mean the communists that you've just said so many people vote for in free, democratic elections?

– Aw, come off it, man. Those Mickey Mouse politicians don't know shit from seawater. It don't matter to the Soviets what they vote. They'd move the tanks in tomorrow given half the chance. From Berlin to Gibraltar. If it wasn't for the US military you guys would have been sucking Russian bear's dick years ago.

– Yuck. How unpleasant, said Jade, just loud enough.

– Say that again, Miss? Said a third man, wearing a vest that showed off formidable biceps.

– I said: how unpleasant.

– You American? This man had a quieter, more controlled manner, and the slow cadences of the South.

– I am.

– Where from?

– West Virginia.

– In that case, I apologize for my friend's lack of courtesy. I didn't realize you were an American. What you doing with this crowd?

– They're my friends, said Jade.

– You should choose your friends more carefully then, young lady, said the old Pamplona hand.

– If I needed advice on my choice of friends I don't believe I'd go look for it in whatever hole *you* crawled out of, replied Jade.

– Manners, please, said the Southern man to Jade, in a tone of mock alarm. Then, switching register to the expert on bullfighting: – Tom, I don't think it's for you to tell this young lady how to choose her friends. She has a free choice in that; this is how we differ from the Reds.

The one called Tom growled.

– Don't answer the question of whether this guy – he jerked a thumb towards Cosmo – thinks it's a good idea that we risk our asses on his behalf, or whether he'd prefer to see Europe being trampled under by the Soviets. He turned and wagged a finger at Cosmo, something that Cosmo hated. – So which way do you see it, buddy? Better red than dead, huh?

Again the restraining hand from Alysa. But Cosmo was halfway out of his seat and more than halfway to losing control. He now had a legitimate target to vent all his loathing against the people who had destroyed his paintings. It didn't matter that these ones were not responsible: it was what they represented that counted, and he was going to oppose that even if it meant swearing to allegiances he didn't have.

– You want to know what I think, *buddy*? If the choice was between communism and being looked after by you and your chums, I'd choose communism every day of the fucking week.

Attempted Moustache was out of his seat now, shouting.

– See what I mean! This mothafucka's a goddam *communist!* Some of my best friends wuz *killed* by communists. He shoved past the table towards Cosmo, who was also on his feet. A couple of the Americans glanced quickly at each other. They were professional soldiers, but they were also on vacation and had been drinking all day, and things were going in a bad direction very fast. It was only seven years since the US had pulled out of Vietnam, and most of these men had seen service there. But this was unsafe territory. They were under instructions not to get involved in discussion of local politics in Europe and both Bull Guru and Attempted Moustache were running close to the line. The Southerner tried to restrain the latter, but he pulled away and squared up to Cosmo. He stood there, red face inches from Cosmo's and prodded Cosmo's chest with an extended index finger in rhythm with his words. The insistent prodding against his clavicle was more than Cosmo could endure.

– I *said*, my best friends wuz killed by goddam communists.

– I heard you the first time, fuckwit. Perhaps they should have thought about that before going to a country where they weren't invited.

Attempted Moustache lunged at Cosmo with a straight left. Cosmo dodged, but not so fast that there wasn't some contact with his cheek. He reckoned the best way to deal with Attempted Moustache was the head-butt. Recovering, he positioned himself for this just as Ruben dived between them, very quickly indeed, and had Attempted Moustache's head in an arm-lock. Then all hell broke loose. There was much scraping of chairs as the other Americans rose, and Cosmo found himself wrestling with Tom, the Bull Guru, who was strong and wiry, but was disadvantaged by his efforts to fight like John Wayne, throwing two punches that failed to land. At close quarters he lacked Cosmo's skill in foul play. Having been foiled in his attempt to gift Attempted Moustache a Liverpool kiss, Cosmo bit his way free of Bull Guru's clutches and brought his forehead down with a crack on the bridge of his nose. With a loud groan, Bull Guru concertinaed to the ground. Meanwhile Ruben had brought Attempted Moustache's head crashing down on the metal table-top with a nasty thud, and for now it seemed that Cosmo and Ruben were holding their own. One of the other servicemen was attempting to help Bull Guru from the floor when Alysa brought a chair down on *his* head. Cosmo was looking around belligerently for someone else to batter. The Military were three down by the time the muscular Southerner stepped into the fray. He was the only person who was utterly calm, and this commanded both Ruben and Cosmo's attention. Neither of them wanted to tangle with this guy. A couple of waiters were also standing close to, and bibulous shouts of encouragement drifted over from the neighbouring tables.

– OK, OK, let's hold fire a minute here. The Southerner turned to his compatriots. – Y'all listen up, guys. This is a nice fiesta and we're here to enjoy ourselves. This incident has gone far enough. We have our differences of opinion, I think we can agree on that. So let's call it off now, before anyone gets hurt bad.

He held first Cosmo, and then Ruben, in his gaze. They recognized the man's authority, though Ruben was clenching and unclenching his fist, trying hard to contain himself. Bull Guru, wiping blood from his nose, heaved himself upright and Attempted Moustache was already back on his feet. The one who'd been felled by Alysa's chair was sitting up, looking groggy.

– Fair enough, said Cosmo, shaking. – Seeing as you guys have had enough. Attempted Moustache tried to make a move towards him, but the Southerner blocked him with an outstretched arm.

– Maybe you'd better leave. And take your friends with you, said the Southerner.

– How come *we* get to leave? asked Jade, as calm as the other. – We were here before you gentlemen arrived.

– Oh Christ, leave it, Jade, muttered Cosmo, who was suddenly sick of the whole thing and just wanted to go.

– No, Cosmo. It's a matter of principle. *They* should go.

The Southerner sighed and looked at his party.

– If it makes the lady happy, we'll go. He signalled to the waiter.

– Only kidding, said Jade, acknowledging Cosmo with a wink. – We were about to leave anyway.

The Americans settled back at their table, and Cosmo and Alysa started to make their way out from under the awning. Ruben spoke briefly in Spanish to one of the waiters, before turning to re-join his friends. As he passed the Americans' table though, he pointed index and little finger at Attempted Moustache and hissed.

– What's that? asked Cosmo, as they started out across

the Plaza del Castillo. – Latino voodoo?

– It means I'm not finished with the fucker.

They headed down towards the town's main park, which surrounds the *Ciudadela* or fortress. A huge funfair, complete with helter-skelter, wall of death and big wheel adjoined the park. Ruben dived into a bar just before crossing the road and emerged with four bottles of wine.

– We're just in time for the fireworks, he said, leading the way through the crowds that milled outside the bus station.

They found a space on the grass and settled down as the display began. It was a dazzling exhibition of pyrotechnics, a perfectly choreographed display of form and colour, kept up at a frenetic pace for a half hour. When eventually the skies cleared, the air around them was dense with the smell of gunpowder. Alysa took a slug of wine and passed the bottle to Cosmo.

– You're something of a lunatic, on the quiet. A most Unpredictable Person. I thought you were going to get yourself killed.

– You were pretty useful yourself, he said, deliberately misinterpreting.

– Ruben was enjoying himself.

– Yes. He rises to the occasion. Cosmo glanced over at Ruben, who glowered back at him. He disliked any implication that he enjoyed violent confrontations, even if this was indisputably true.

Cosmo leaned back on the grass, staring at up at the stars.

– Don't think I'm going to make it back to the hotel tonight. Too much Alternative Activity. Maybe stay away from the Plaza del Castillo for a while though.

He picked up the wine again and took a long drink. The groups which had assembled in the park to watch the firework display began to drift back towards the town centre. Cosmo was not at peace, not with the world and certainly not with himself. The loss of his work in Xania rankled anew, and he had now begun to think of it in terms of financial disaster as well as deep spiritual insult. He had always relied on his paintings for money, and many would have considered him fortunate to indulge that passion as a source of income. But it was something he had never had to think too much about, until now. The underemployed, pragmatic side of his nature began to stir, reluctant and angry. He had lost the appetite for painting and needed something, somebody, to blame. He watched Alysa's face as she sunk into sleep beside him; the perfect calm on her perfect features: the face of an Egyptian princess, he remembered thinking to himself, long ago in the Lyrakia. He played absentmindedly with a strand of her hair and she began to stir, gasped, and turned on her side. Ruben was already asleep, head resting on his forearms, knees tucked in. Only Jade remained awake. She had been watching him, he realized, as he watched over Alysa and touched her hair. He could not fathom Jade. At times he wondered if she was simply bored.

– You not tired? He asked.

– Yes, I'm tired. She was rolling a cigarette, or rather, Cosmo realized, a joint. – I was going to have a smoke, then try to sleep.

– You been having trouble sleeping? It doesn't show.

Jade's eyes were very green. They were reflecting moonlight in a way that made Cosmo feel dangerously vulnerable.

– No, I never have trouble sleeping, she answered.

She finished rolling her joint and lit up. She took three drags and passed it over to Cosmo, who had to lean over Alysa's sleeping body to collect it. Cosmo inhaled deeply: it was strong, rank-smelling weed.

– You enjoying the fiesta? He asked, feeling chatty once the marijuana was in his blood.

– Bits, she said. I like the partying bits a lot, don't like the bull thing much though, as I said. Too macho. But then, it's funny, because I rather enjoyed the brawl. So yeah, I like bits of it. And I like this bit.

– This bit?

– Sitting here. Talking. Smoking the herb. The company.

Cosmo handed the joint back to her.

– You're a very confusing person, Jade.

– Am I? I don't think you'd find that was true.

– If?

Jade laughed; a full-throated, then almost-dirty laugh, that trilled off into a lighter, more girlish sound. A laugh in three movements, thought Cosmo.

– Don't try and catch me out, Mister Bull Painter.

– Hmm. Is that a compliment or a description?

– A description. Like once a tailor was called Mister Tailor. Or a smithy Mister Smith. In Olden Times. And you paint bulls.

– A cooper made the bendy bits for barrels. Mister Cooper.

– They're all men's jobs.

– Women didn't have jobs. They had babies.

Jade looked at him sweetly, refusing the bait.

– At school, she said, back in good old West Virginia, there was a kid whose name was Smellie.

– Poor bastard.

– You'd think, she went on, that with every other immigrant changing their name, it wouldn't be too much to change your name to, like, Smalley.

– Or Smiley.

– Indeed. Or Smiley.

– I paint other things than bulls, you know.

– I know. I was teasing. Mister Bull. There *was* a Mister Bull, ran the hardware store in my home town.

– And a Captain Bullshit?

– Uh, that title's taken, I regret to say.

– By whom?

Jade jerked a thumb at Ruben's reclining body.

– Harsh, said Cosmo.

Jade didn't reply. She frowned and stubbed out her reefer, laid her head on her woollen Cretan *sakouli*, and called over to Cosmo. – If anything exciting happens, wake me, will you?

– Sure, said Cosmo, and blew her a kiss from the palm of his hand. She smiled and closed her eyes.

21. *An Unpleasant Confrontation*

Cosmo woke up in the cold, struggling against a dream that was washing him downstream through red streets that he dimly recognized as Pamplona. Ruben was shaking him. Cosmo had no idea how long he had been asleep. At his side lay three empty bottles.

– You coming along? We're gonna find a cosy bar. Then to the running of the bulls.

Cosmo groaned and turned on his back. The world spun around him, curiously large and frighteningly distorted.

What was that about I wonder where did my soul travel in the time between chatting with Jade and now why am I so radioactive I mean reactive I guess if you don't react you're dead Jade has beautiful legs too and why am I responding have I been completely blind or am I just falling apart a blown thing a leaf ouch my head hurts is that a hangover or where I butted the bull-man I can't have a hangover you have to stop drinking to get a hangover I'd better have a blast of something wonder if Jade has more of that weed if I look up through the branches of this tree I can see the moon very shiny and nearly full and if all the chaos of this fiesta were distilled into a single pill how big would it be the size of the moon framed between my finger and my thumb like that and who would play the music shit what is going on and how is it that I cannot tell whether Alysa is telling the truth maybe just as well Ruben now seems to be enjoying himself ah good he's rolling up a smoke thanks mate you read my mind now I only have to lean on an elbow and ah there's some wine left in this one thank you I'll have some of that too oh dear not such a brilliant idea señor flute for now you must attain the vertical

Jade and Alysa were already standing; in fact they were dancing. They faced each other, shimmying sinuous and slow in a way that Cosmo, alerted by some remnant of his dream, found acutely emotional. He tried to connect what he was seeing, this dance, this expression of timelessness, these two women shadowing each other's movements with such spontaneous grace, but he could not find it within him, could not reach the place the dream had retreated to. He was wary, and his psychic antennae were sharp, in spite of the drink: the dream was nagging at him gently even as it loosened its last lingering touch on his consciousness. In the distance someone was playing the Galician pipes in an impromptu recital, the lilting melancholic drone carrying across the park, over the many human forms that lay in clutches under the trees and around the edge of the nearby battlements.

In the old quarter they wound up in a bar with a crowd of Basques. There were musicians, too, playing reels, or something like reels, and there was frantic dancing, very different from the dance Cosmo had just been watching. He still felt emotionally laden, but attributed it, at least in part, to the prolonged drinking. One of the Basques handed him a brandy, and another presented him with a spliff. He took a couple of drags and passed it on to Ruben.

– What happened to pacing yourself? Asked Ruben.

– Bollocks, said Cosmo.

One of the Basques was interrogating Alysa, evidently impressed by her hair, which Jade had plaited while Cosmo slept. There was a slight language barrier.

– Wales?

– Wales, *Pays de Galles*, Alysa tried French.

– *País de Galles. Tu eres Galesa? Verdad*?

– *Galesa, si*, Alysa managed.

– *Muy bueno. Gente Celta. Nunca he visto una Galesa tan hermosa.*

– What's he say? Alysa asked Ruben.

– He says he's never seen a female Welsh so beautiful.

– Ask him if he's ever seen a female Welsh in his life.

Ruben did.

– He says no, he hasn't.

– Not even Bonnie Tyler?

Ruben translated.

– He's never heard of her.

The Basque who hadn't heard of Bonnie Tyler swept Alysa away, leading her to the middle of the pub, which served as a dance area. There was cheering and clapping as Alysa began to dance with the man, improvising along the lines of the generic reel or the Spanish *jota*, with arms high and swirling moves and high jumps. Jade joined in, taking one of the young Basque men from the same group with her. Cosmo turned back to Ruben.

– I like these people. They possess style and lubrication. They are hairy, but not excessively so. And Alysa, she can fling a leg.

– It's good to see her dance. She's been kind of withdrawn since the house got raided.

Cosmo sighed, non-committal.

– Maybe she blames herself, he said.

– You think? Some women do that. Always blame themselves when things go wrong.

– Whereas she should be blaming you, right?

– Drop it, Cosmo.

– Sorry. It slipped out. I guess I'm still angry.

– That's OK, *cabrón.*

– Yeah but I'm still sorry. Fuck it. And letting go at those Americans was just dumb.

– Forget it. I was beginning to enjoy myself.

Someone pushed a plateful of hot tapas along the bar towards Ruben and Cosmo, gesturing to eat. Ruben thanked him and they helped themselves to the food.

– You still getting along with Jade?

– Why you ask? Ruben chewed on what looked like a sparrow in batter.

– Just. You know. A feeling. Looks.

– Hmm. Ruben spat out the sparrow's foot onto the floor.

– You don't have to answer.

– I don't mind you asking. You're my pal. But no, we aren't doing so great. All that stuff about the bunker. She said I was *intransigent.*

– Intransigent?

– Yeah. And another word. *Incorrigible.*

– That's rough.

– Intransigent I had to think about. Intransigent is OK. Incorrigible is not so good.

– It's rough.

– Yeah. So I dunno. We get on fine most of the time. Hey, what am I telling you this for?

– Cos I'm your pal?

– Right.

There was a pause.

– I think she likes *you*, man. Ruben was looking straight at him.

– Oh, come on, man. This I can do without.

– No. It's obvious. Looks. Like you said. I've seen her watching you. But it's not a problem. I started off too well with her. Maybe I can't keep up the uh. What's the word? Momentum.

– That's sad.

– No. It's the way I am, I guess. I lose interest too quick. No sticking power.

– Hell, I can't help you there. My attention span is, like, zilch.

– Women like you in a different way to me. They just want my body. I mean, you can't blame them, hey? Ruben made a self-deprecating little laugh. – But from you they want your soul.

– Shit, is that an improvement?

– I couldn't say. But while you were in prison, it was like the whole household was pining. Alysa and that Pascale, Christ! What do you do to these women? And Jade going on at me how I should be doing more to get you out. We did everything we could, swear to God, man.

– I believe you.

Cosmo hadn't known Ruben to lower his guard in this

way before. He never showed himself to be vulnerable. Cosmo wondered just how sober his friend was. This fiesta was not conducive to sober assessment of anything or anyone. Ruben didn't appear to be too drunk, but it was often difficult to tell with him.

– But you don't get it, do you? It's like you were the essence of that house, the *epicentre*, man. I mean we found it together and we shared the rent, but it always felt to me that it was *your* house. It was where you did your art. When I saw what they'd done to your pictures I didn't want to live there no more. Like they'd ripped the secret heart from the place.

– I'm moved, Ruben. You're moving me.

Ruben looked at Cosmo sharply.

– No bullshit, said Cosmo. He put his arm around Ruben and kissed him on the cheek.

– We breaking in on something? said Jade, bouncing back from the dance floor.

– Just a love-in, baby, said Ruben, putting his free arm around her shoulders. Alysa joined them.

– That is some shit-kicking music, said Jade, and did her Lady Brett Ashley impersonation in faultless Anglo-aristocratese: – I say, can a chap get a drink?

Cosmo ordered more brandy, and passed the small balloon glasses around. He bought for the Basque men who had been dancing with Jade and Alysa and for the man who'd given them the tapas. It was hardly necessary: there were rows of drinks in front of them now they had been adopted as a part of the Basques' circle. One of the men, who had been dancing with Jade, spoke English.

– You run with the bulls?

– We watch, I think, answered Jade.

– Better to run. And then you can watch yourself on TV later.

– Yeah, well, I'll think about it.

Alysa, looking flushed and happy, stepped over to Cosmo: – You want to dance?

Cosmo looked her up and down.

– No. You dance like a Russian.

There was an excruciating moment's silence.

– *What?* What's that supposed to mean?

– You know. You just lack the felt boots and the woolly hat.

– That's not what you mean at all. Wanker.

– Work it out for yourself.

– No, Cosmo. I won't accept that at all.

Cosmo turned his back on her, then swung around again, face livid. He was feeling drunk and vindictive. He realized he couldn't justify himself, but he was burrowing deep into a suspicion that had been plaguing him for days. His voice was low and contained, almost a whisper, but crackling with repressed anger.

– Tell me then. Tell me that you have nothing, absolutely *nothing* to do with what happened back in Xania. Tell me that you told the KGB to go fuck themselves. Because, you know what? Nobody just walks away from an approach like the one made to you. Nobody. This guy, Michalis, the one who told you about your father, he was sent to recruit you, yeah?

Alysa could not contain her surprise and shock.

– Michalis? Who said his name was Michalis?

– No one. I guessed. It came to me in a dream. Was it?

Alysa nodded, eyes on the floor.

– And so you told him No Way, Fuck Off, Whatever?

Alysa looked at him, eyes imploring him to stop.

– Bullshit! Nobody walks away. They were onto you, weren't they? That Michalis, the one you met in the States; he had a half-chewed ear didn't he?

Alysa nodded, silent.

– And when I told you the story I heard from Stratis in jail, you seemed very interested all of a sudden. Weird, the guy's name being Michalis. So, I reckoned, my pal Stratis' story was some kind of allegory, yeah – something that *almost* happened. Or *might* have happened. And then, guess what, I discover there's someone hanging around Xania with half an ear. Odd, wouldn't you say? It's not every day you meet a one-eared dead person walking around in a YALE sweatshirt and a baseball cap. And if the KGB were onto you, it's likely that the Yanks were, too.

– That doesn't follow. Her voice quiet, small.

– No? The place got trashed. My work got trashed. Maybe I was too hasty back there in Xania. If it wasn't the Yanks seeking revenge for the bunker thing, a bit fucking obvious on reflection, then who the fuck was it? Any ideas? A Russian agent in Xania giving you a hard time for not doing what you're told? Now *there's* an interesting possibility.

– Cosmo. Stop it. Please. I don't know for certain who wrecked your house, any more than you do. If I told you that Michalis had followed me to Crete, you'd blame me. If I didn't, you'd find a way to blame me anyway. I can't win. You've already made your mind up, you bastard.

Fighting back tears, she walked out of the bar, head high.

Jade, who had been talking with Ruben and the Basques, turned to Cosmo:

– What's going on?

– Nothing. She left.

Jade ran out into the street, but returned shortly, without Alysa.

– I can't see her. It's impossible to find someone in these crowds.

– Fuck it. Leave her be.

– What? Cosmo, are you out of your mind? This is Alysa we're talking about. She's with us. She's with *you*.

Cosmo took a gulp of brandy and looked at Jade.

– Wrong. She's on her own. We're all on our own.

Outside daylight was forcing an entry into the narrow street.

Five minutes before the rocket was fired to mark the start of the *encierro*, Cosmo, Ruben and Jade were installed on the wooden railings that look out on the final stretch of the running, where the bulls turn left at the *Telefonica* building and head towards the Plaza de Toros. Here the runners and the bulls pass through a tunnel and out into the ring, where the bulls will be ushered into their stalls beneath the stadium. The tunnel is a notoriously dangerous part of the course, since it creates a bottleneck where many people are running in a confined space, and there is sometimes a pile-up, with serious consequences for the runners who fall or whose way is blocked by others who have fallen. By the time the bulls and the runners have reached this stage they have covered nearly a kilometer of the narrow cobbled streets from the corral. People who fall here may be tired or over-exerted; it is foolishness to attempt to run more than a short stretch of the run with the bulls, since they keep up a pace which the runners cannot match.

It was a crystal bright morning, the sun newly risen,

with a sharp bite to the air. Ruben rubbed his hands in the chill and drank from a wineskin that one of the Basques had presented to him for safekeeping while he and his friends set off for their starting point near the corral. He lifted the skin high above his head and squirted an arcing parabola of red wine into his mouth. He rubbed his lips on his sleeve and passed the wineskin up to Cosmo, high on the thick wooden barrier, straddling the upper beam. Jade was standing on the lower beams of the fence, peering down Calle Estafeta from which direction the runners would emerge. When the second rocket was fired the crowd pushed forward in anticipation, even though it would be a good ninety seconds before the bulls reached this part of the course. But already, from here, they could hear the noise from the streets of the old town, and a thunderous echo, as many hundreds of runners set off in the company of the bulls and their minders, the harmless steers who are released alongside them.

As the crescendo drew nearer, people strained forward again to catch sight of the first runners. They hove into view of a sudden, running at speed, and almost immediately after them came the bulls; three, four sturdy black beasts, angered, excited, goaded, scenting the panic and excitement, themselves subject to who knows what terrors at being released so rudely into streets packed with human beings. The animals' knowledge of people was very limited, having lived their lives in the wilderness of a vast Andalucian estate: suddenly this enemy was all around them, provoking, shouting, roaring, running. Those who liked to run the gauntlet whacked the bulls' rumps with rolled-up newspapers, the kind of baiting that Tom, the American of the night before, had warned his apprentices about. As the bulls approached, Cosmo could see the fantastic musculature of their necks and chests, hear the hard pounding of their hooves on stone, smell the steam from their nostrils and their hides, the tremendous exertion and power and beauty deployed with such ease. Jade gasped out loud next to him. One bull, forced by the momentum of the race, veered towards their railing, almost crashing into the barrier just below her, before swerving and skidding, pausing for a moment to orient himself, then joining the other bulls for the final dash into the tunnel. In the instant that the bull stopped and turned, looking around, his eyes lingered for what might only have been a second on the people hanging onto the barrier. Cosmo saw his confusion, but more, his refusal to submit to that confusion, his determination that the enemy should not evade him, and the bull downed his neck and shook his head with an eager snort, and the frothy effluence on his nuzzle was reflected in the sunlight. Then he was gone, with a clatter, pursued by runners, who in turn were attempting to avoid the two remaining bulls that had lingered a little way behind. These two bulls were accompanied by more runners than the first four, which had been going at a greater pace. The quantity of people forced several runners to flatten themselves along the side of the barriers fronting the street, just below Cosmo and Jade. One of the bulls, a huge brown animal, swerved, with lowered head, horns at the ready. The horns were long; longer than Cosmo had imagined, and they tapered to needle-sharp points. The bull smashed into the lower back of one runner, catching him with his shoulder, rather than his horns, and the runner spun into the air like a child's doll, landing face-down on the road. The injured runner, who may only have been winded, pulled his hand over his head, curled into a foetal position and waited for the danger to pass. Meanwhile, the brown bull had caught a second runner against the barrier itself. This time there was blood, as he gored the runner through the thigh with one of his horns. Cosmo saw the dagger point enter the flesh. The runner pulled away at the moment of impact and now clung to the barrier grimly, his face riveted. Ruben, thinking quickly, reached down an arm and heaved the man, who was quite small and slim, to the safety of the barrier's top rung. By now the bull had moved on, giving a disconsolate snort, and the run was over, a few steers bringing up the rear along with the onrushing tide of slower runners.

Within seconds of rescuing the wounded runner, Ruben was passing him down to the Red Cross team who had materialized behind them. The man was propped against the upright of the fence and given First Aid by the paramedics. He was in a state of shock and, apart from muttering repeated thanks in Ruben's direction, barely recognized what was taking place. But he did not appear to be badly injured and the wound, while bloody, had only punctured the outer thigh, not the dangerous inner part where the femoral artery flows.

The Basques who had run with the bulls returned and invited Ruben and the others to take breakfast with them. They sat on wooden benches in a big cafeteria and drank coffee, dunking *churros*, and talking rapidly in Spanish with Ruben. It had been a very quick *encierro*, they said, and there had been few incidents or injuries. Essentially, Cosmo thought, this was more to do with luck than any kind of planning. It seemed ridiculous to him to confront a force of nature, a bull, with any effective strategy for evasion. Jade concurred, adding that the only sure way to avoid getting injured was not to attempt an early morning sprint with a 500-kilo bull. She conveyed this to the Basques, via Ruben, and they said that no doubt she was correct, but that wouldn't stop people from wanting to run.

The Basques said goodbye, hoped they would meet again in the bar of the night before, their favoured drinking place, and left Ruben with the wineskin as a memento. Jade said she was tired and wanted a hot shower, and the three of them made their way slowly through the streets towards the Hotel Eslava. The way back was again packed with people, with early bands parading, banging drums, blasting out distorted tunes on trombones and trumpets, drunks staggering into one more bar before crashing out senseless on the pavement; all components in the irrefutable logic of the fiesta, to carry on partying as though the opportunity would never come again.

22. *Broken Glass*

Back at the hotel, there was no Alysa. Her things were still there though, so Cosmo figured she hadn't simply taken off. He fell onto the bed exhausted, but could not sleep. After an hour he gave up trying, slipped on his shoes, and wandered out onto the street. In Bar García he stopped off for a beer and ate some tapas. The adrenalin of the fiesta was like a riotous contagion. Many of the people who came into the bar wore the marks of extreme exhaustion, yet they were fired up with a frenetic energy that enabled them to spend days on end without sleep; driven by the relentless dynamic of the fiesta itself. The continuous honking of trombones and yelping of trumpets playing the same tunes over and over, the anthems of San Fermín with their tinny and ribald cadences, reminded Cosmo of Big Top music from visits to the circus he had made as a child. He shared a few beers with an Irish couple from Galway, then left. The bar was dark and air-conditioned, so exiting onto the bright streets in the heat of the day came as a shock. Cosmo had left his sunglasses in the hotel room, and covered his eyes against the glare. After fifty metres he ducked into another bar, scanning the tables for any sign of Alysa. He ordered an *anís* and emptied his bladder in the latrines of a luxurious marble washroom. Back in the bar, he perched precariously on a stool, enjoying the comings and goings of groups of revellers in varying stages of exuberance, then played table football with a threesome of holidaying Catalans. He drank several more servings of *anís*, and by the time he left the bar, it was late afternoon and Cosmo was not sober.

When he returned to the hotel room, Alysa was sitting in bed, propped up by pillows, staring into space. She had showered, and was wrapped in a towel, smoking a cigarette. Her face was sullen and she didn't respond to his greeting. Cosmo, caught between conflicting surges of vindictiveness and compassion, remained silent. He realized, with a vague sense of shame, that he had no desire for her, that he was spent – and not just in a physical sense – and he was tired of her company, which until so recently had exhilarated and excited him like no other. He was angry with himself but could not force himself to want her, or even want her around. Then, his anger waning, he began to overcompensate, trying to comfort her, to coax her into speaking, but failed even to convince himself, and she brushed him aside, turning her face towards the door.

He needed to use the bathroom, and while there, decided to take a shower. He spent a long time under the spray of warm water, wondering, with some confusion, how best to approach her. Although he had been aware of a gradual disintegration in their relationship, they had, till now, managed to gloss over the cracks; but today he had provoked a further, possibly terminal dip, which he wasn't sure he had the will to repair. His harping on about her possible connection with Soviet state operatives hadn't come as a sudden illumination, but in the light of it he now felt that he could better understand her mood swings since the night the house was raided and his paintings wrecked. He had never got an answer to his questioning beyond a general reply that she was 'a bit down', that she felt badly about his loss. Then that one time, in a torrent of emotion on the boat from Piraeus to Brindisi, she had expressed anger at his interrogation. So he had stopped asking.

But when she had stalled his earlier questions, saying she was feeling low, had she not simply been playing the only role left to her short of full confession? He was not convinced by her, and in particular by her claim not to have been with Michalis on the night of the rally. Moreover, he harboured a strong suspicion, as he had intimated in the Basque bar, that she had been and still was in some way responsible for Michalis' presence in Xania, and whatever task it was that he had come to carry out. When he emerged from the bathroom, drying his hair roughly with a towel, he asked her again, quite superfluously, what was the matter, and the manner of his asking was not pleasant, but sounded like another veiled accusation.

– You *shit*. I have nothing to tell you, she said.

She sat up, and only then did Cosmo notice that there was a bottle of brandy on the floor, on Alysa's side of the bed, with a half of it gone. She picked it up and drank straight from the bottle, and then fumbled for Cosmo's cigarettes on the little table at her side. Her hands were shaking as she lit the cigarette.

He leaned over towards her, in an attempt to secure the brandy bottle. Alysa, muscles tensed, as if acting on reflex to a perceived threat, punched him hard in the mouth. He recoiled, hand to his face, and swore.

– That's for insulting me in the bar, she said, as she braced to deliver another. From her intonation, Cosmo guessed it was to be the next of a sequence. Blood began to seep between his fingers, but he was weary, and did not feel up to hitting her back.

– Hang on, hang on here. Cosmo's tongue flickered over a wobbly tooth as he spoke. – What are you so worked up about? Blood had dribbled onto his chin, and he smudged it with the back of his hand.

– What? You shit you fucking arsewipe I'm going to fucking hurt you. Alysa was out of the bed and on him. She punched his face again and pushed him against the wall. He lost his balance, slid to the floor. Alysa tore away his towel and punched him between the legs before scratching with long nails at his groin. He pushed her away, covered himself, shouting.

– Mad fucking bitch.

Cosmo, doubled up, naked on the floor. Alysa, standing tall and naked, sneering down at him. He looked down at his wounds. There were deep pink welts up his inner thigh.

– Don't think I haven't figured out how you operate, you *hypocrite*. She was kneeling in front of him now, eyes narrowed, right arm lowered, but poised. – Here's your choice: you either believe in your story about me and the Russians or you believe mine. I know that by turning them down I was risking a lot, maybe my life, but I never intended for you to be hurt, or your precious work to be destroyed. I was not a *party* to it. You understand that, you selfish prick?

Cosmo shrugged, wiping blood from his mouth with the back of his hand.

– But that's not really what's at stake here, is it, shithead? Not what's *really* bugging you!

She took another swing at Cosmo, who shied away, her fist catching him near the eye. But she punched hard, and his head knocked back against the wall. He tried to stand, or at least to put some distance between himself and her, but from a squatting position, she struck out deftly with her right foot, making full impact with his shoulder. He heard something crack and felt a searing pain. She had told Cosmo about her training in martial arts, but right now that information only fed his suspicions about her training as a KGB operative.

Cosmo slumped back against the wall again. He was strong enough to take her on, close to, and wrestle with her, even if he lacked her skill, even with a wounded shoulder. But he lacked the will to fight and his background had instilled in him the stubborn belief that a man never hit a woman, however much mental violence he might exert.

– The whole story. The *whole* story, goes like this, Alysa went on, crouched in front of him like a panther. – You are weary of your black bitch - *Don't* deny it! She screamed at him, as he began to mutter in contradiction. – So you take up this line, about me and my father and the communists, not as if it was news, cos it isn't. I *told* you, you little fuck, I *told* you myself, in so many words, and in confidence, soon after we met. Up in the mountains, yes? Remember? I wasn't hiding it from you. I wish to God I hadn't told you. But I didn't want secrets between us. Concealing stuff. Unlike you. That story you told me from prison. Jesus, who *was* that guy? What the fuck was all that stuff about the eyes? Did you make that up? She shifted the weight on her feet, but was still in a combat position.

– So you're getting tired of me, and you have been since

you shagged Pascale. Yes, I know, I was responsible for that. But variety is what makes you tick, isn't it Cosmo? The spice of life. It *pleased* me to offer her to you. Can you understand that? It gave me pleasure. You know that feeling: taking it to the edge. Not holding back? Seeing just how far you can take things? I know you do. I mean, I'm surprised you didn't take on Lucas, too. I know you wanted to. He would have, like, rounded out the picture nicely. And everything has to look good in your pictures doesn't it? We're all figments of your fucking art. We all end up in a fucking painting, one way or another. So, out of interest, why didn't you fuck Lucas? Enlighten me. It wasn't out of prudery, that's for sure.

Cosmo looked up at her, sly, adapting to her mood. Blood dribbled from his chin and onto his chest.

– He never asked me to. Unlike you.

She was poised to hit him again, but lowered her fist this time. The towel had come loose when she first attacked him, and she looked down and shook her head, her long plaits swinging about her bare shoulders. Cosmo pulled himself tentatively up against the wall and Alysa gathered the towel around her and walked to the bathroom, her fury abating. She returned with a glass and half-filled it with brandy. She sat sipping it on the bed, determinedly avoiding eye contact. When Cosmo reached over and took the bottle, she ignored him. The brandy stung his cut lip, but the warm rush of liquor immediately restored him to relative calm, and a question began to form on his lips.

– I want to ask you something.

Alysa raised her head, looked at him without expression, and said nothing.

– Did you know that Nikos was going down into the bunker that night?

She shook her head, and spoke wearily.

– *What?* You want to talk spy stuff now? Don't you think you've made enough stupid remarks for one day?

– I need to know what was going on in Xania. Don't you understand? If I have got it wrong, well, shit, I'm sorry, for what it's worth. But I think we might talk rather than you just batter me. It's a bit one-sided. He rubbed his left shoulder emphatically.

Alysa let out a short, sarcastic laugh.

– That's the problem. You've got it right, just about. As for Nikos, I can't help you. Oh hell, what does it matter now? She adopted the tone of an inquisitor at the McCarthy witch hunt trials: – I am not now nor have ever been a member of the communist party nor am I now nor have I been in the past on the payroll of any intelligence network opposed to the interests of the free world. Will that do? Will that *suffice?*

She lit another cigarette, took a drag, then made a face and crushed it in the ashtray, stubbing it repeatedly with fierce concentration while she chose her words.

– I don't want to talk to you. I really don't want to. I'd like to beat you up. You know that, don't you.

– Yeah, I know that, said Cosmo, containing a sudden and inappropriate desire to laugh. She had spoken as if merely relaying factual information.

– But it'll do me good to clear the air. For myself. Then I'll never have to speak to you again.

Cosmo nodded and took a swig of brandy, not trusting himself to reply.

– There's no harm in you knowing this, I guess, since Nikos is dead, as far as I can judge. He *was* working for the Russians, but he went rogue, off beam. As a Cretan with a sick father, he managed to get himself posted to Souda, which was where Moscow wanted him. But he was, as you know, a liability. He became more and more eccentric, was indiscreet, kept getting arrested by the navy police, became diverted by his tourist terrorism thing. Moscow was losing patience. They probably wanted him liquidated. That's the way they do business. As I understand it, Michalis was sent to intervene, to see if Nikos could be salvaged.

I had told Michalis I was coming to Greece: I needed to do some research for my thesis. But I also told him, back in New York, that I was not tempted by the lifestyle of a professional spy. He laughed and said we'd see. I was adamant. He was insistent, resourceful, patient. I think he was fond of me though, in a paternal sort of way. I think he was loyal to my dad, and if it had been anyone else who had tried to recruit me, I would probably be at the bottom of the Hudson River now with cement boots. In the end he seemed to acknowledge that I was serious. When he turned up in Xania I was worried. I was frightened, to be honest. The night of the rally, just before you went out, we had a row, remember? I was feeling shit, knowing I had to go and meet him and Nikos and wondering how I could do it without you or Ruben finding out. Funny, huh? I met him briefly, as you saw, told him that he could not keep trying to use my loyalty to Dad to count on me doing any work for him. He smiled, seemed unfazed. Same attitude: he believed that with time, and no doubt a little pressure, I would come around.

– And Nikos? He was with you and Michalis. Yet he was down in the bunker at the same time as us. He must have known another entrance.

– No doubt. He certainly fooled Michalis. He acted dead straight with Michalis, never mentioned a thing about his plans for the bunker, obviously. But he was totally out of control, as it turned out, and that just put more pressure on me.

– How come?

– With you and Ruben playing at Batman and Robin down in the shelter, I was linked to the whole story. I became visible to the authorities. That was not good, according to the plans that Michalis still had for me as a trainee spook. He didn't like the fact that I was living with you and Ruben, thought you were under CIA surveillance, which you were, for quite a while, thanks to Ruben and his camera. Next thing, he began hanging around closer to the house. That's when I got worried.

– You haven't explained how you found the shelter.

– Nikos told me. He talked too much, that was part of the reason they wanted to be shot of him. Or to shoot him. So I guessed that was where you were headed that night. I ran back and woke Jade, and we set out after you. You must have taken a detour, because when we passed Café Costas Jade saw you making your way along the harbour, which was convenient. It allowed her to think we'd spotted you purely by luck.

Cosmo listened in silence, taking it all in. He still wasn't sure how much of this he believed. Alysa was talking to him, at least, but her eyes remained averted and her voice was cold.

– And Courtney? Did this guy Michalis kill Courtney? *Torture* him?

– I don't know for sure. But I suspect it was Nikos and Michalis. Unless there's another person in the network that I don't know about, which is perfectly possible. Michalis didn't exactly volunteer information.

– Jesus. Poor Courtney.

– Yeah, well, that was what did for me. I knew I couldn't work with these kinds of people. And *Courtney*, poor dab, he didn't need to die, let alone in *that* way. He knew fuck all. Worse than that, he was a black man, a *brother!* How could they justify that in the war against the oppressed? He was just a pawn. He didn't stand a chance.

Cosmo took a long swig of brandy and lit another cigarette from the stub of his last.

– How come you could risk coming here? Won't they come after you, I mean, wherever you go? Isn't that what happens in these things. They hunt you down.

Alysa laughed tersely, but again, without good humour.

– You've been reading too many cold war thrillers. If I had already been on their payroll, if I had somehow let them down, then yeah, I'm sure they would. But they had nothing on me. Michalis, because of his loyalty to my dad, he wouldn't have taken it that far. That's what I was counting on: he'd let me go. But my freedom came at a price, with him making a nice mess first to show me how I'd hurt his feelings.

– So what you're telling me, in a roundabout kind of way, is hey, my buddy Michalis trashed your house, correct?

Alysa nodded. – It seems that way.

She appeared reflective now, her anger dissipated. Cosmo, by contrast, was experiencing a renewed onslaught of blind rage, and fought hard to control it.

– Those two guys on the quay at Souda, the two American spooks: they weren't guilty at all! If anything, they were watching my back, because they had wind of KGB interest being stepped up in the area; and because of my involvement with the explosions at the bunker I was under continuous surveillance, right?

– I guess so.

– Let me get this straight. The KGB trashed my house and destroyed my paintings because *you* wouldn't play spy games for them? Just like I said in the bar this morning?

– That's about the size of it. I'd say I was sorry, but that makes it sound like it was my fault. I *am* sorry, of course, but what the fuck could I have done to prevent it? Tell me that.

Cosmo sat in silence, his emotions shot to pieces.

– You know what depresses me about you Cosmo. What makes me really sad about this whole sorry fucking saga?

She didn't wait for a reply.

– What really makes me sad is that you haven't got the guts to tell me the real reason in the bar this morning, that you want done with it, that you're through with me, and I don't know for sure whose life you want to fuck up next but I'd venture a guess. And of course, she's eager for it. Any fool can see that. Christ, you *deserve* each other! Ruben can see it. He's man enough to acknowledge what he is. With Ruben you get what you see. But not with you. You have to camouflage your story. So you bring up all this stuff about dancing like a bear. Sideways stuff about me being in with the Russians. Information, which, as I've said, I fed you in the first fucking place. God you make me want to fucking *hurt* you.

Cosmo was not so dull as to deny that Alysa had hit a vein of truth: his quip in the bar had been unnecessary, even infantile. But he could not acknowledge that he had acted as deceitfully as Alysa had suggested. The thing with Jade he had only been dimly aware of until the previous night, a vague attraction that he had felt towards her from the outset, but because of her pairing with Ruben, had never followed up. True, the way she had been flirting with him in the park, playfully intent, had aroused his interest, but he had no idea that his own behaviour around Jade was so transparent. The accusations he had made in the bar about Alysa and the KGB were fumbling and vindictive, he could now see, but, hell, he was drunk, they were all drunk: this town, this fiesta was a catalyst for drunken outbursts. The instinct that he was so proud of following now presented him with an agonizing double-bind: he suddenly wanted to take Alysa in his arms, to forget all this, to ask forgiveness. She looked so lovely to him just now, her angry black eyes burning holes in his heart, the elegance of the outstretched right leg, the beauty of her feet – why had he not dwelled upon her feet before, he wondered as he stared at the right one, the one that a few minutes earlier had smashed into his shoulder? He sighed, feeling the first stirrings of a complicated desire, and looked up.

Alysa was on her feet again. She stood over him, close. His head was at a level with her thighs. He wanted to bury his head between her legs. He wanted all this mess, all this poison to be washed away. His heart was pounding below his ribcage and sweat drenched his face and body. But he didn't move from his place on the floor, against the wall. There was a brief moment when she looked at him, and her eyes softened and acquiesced, and he wondered if what he wanted, she wanted too: and by doing so could they undo the damage they had brought about, scour out the poison? Was sex enough to grant them a reprieve?

And then the moment was gone. He sat, rigid against the wall, watching Alysa as she got dressed, feeling himself fill with an almost unbearable longing, but, simultaneously, refusing to give her the pleasure of having somehow won, of having vanquished him. He watched as she slipped into clean white knickers, as her long brown legs eased into jeans, and he watched the golden double-axe pendant swing between her breasts as she crossed her arms and pulled a white tee-shirt over her head. He watched as she sat on the bed and pulled on her trainers. He watched as she slipped a cascade of fine golden bracelets on her wrist, before turning with an almost imperceptible sashay, a parting gesture of swagger and bravura; and he was still watching when she paused on her way to the door and took a last slug from the brandy bottle before lifting it at arm's length and letting it drop on the hard tiled floor.

– All gone, she said.

The bottle shattered and broken glass splintered across the room in fine shards, then the door slammed shut behind her.

Cosmo crawled onto the bed, and in spite of the voices in his head and the uproar from the streets below, he was drained by the excesses of alcohol and emotion, and sank into a deep, turbulent sleep.

23. *Mostly Jade*

It was evening when he woke. Crossing the bedroom, trying to avoid the splinters of glass scattered across the floor like quartz, he took another shower, this time a cold one. He looked in the mirror: a swollen lip and some reddening about the left eye. Although his left shoulder ached, it only hurt him when he moved awkwardly. He needed to think straight, but this fiesta was not designed for straight thinking. In spite of having slept, he was hardly sober, and definitely he was hungry. Thinking could wait. He was always confusing the need to think with the need to eat. He sat on the bed and got dressed: Greek army pants and a sky blue shirt, sneakers. When he was done, he went downstairs to the hotel lobby.

Jade was at the bar, talking to an elderly woman. He wondered how much Alysa had told Jade about her past. He wondered if she knew the story of Alysa's father. His guess was that she didn't. She was an American girl from a privileged background. She would have provided good cover for a Soviet agent, had Alysa taken up the offer from the man called Michalis while they were dorm mates. And with that thought came another: what if Alysa's denial of her role in any espionage was simply a double bluff? What if she *had* accepted the offer made to her by Michalis, and that the fury of her denial were that of a person who protested too much? Could Alysa really have been that cynical? Could all her loves and friendships be subordinated to her role as an intelligence operative? Cosmo simply had no idea. He was afraid even to speculate. He had, he realized, accepted her version of events up in the bedroom, but that acceptance was motivated, at least partly, by obscure sentiments on his part: he had wanted her to be innocent, even if it showed him in a very poor light.

But his attention now shifted towards Jade. She was looking at his face with a concerned expression, but thankfully did not ask him to explain it. He thought: *she has already guessed.*

– Hullo, he said, and kissed her on the cheek. Gently, she lifted a hand and traced her fingers along his swollen lip. As she leant forwards, he lingered an instant, smelling her hair. There was movement inside his jeans, stirrings against the cloth. He looked away, and took a stool at the bar.

– Hi, Cosmo. Let me introduce Mrs Barbara Schlesinger. Mrs Schlesinger; Cosmo Flute, the famous painter of bulls.

Cosmo glanced at Jade and shook the old woman's hand. It was frail and freckled and felt as though it would crack in his if he exerted much pressure.

– Mrs Schlesinger was telling me she has been coming here on and off since the nineteen twenties. That's right, isn't it?

– Since 1923. I am now eighty-one years of age. Born with the century. I used to come over regular, when Mr

Schlesinger was alive, God rest his soul. But I fear this may be my last trip.

She smiled at Cosmo, the ingenuous smile of a ten year old.

– May I buy you a drink? asked Cosmo.

– No thank you, but you two go ahead. I am with a party. We're just waiting for dinner to be served. At my age Spanish eating hours play havoc with the digestion.

– I'll have a Bloody Mary, thanks, said Jade.

Cosmo ordered two from the immaculately groomed barman.

– Forgive the question, please, Mrs Schlesinger. But having come here for all these years, I suppose you must have known Mr Hemingway.

The old lady appraised Cosmo coolly.

– I did indeed. He was a frightful man, a boor and a bully. Terribly rude. Oh, here are my friends. Nice to meet you, Mr Flyte; Jade. We'll chat again, I hope.

Mrs Schlesinger gathered her walking stick and moved across the room in a dignified way towards a group of middle-aged and elderly Americans who were hanging around impatiently by the entrance to the dining-room.

– Before you arrived, said Jade, she told me she had known the real Brett Ashley. Isn't that exciting? I asked her if the real Brett Ashley really said 'I say, can a chap get a drink' and 'I'm rather tight.'

– And did she?

– She couldn't remember. Said it was quite possible. Everybody, all the British aristos, talked like that in the twenties, don't you know? She also said I looked very much like her.

– Like Mrs Schlesinger?

– No, you idiot. Like the real Brett Ashley. Her name was Lady Duff Twysden. An original flapper, or is it slapper? Mrs Schlesinger told me.

– No kidding?

– Scout's honour.

Cosmo started playing with his lighter.

– Where's Ruben? he asked.

– Good question. Afraid I can't help you though. We had a little to-do. A barney, as the Brits say. I like that. Makes me think of Barney Bear.

– You're tight, Jade.

– Nonsense. I am never tight.

– Hey ho.

– Just what precisely does that *mean*, Cosmo? Hey ho?

– Oh, you know. Hey ho.

– In the context it could mean practically anything. Now then, Jade started, sipping at her Bloody Mary, – what are we going to do about our respective lovers?

– Now I don't know what you mean.

– Don't you? How disappointing. I thought we might help each other out. You know Ruben pretty well, hey? Best buddies an' all. And I know Alysa as well as . . . hang on. I believe I'll retract that. In the past week or two I've come to realize that I don't know Alysa at all.

– Look, can we pass on this topic? Alysa and me have just had something of a barney ourselves.

– Oh? Jade's face contorted in an effort to look concerned, then lit up with the tremor of a smile. – So it's you and me, huh? You want to do dinner?

They moved into the dining room, which was empty other than the party of Americans that included Mrs Schlesinger, and chose a table next to the window. Half way through his starter, Cosmo, who had always been indiscreet, decided to test the waters with Jade, to see if she had any inkling of the real cause of Alysa's distress.

– Tell me, Jade: when you knew Alysa in the States did she ever do anything or hang around with people who aroused your suspicions, you know, about what she was up to?

– Huh? Can you put that in English?

Cosmo sighed, and wiped his mouth with his napkin.

– I'll try, but it's going to sound weird. For starters though, did she ever talk to you about her father?

– Very little. I knew he had split with Alysa's mother, and that he'd been in the USA when he died.

– Nothing else? She never talked to you about her dad's allegiances, his politics? Never told you what he did in the Greek civil war?

– No. Nothing like that.

So he told Jade what Alysa had told him of her past, of her father's involvement with communist partisans in World War Two, of his flight from Greece and subsequent exile, of his involuntary departure from Cardiff when she was a child, of the approaches made to her on behalf of the Soviets while she was at Princeton, of her refusal to collude with them, of her suspicions that she was being watched, and of her guilt at having brought about a revenge attack on Cosmo and Ruben's house in Xania and the destruction of Cosmo's paintings. He told her how Alysa had reacted when they had stumbled upon the execution place in the olive groves, and Cosmo had gone back and found machine gun bullets littering the topsoil. Jade listened in silence. He left out nothing, apart from Alysa's suggestion that he and Jade were flirting with each other. When Cosmo had finished talking, she stared blankly at him and said.

– Well, she's quite a gal. I mean, I had no idea.

Cosmo had the impression she was hurt, but was trying not to show it.

– And your face? Alysa did that to you?

– Yeah, but I probably deserved it.

After eating, Cosmo went upstairs to see whether Alysa had returned, but the room was empty. He made an effort at sweeping most of the broken glass into a corner with a newspaper, and went back down to re-join Jade.

– Alysa's out. Ruben too, you said?

– Yeah. Maybe he's gone to pick a fight with someone else. I was, uh, a little harsh with him.

– So, shall we go after them?

– We could go out. I don't know if we should go *after* them. I've had enough crap for one day.

– Alysa's pretty fucked up right now. And I haven't helped.

– I should say.

– And I'm not sure I can help her anyway.

– Do you think I haven't been trying? She cuts me off whenever I ask. She accused me of prying last time. Easy to see why now, of course. So I've given up asking. But it's scary.

– How do you mean, scary?

– *She* is scary. Like I said before you told me all that stuff, I feel like I don't know her any more.

They set out in vague pursuit anyway, walking together through the teeming streets, checking the bars along the way to the Plaza del Castillo. They looked in the Iruña and made their way to the Basque bar of the night before. There they found the men they had breakfasted with that morning, shared a few drinks, and heard that Ruben had been there earlier, but had left with Alysa not long ago. They had not said where they were going.

It was a warm night. As they wandered with decreasing enthusiasm for their task, Jade took Cosmo's arm.

– We could just buy something to drink, and sit in the square with the winos, she suggested. – There, at least we'll have a view.

They stepped into a bodega and Cosmo bought a bottle of brandy, a mixer, and plastic cups. When they got back to Plaza del Castillo, they headed for the bandstand. Cosmo poured drinks, while Jade sat on the steps and rolled a spliff. She looked up.

– Call off the search, huh? I guess we have to settle for a private party.

Around the bandstand and on the paved surface of the square itself, a dozen people lay sleeping, mostly dressed in San Fermín white, sullied with evidence of five days' carousing. Above the park, the nightly firework display had just begun and the air was loud with explosion. Cosmo found himself sinking into a state of almost catatonic resignation, which, compounded by the powerful weed and the brandy, soon led to the most vivid imaginings. The bandstand began to resemble a time capsule, in which he and Jade were the sole survivors of a world in which the religion was worship of the bull and the vine, and the presiding god had driven the inhabitants to a state of perpetual dementia. Meanwhile, in the more immediately visible world, an occasional reveller would stop by and hail a greeting, or offer them a drink, or take a slug of theirs. Everyone shared the condition of a recognizable and temporary insanity, and it was this recognition, of a time apart from the everyday, in which almost everything was permitted, that made for the fiesta's common purpose. For Cosmo, it was a celebration of Dionysos, the god whose triple sacrament was drunkenness, madness and tragedy. Drifting on the margins of consciousness, he began to fantasize a bizarre kinship with the figure of Dionysos himself.

Time takes on a different aspect during a fiesta. Everything is in a state of suspension because the rules of everyday conduct and routine by which people normally measure their lives also form the basis of their belief in time as a linear passage. In fiesta time these rules do not apply. Time becomes circular, a constant recycling of variations on a theme, fragmented, one thing not following on from the next but concurrent with it, overlapping, fluid. The fluidity of time is made visible, and the delicate circuitry of human souls responds in kind. At a time of such intensity of emotion, the electrical sparks that are thrown off shine brighter in significance than at other times.

The fireworks in the sky had died away, but their ascending rhythms and eruptions of bright light continued to drip like neon over Jade and Cosmo, and she pulled closer to him, resting her head on his shoulder.

Cosmo dozed off, and found himself in a dark house with many rooms. One of the doors would not open. Ruben, draped in an animal skin, was hammering at the door with a bone, a human femur. The door gave way and a blinding light shone from the interior of the room. Nikos stepped through the light, wearing his bull's head and carrying in his arms the limp body of Courtney. There was a red gash across Courtney's throat and his head lolled to one side.

Cosmo turned away and fled down a dark corridor, where the ground heaved beneath him, vines shooting from the packed earth and pulling at his ankles. He fell, but continued trying to drag himself forward. A crone approached, long white hair loose about her shoulders. She was carrying a book. She stopped beside Cosmo, knelt, and told him that she too had been in Tangiers. Her kiss lingered on his lips with the taste of sour cherry. When he looked at her again, she was Mrs Schlesinger, walking steadily away down the corridor on her stick. The stick clacked on the dry floor. His ear was to the ground.

He awoke with a start. Ruben was standing over him. He was barefoot, and tapping the stonework of the bandstand with one of his shoes.

– Just getting the gravel out, he said, in a thick voice.

Cosmo loosened himself from Jade, who in turn woke up.

– Getting cosy? asked Ruben.

Neither Cosmo nor Jade bothered to reply.

Ruben reached for the brandy and drank straight from the bottle.

– Have you seen Alysa. We heard you were together.

Ruben nodded, swilling the brandy around his mouth.

– We were together; then I got talking with a Uruguayan I'd known in Buenos Aires. The world is a handkerchief. Alysa went dancing.

– Dancing, that figures. Where?

– Iruña.

Cosmo was on his feet.

– Let's go find her.

Ruben shrugged, and the three of them crossed the square to the Café Iruña. Inside, the place was a cauldron. The floor was scattered with empty plastic cups and wine stains and sawdust. The music was loud. Human forms leaped and twisted in wild varieties of dance. Cosmo spotted Alysa at the far side of the room and made his way past bodies that bumped and toppled into him. When he caught up with her she didn't stop dancing, but grabbed his hand and made a full pirouette, then letting go of his hand, pushed him away. He fell against the next dancer, regained his balance and stepped over to her again. He had to shout to make himself heard.

– You want to get some fresh air? Maybe talk.

– Nothing to say, she shouted back. *Nada de nada.* And turning her back, danced away from him.

– Cosmo shrugged, and went to the bar. He bought a beer and watched the dancing. His eyes kept returning to Alysa, and as he watched her dance, he was reminded of the music he had listened to that night weeks ago in his studio, and the girl who danced herself to death in *The Rite of Spring*. That was the night he had found her in bed with Pascale. She had watched as he made love to Pascale, and he knew she had relished it, marvelled in the sight of their joined bodies, in a pained sort of way. He wondered if this observer's role, this voyeuristic tendency, was part of her substance, what kept her alive. She was, after her fashion, the star adept of Deep Hanging Out, because she made sure she did not connect, did not attach, could even afford to inflict little cruelties on herself just to test her strength of purpose.

Jade and Ruben were further down the bar, arguing. Cosmo didn't want to hear, and decided to keep away, but in spite of the noise around him, he could still make out their raised voices. The bonds of love and friendship that had linked the four of them together were frayed, if not already sundered. He sipped his beer and looked around. This place was the hot engine-room of the fiesta right now, and looked ready to combust. Then he caught sight of the American, Attempted Moustache, crossing the dance-floor with three foaming beers cradled in his hands. He glanced across at Ruben, and saw that he had noticed him also. He moved down the bar. Attempted Moustache reached the end of the bar before Cosmo, and Ruben moved sideways just as the American passed him, barging into him and sending the beers tumbling to the ground. Attempted Moustache stared a long time at the spilled drinks, and then turned towards Ruben.

– Shit, was that me? Ruben said, shaking his head.

Attempted Moustache was still staring. He seemed so drunk that Cosmo was not even sure that he recognised Ruben.

– That is so, fucking, infantile, Jade shouted.

Ruben was grinning at Attempted Moustache, who mumbled something, then hollered at Ruben what sounded like *allthamothafuckingodslaterbilge*.

Jade yelled back, – Sorry about him. Let me buy you more beers. Attempted Moustache focused on her unsteadily and attempted a smile.

– You aren't going to buy that cretin drinks? Ruben shouted, horrified.

– Watch me. Jade's face was set, disdain spread like lacquer across her features. When Jade's back was turned, Ruben put his arm around the American's shoulder and, leaning to say something in his ear, very deftly and swiftly administered a blow to his jaw with his free hand. Attempted Moustache fell sideways, his head hitting the ground with a crack.

– Oh dear, said Ruben, standing over him. – That's

too bad.

Then Jade was back, screaming and remonstrating with Ruben. People kept piling into the Iruña, stepping over the prostate form and moving towards the dance floor. Ruben threw his hands up in the air, in mock surrender, and backed through the door. Jade stood next to the bar, fuming. Her eyes followed Ruben as he disappeared into the crowd outside.

– Why does he do that?

– It's in his blood I guess. Why does *she* do *that*? He gestured over to where Alysa continued to dance like a thing possessed.

Jade looked at her and sighed. She said the sentence slowly.

– She dances because she's sad.

Cosmo grunted, and took some beer.

– Can't taste this stuff. Got the brandy?

Jade fished in her bag and nodded.

– Let's go outside. Difficult to breathe in here.

On the way, he checked on Attempted Moustache, and helped him to his feet. Attempted Moustache stood up briefly, swore at Cosmo, and then sat down again, landing in a heap against the wall. Cosmo left him there.

Outside, they sat for a while on the kerb at the edge of the square, with a view of the Iruña. They saw Alysa leave the bar with a group of strangers but did not follow her: instead, they found a vacant bench and smoked some more ganja. Jade lay on her back with her head on Cosmo's lap and before very long the night sky began to be flecked with grey and pink.

– Come for a walk? asked Jade.

They followed the narrow streets towards the cathedral, and then down some steps, and along the battlements. Jade was huddled close to Cosmo, and he felt the contours of her body against him in the chill dawn air, nestling against his ribs. They left the path silently and were on a steep grassy incline. Below them lay the river, a dark serpentine mirror that had swallowed up the night and was reflecting its blackness back at the changing sky. The sudden quiet after the turbulence of the Plaza; this breach in the aperture between day and night that engenders possibilities unknown to either; the tension within their bodies that seethed on the brink of hot explosion; all of this conspired with the inevitability of a stone thrown from land to water, its trajectory delimited and fixed in flight between one point and the other, where the stone drops with a splash into deep water and leaves a kinetic imprint of concentric circles rippling across the surface; and they silently acknowledged the fixed purpose of their departure from the Plaza, stopped walking as they passed a dark, cave-like enclosure set into the thick walls of the battlements, and were in each others' arms with a rapaciousness that seemed driven by a force of destiny. Thrust against the hillside in that dank and mossy recess, they tore at each others' clothing, desperate collaborators, their desire fuelled by the heady stimulant of betrayal and, minutes later, their climax echoed in awful caricature by the cawing of the crows that circled the treetops below them.

They held each other close, filled with something approaching terror at the suddenness and intensity of the encounter. The absolute physical release, now that it had been expressed, was convoluted by a reluctance to accept that this act inevitably signalled the end of one thing or the start of another.

24. *The Tunnel*

Slowly, in the swelling light, Cosmo and Jade made their way to a café just behind the Plaza and drank strong coffee as the white-clad runners prepared for the morning *encierro*. The sun was cresting the rooftops to the east, and there was a chill to the air. Cosmo sat wild-eyed at the table, smoking. He had ordered a brandy with his coffee, but had drained the glass at once, and was re-filling the balloon glass from his own bottle. He *needed* to drink more: his body screamed out for it, but his mind had long since overreached tolerance point. He had entered that phase of continuous drinking where wild things lurk, and the power of the brain to shape thoughts or meaning into recognizable forms was dissipating fast. Someone pushed against their table as they passed, almost knocking it over. Cosmo cursed and steadied his glass. He watched Jade as she rolled a spliff.

– You OK? He asked her.

Jade nodded, concentrating on her task, then looked up at him.

– What are we going to do?

– Shall we watch the running? asked Cosmo.

– That wasn't what I meant, but yeah, if you like.

– It's what I came for, I think. To see the bulls run.

But even as he said it, Cosmo knew that he didn't care for the role of spectator. Jade lit up her joint and crossed her legs. She blew out smoke at Cosmo.

– So. D'you think you'll go back to live in Crete.

– Dunno. I doubt it. I'll have to go and sort out the house, the rent, all that shit. But I was thinking of going to Paris for a while. Then maybe do some travelling. Mexico, Guatemala, Nicaragua.

– There's a war in Nicaragua. Did you know that Ruben is talking of going there, to fight the *Contras*?

– Is he? Cosmo sat up in his chair. Christ! He mentioned it a while ago, but I didn't think he was serious. You mean to actually fight, or to take pictures?

– Can you do both? I don't know. No doubt Ruben thinks he can. Yeah, he's serious.

– And he knows about guns and stuff, added Cosmo vaguely. He did his military service but I get the idea he was acquainted with firearms a while before that.

– Me too. Jade passed the spliff on to Cosmo.

– Maybe I should join him, he said.

Jade laughed. – Aw come off it, Cosmo. You're not cut out for that kind of thing. You're an artist, not a warrior.

Cosmo laughed out loud. When he answered, his speech was slow and slurred.

– Wrong. I am Dionysos. One of the immortals. I'm undercover at the moment though, so don't tell anybody.

Around them, late arrivals hurried to the start of the *encierro,* or to find a place to view the spectacle from the wooden barriers that line the run. One passer-by dropped a firecracker near their table. It hissed and sizzled, exploding in an erratic sequence of sharp cracks. Cosmo looked up, startled.

– Fuck it, let's run with the bloody bulls.

– Cosmo, take a look at yourself! Are you out of your mind?

– Probably.

– Hmm. I can't say I wasn't expecting this. I mean, why come all the way here and not join in? OK, if you like. But I'll just watch, thank you.

– Feeling that reckless, huh? How about we run with the bulls, get some breakfast, and see if we can't find somewhere else to stay? Maybe we could spend more time doing what we just did, but in more comfort.

– Maybe we could. But I'm not running with any bulls.

They began walking towards the Town Hall and Mercaderes Street, but they were not as early as the day before, and the prime positions on the barrier had been taken. There was still time before the run was due to start, and they made their way through the crowd to find a spot where it was possible to slip through the barriers. After the second rocket was fired, and the wall of noise began to engulf them from the direction of the corral, they were pushed forward by the surge of the crowd, and pressed against the wooden fence, with a limited view of the runners as they came into sight. Again the leaders passed by them, having negotiated the sharp curve into Estafeta Street, with the first bulls not far behind. There was some delay before the main body of runners caught up, with the three remaining bulls clattering over the flat cobbles. Amid all the shouting and cheering and mayhem, Cosmo saw a fat man fall right in the path of a charging bull. The bull dipped its head, and without dropping speed, picked up the man on one horn, hooking his sweatshirt, and dragging him along for twenty metres before dumping him unceremoniously when the shirt finally ripped apart. Then, on the other side of the street, head high, hair in a red bandana, Cosmo saw Alysa. She was laughing, in her element, and running gracefully and at speed. Out of the corner of his eye he saw Ruben too, just to the rear of Alysa. He yelled at them, pointlessly, and slipped between the barrier slats and into the street. Someone shouted after him to stop, that he could not join the run here, but he wasn't listening. The flash of crimson had ignited something in him, an epiphany – and he knew exactly what it was: his dream that night while sleeping in the park, of being washed down the narrow streets of the city on a tide of blood. He knew what it meant. He had been dwelling in the Cretan myth, the story, for so long, had ingested and drunk the myth so thoroughly that it all made perfect sense to his addled resources: Alysa was to be sacrificed to the god of sundering and tearing apart, of blood that flows, to the god of chaos and of delirium, the god of bulls. With a frantic energy, Cosmo sprinted after the crowd, and heard behind him the pounding of hooves as the one remaining bull and its steers closed up on him. He could smell them, the wild smell of animal hide and dust and dried grass, and even against the backdrop of noise he could hear the breathing of the bull right at his heels, as it broke past him, horns passing inches from his elbow. A few other runners were alongside him now, and ahead he could see Alysa, conspicuous in her head-band, as the route passed the *Telefonica* building and turned left towards the Plaza de Toros. He shouted after her, but to no avail.

When he approached the tunnel that formed the entrance to the arena, Cosmo saw a black bull, isolated, pacing with a curious indifference around the entrance. The bull turned to face the throng of runners that included Alysa and Ruben as they ran towards the tunnel, and in doing so caused the bull which had overtaken Cosmo, flanked by steers, to swerve aside. Runners scattered, and several fell, forming a bottleneck in the tunnel itself. Amid the shouting and screaming, Cosmo saw the lone bull dip and swerve at Alysa - who sidestepped the horn with a skip and a jump - and head towards the heap of humanity caught there.

Cosmo was panicked. As he came towards the tunnel his limbs seemed heavy, his movements sluggish. He had run four hundred metres and was sweating and out of breath. He felt clumsy: he did not flow with the rhythm of the other runners, and he had the strange sensation that a bomb was about to explode somewhere in the vicinity of his heart.

Inside the tunnel, he stumbled and tripped over an extended leg, poking out from the fallen mass of bodies. People were clambering over each other, attempting to crawl their way to safety or trying to become invisible by pressing themselves flat against the wall. But it was a tight passage; the tunnel was dark, one-way, and offered no protection. The bodies formed a small mountain of writhing human matter. The bull, which had moved into the tunnel and was testing the human mound for give with one of his horns when Cosmo fell, was stopped short by this new casualty. He twisted, to retrieve his horn, but it was caught, and he shifted his weight so that the man he had been prodding was now balanced on the ridge of his horns. He nudged him disdainfully back onto the heap and went, head low to the ground, for Cosmo. He scooped him up in a single movement and tossed him to one side, then steadied himself. The bull snorted, and Cosmo felt the thick breath on his face as the beast turned his great head and drove and twisted his right horn under Cosmo's rib-cage. The horn entered the abdomen violently, just below the umbilicus. It tore through skin and subcutaneous tissues, the peritoneum and small intestines, up through the transverse colon and stomach, rupturing the splenic artery on its way through the diaphragm and, finally, pierced the heart.

In the seconds that followed, there was much commotion. Ruben and one of the uniformed stewards were trying to lure the bull away from Cosmo's limp body. Blood had streamed into a pool beneath him, strangely orange and viscous, and bubbles were foaming at the corner of his mouth. The steward was pulling at the bull's tail. The bull stood guard over the body, tossing his head. Then Alysa was there, leaning over Cosmo, impervious to the danger, while Ruben whacked the bull with a long stick that the steward had dropped in the tunnel. The bull turned and cantered into the arena, flicking his tail.

A frenzy of voices, paramedics, helpers, gawpers. Alysa held Cosmo's head in her arms, but he was choking blood now, his head rocking from side to side. A medic was trying to staunch the wound in his abdomen, but Cosmo was losing too much blood for this to make any difference. His eyes were glassy, deep tunnels that led away into unknowable panic, and he was trying to speak but no sound came from his lips, just mute labial movements and a trickling of blood.

So this is what it is like this is how it ends not with a bang but a crash and a howl and darkly through glass anybody there the air is suffocating nose blocked hard to breathe blood dirt sand sawdust mouth grit lungs pumping dying fish on the quayside thrash like that oh where Tassos would go and buy for the Unspeakable Igbar too sometimes and I remember the White Mountains in the colours time before sunset and the olive trees and the heaps of oranges at the roadside and the giant who slept each night beside his stack of watermelons on Melhidissek Street who one night caught Ruben stealing a watermelon and chased him with a broom and in Paris in Papa's home the ceilings were high I would lie in bed and the vault of the room was the sky and eternity and I was alone on the earth that was when I was a child I'll never have children and is that all is that all someone is calling someone wants to take me with them to go with them who is that oh Alysa it's you sweet girl who dances when she's sad and oh there are tears she's saying something I don't know what saying something to me and I can't hear I realize I can't hear a thing and it's as if I hadn't noticed that I couldn't hear I feel so tired so done in this fiesta is a killer and there's something tugging at me at my memory no at me some pure gravity pulling yes pulling

Alysa was cradling his head in her arms; she knelt and spoke to him in whispers, words meant to comfort, meaningless words conjured from the air, anything just to speak to him, to make those sounds that he would recognize, perhaps, as words. With a furrowing of his brow, an extraordinary effort of will was taking place as Cosmo sought through a cyclonic storm of neurons for the correct formulation of a word or phrase; a word or phrase that would be his parting gesture, his final utterance, and the air about them was heavy with the stench of blood and a fly had landed on Cosmo's face and Alysa swiped at it with her free hand, but the fly returned with a furious loud buzzing, as if angered by Alysa, prematurely asserting its divine right to sit and vomit on the deceased; this turquoise fly rubbing its forelegs together over the body of her dying lover; this beautiful crumpled wreckage of a life. And as he stared up at her and the word or words could not find expression, the effort was too much, whatever words were in the process of being formed or uttered were left definitively and forever unsaid, because the tunnels that were his eyes became cloudy and unfocussed and the bubbling of blood from the side of his mouth spilled like soup down his cheek, and his whole body tensed as if preparing for a high dive or some other momentous physical act.

By the time they had brought a stretcher for him to be taken inside an ambulance, Cosmo was already dead. Jade ran into the tunnel and into Alysa's arms and the two women hung close to each other in their shared grief and terror. Ruben was standing with a paramedic, gesticulating furiously at the ground, at the blood that flowed down the concrete ramp and had already been absorbed by the sand marking the edge of the arena.

Historical note

The invasion and occupation of Greece (1941-44) shaped the political forces of the country for the remainder of the century. Under Nazi rule a fierce resistance was launched across the country, which was suppressed by the occupiers with the utmost brutality. Despite this, the Greek partisans were so successful that the liberation of their country was complete even before the landing of allied troops at Piraeus in October 1944. Anti-Nazi partisan groups, of all political hues, had received aid from the Western allies during the resistance. However, with the German, Romanian and Bulgarian occupying armies gone, British and American aid now favoured a conservative political agenda. As with Italy in the same period, the allies sought to undermine the establishment of a leftist government, to prevent the Soviet Union from strengthening its influence in the region. This antipathy to left-wing groups meant that allied support was extended to the country's new militias, composed of democratic nationalists together with Greek monarchists, fascists, Nazi collaborators and common criminals.

A long civil war in two parts both coincided with and followed the occupation; the first part (1942-5) culminating in the restoration of the Greek monarchy after a plebiscite – rigged, according to its critics – and the second (1946-9) with the destruction of the ELAS (pro-communist) army that had formed the bedrock of the Greek resistance to fascism in large areas of the country since the Nazi invasion. ELAS leaders were shot, imprisoned or went into exile. The figure of a half million dead left by the occupation was compounded by an estimated eighty thousand dead in the civil war and over a million and a half displaced, destitute or refugees. By preventing a communist government in Greece, including Crete with its Souda Bay naval base, the West scored a strategic geo-political victory: it disabled the encirclement of Soviet influence around Middle Eastern oil resources, including the Persian Gulf area. Greek leftists, who had fought the Nazis fiercely and suffered harsh reprisals, felt an intense sense of betrayal, since the success of the Greek Right was in large part dependent upon American military aid provided under the Truman Doctrine. During the Cold War (1945-89) Greece was a member of NATO, and host to US military installations. Among these, Souda Bay was, and remains, the key base in the Eastern Mediterranean for the U.S. Sixth Fleet.

In 1967 a military coup led by a group of Colonels, and supported by the CIA, took power and held it until 1974. The US Ambassador to Greece, Henry Tasca, called that military government "the most anti-communist group you'll find anywhere." The Colonels' regime ended after a last-gasp attempt to secure enosis (union) with Cyprus ended in disaster and a viciously suppressed student uprising in Athens attracted international condemnation. Shortly thereafter a referendum abolished the monarchy. By 1981, when the events in this novel take place, Greece was a stable democracy with a centre-right government and had applied for membership of the European Community.

Author Biography

Richard Gwyn was born in Wales and grew up in the village of Crickhowell. *Deep Hanging Out* is his second novel: he is also the author of *The Colour of a Dog Running Away* and several collections of poetry and very short stories. His website can be found at www.richardgwyn.com.